A Rose From Blighty

"It's clear you've never been on a platform that was invaded by police," Louise said, voice low and passionate. "Maybe when you've been seized, thrown about, had your breasts twisted till you could scream with pain, it will change you. I can tell you, childhood is left behind. You grow up *fast*."

She saw Aunt Gertrude's jaw drop, face ablaze, but there was no joy in making her speechless. The burst of smoking temper cooled and dwindled almost as quickly as it had come. Louise stood up quickly and had to grip the back of her chair to steady herself, her whole suffragette experience concentrated in her head, jamming the wheels of her mind. She could scarcely think. The walk to the door seemed like a hundred miles. As she closed it, a great flood of envy swept through her.

It wasn't fair! Pete was out there, flying free. *Involved*. While she was trapped. Just because she was a woman . . . oh damn him . . . damn Aunt G . . . damn everything!

Marjorie Darke

A Rose From Blighty

Lions
An Imprint of HarperCollins*Publishers*

Words from *Rose of No Man's Land*
(Caddigan/Brennan) are reprinted by permission
of CPP/Belwin Inc. International Music Publishers,
Copyright © Leo Feist Inc.

Words from *There's a Long Long Trail*
(Stoddard King/Zo Elliott) are reprinted by permission
of West's Ltd, administered by B. Feldman & Co. Ltd,
London WC2H 0EA, copyright © 1913

First published in Great Britain by HarperCollins 1990
First published in Lions 1992

Lions is an imprint of the Children's Division,
part of HarperCollins Publishers Ltd,
77/85 Fulham Palace Road, Hammersmith, London W6 8JB

Copyright © Marjorie Darke 1990
The author asserts the moral right to be
identified as the author of this work.

ISBN 0 00 673543–6

Set in Garamond
Printed and bound in Great Britain by
HarperCollins Manufacturing, Glasgow

ACKNOWLEDGEMENTS

I wish to thank all those people who so willingly gave their time and expertise in helping my research into various aspects of the First World War:

the staff of the Royal College of Nursing Library, and Helen Thomas in particular;

Margaret Poulter of the Archives Section of the British Red Cross Society;

Nigel Steel of the Department of Documents at the Imperial War Museum;

Sue Wooldridge who, with permission from the Coventry Museum of Motor Transport, provided information and photographs of vehicles of the period;

Dr Sylvia Darke for sharing memories from her wide medical experience;

Patricia Oakley for her reminiscences.

I also wish to mention that splendid book *The Roses of No Man's Land* by Lyn Macdonald, published by Michael Joseph, which was invaluable to my understanding of nursing and hospital life both in England and overseas during the war years 1914–18.

~ PART 1 ~

LOUISE and PETER: 1914–1916

~CHAPTER 1~

Toasted muffins! The mouthwatering buttery smell rose up from the hearth where firelight flickered on the brass fender. A pot of tea sat under a blue quilted cover. There were delicate madeleine cakes and butterfly biscuits on the little table. Outside, the winter gale howled and battered at the windowpanes. But it was warm in the old nursery. Warm and safe. She sat down cross-legged on the hearthrug . . . then suddenly, and quite naturally, she wasn't sitting on the floor but on her bicycle. Freewheeling downhill into Birmingham. Summer wind made streamers out of her loosening hair. The placard on her handlebars billowed like a sail. VOTES FOR WOMEN! Her skirt flapped. Wheels spun. A thrilling sense of freedom coursed through her body. Oh it was good, wonderful to be outside. On and on, cruising unfettered. She felt like a bird, on and on . . .

A sharp bar of sunlight coming in through the high cell window sliced across Louise's face. She shifted on the lumpy mattress, trying to sink back into the dream, but it was hopeless. The scent of hot butter changed into the sour mustiness of prison bedding. Sleep vanished, letting in a flood of disappointment. Her empty stomach knotted. Opening her eyes she saw the heavy door begin slowly to open.

They were coming for her again!

She clutched the thin blanket with both hands, whispering: "No," then shouting: "I won't . . . NO!"

"Dreaming again, Marshall?" The wardress, broad with powerful shoulders and a long face that drooped into loose jowls, set down the usual stale little brown breakfast loaf and mug of thin tea on the scrubbed table top. Her small eyes, set in a fretwork of lines, darted glances round the cell.

Louise didn't stir.

"You'd better rouse yourself and get dressed," the wardress ordered. "And mind you leave everything shipshape. There'll be an inspection before you can go."

"Go? Where?" Anxiety hummed and fretted in her head.

The wardress shrugged. "How should I know? Home, I suppose. You do have a home? Yes – a posh town house and summat in the country too, I daresay. Your sort would."

"I'm to be . . . released?"

'How else could you go home?"

"They think I might die then." She did feel horribly weak.

The woman shot her another glance that was not unkind. "Don't talk silly. It's because of the war. You'd do yourself some good if you ate your breakfast. No need to starve yourself now."

Louise repeated stupidly: "War?"

"Yes, war. Us and them Germans." Impatience in the hard voice. "I'd've thought you with your eddication would've known. Didn't you pick up on the gossip? News usually travels fast in Holloway." The wardress sniffed, then blew hard down her nose as if to get rid of a bad smell. " 'All Suffragettes to be let out of prison. Unconditional release.' Them's the orders."

Her mind would not work. Muddled random thoughts flew about like litter in the wind.

"Four days ago now," the wardress continued. "Papers have been full of nothink else since. Nothink but war, war, war." She laughed shortly. "You could say it's brought luck to some, such as yourself."

An uneasy suspicion crept in. What if this was another of those Cat and Mouse tricks, just to get her to eat? Louise began shouting down the intolerable idea:

"You won't catch me like that! I won't break my hunger strike! I won't . . . I won't . . . d'you hear?" Energy spent, she sagged back against the mattress.

"I should think everyone down the row can hear you! Please yourself – but if you ain't dressed and the place cleaned in a half hour, there'll be trouble. Don't say I didn't warn you." The woman moved towards the open door.

"If it's true, where are my own clothes?" Talking was difficult.

The wardress glanced briefly over her shoulder. "They'll be brought."

The door slammed. Keys rattled. Heavy footsteps retreated along the passage. Nothing remained except the echoing shouts of other prisoners and the chirruping of a sparrow on the ledge beyond the cell window-bars.

Trembling, Louise looked round the drab little cell, then back at the window, trying to assemble her thoughts. Exhaustion bound her to the bed. How long she lay unmoving, she didn't know. At last, using all her willpower, she sat up. Dizziness swept over her and she clutched the edge of the mattress. When the spasm passed, she opened her eyes and saw the mug of tea. Thirst was a torment, but the idea of giving in was an agony. She was still struggling to come to a decision when the wardress returned carrying her clothes. Glancing at the untouched breakfast, she dumped the bundle on the bed, with a warning:

"Twenty minutes left!" and marched out.

Something in the hard voice and the sight of her own clothes convinced her that she really was about to be released. Louise took the mug with shaking hands and sipped. The tea was tepid – thirst-quenching and sickening at the same time, but she persevered. When it was finished, she dressed slowly, then splashed water from the little tin basin over her face, dried herself and did what she could with her hair. She needed a rest before she could empty the water into the slop bucket, and another before tackling her bed. Just as she finished, the door swung back again. This time a senior wardress came in, a tall angular woman with a sour face – the other remained standing at the door. Willing herself not to faint, Louise waited while the inspection was made.

"It'll do, I suppose." The senior wardress pursed her thin lips. "Come along."

"Am I the only one to be released?"

"For the present. Not that it's any of your business."

It was very much her business. There had been at least three other Suffragettes in Holloway when she came in six weeks ago. But Louise was too fatigued to argue. She went on to the landing, bunching up her skirts which persisted in slipping down from her starved waist, and was steered down the iron staircase. Then she was made to wait, though they did give her a chair to sit on. Eventually, formalities complete, she was pushed towards the reception desk.

"One handbag, black leather. Two guineas, three shillings and a tanner. Tortoiseshell comb. Book of paper poudre. One handkerchief. Sign here." The woman behind the desk laid out Louise's belongings, pushed a receipt towards her, inked a pen and held it out.

Louise wrote her name in trembling letters.

The woman leaned forward. "Good luck, miss!" No more than a whisper, but the first kindly words.

Louise stared, saw a faint smile, but could not respond. As she returned the pen, the first glimmer of excitement touched her. I'm leaving, she thought, they're really letting me go! In a daze she watched keys being turned in the several locks. At last the door opened, light burst in and she stumbled through into free August sunshine. Without a word, the wardress slammed it shut again and locked her out.

The hot dusty London air was as potent as wine. Beyond the forecourt a coster's cart trundled along the road. An omnibus rumbled by, pulled by sweating horses. Delivery vans passed. A boy on a bicycle swerved to avoid a cat and almost collided with the Maudslay car she knew so well that was parked by the kerb.

She frowned, fighting giddiness.

Everything had a newborn clarity, almost more than she could take. The distant images kept this clarity, while those nearer seemed strangely indistinct. She saw Mary Grant among the Suffragette reception group who were moving towards her. They were waving. Cheering . . .

And then her head cleared. She could see everything. Less than six yards away, standing close together, was her brother, Peter, with Emily. Two people who mattered to her more than anyone else in the world. She had never realized before just how important and special they were to her. Now it was as obvious as the green of grass.

"Lou!" Peter rushed forward. She was swamped in a great hug. "Oh Lou, this is so good. How are you?" He held her away. "They've made you into a peastick!" and hugged her again.

She was glad to lean against his chest. "I'm . . . surviving!" Tears of weakness ran down the sides of her nose. Someone grasped her hand. She blinked and was looking at Emily . . . dear Emily, red in the face, with that pugnacious yet tender expression she knew so well. Her good affectionate unchanging friend! She felt the pressure on her hand increase.

"Yo'll be all right now, love – all the comforts of home. But yo won, Lou . . . yo beat 'em!" The rest was smothered as Peter put out his arm and scooped Emily into the embrace. For a moment the three stood huddled together.

Through her floundering astonishment, Louise was aware of surrounding voices; other hands touching her.

"You're a heroine! . . . Wonderful to see you free at last . . . We've planned a celebration . . . Are you well enough to celebrate? . . . There's a meal waiting . . . "

Drumming filled Louise's ears. She heard Emily say urgently: "She ain't well, Pete, yo'd better get the car started up. I can carry her. Let's get her back to Holland Park quick." Then everything solid withdrew to a great distance. She felt herself lifted and cradled, had an impression of sunlight sparking off brass headlamps, then . . . nothing.

~CHAPTER 2~

"You mustn't despair, Louise." Mary Grant settled her pince-nez more securely on her short nose.

"I'm not!" But she was and knew it. Three weeks of illness had left Louise low and moody. She smiled rather grimly. "I seem to have changed one sort of prison for another. Aunt G has been such a dragon, keeping everyone at bay, and with the doctor backing her, can you wonder I'm scratchy?" She caught Emily's steady watchful gaze, and yearned for Mary to go. But she was off again:

"The Red Cross and St John Ambulance Brigade are joining forces. There will be plenty we can do to help the war effort – first aid, preparing dressings and bandages, knitting . . ."

"Women's work!" Louise interrupted. She wished Mary would stop making the best of things. "It never changes, does it? Make jam and babies. Roll bandages. Keep the home fires burning and whatever you do, don't interfere. If only I was a man!"

"It ain't worth tuppence thinking like that." Emily took part in the conversation for the first time. "What's the use of wanting to be somebody else? Anyroad, yo've more to offer that's worthwhile than most folks."

"Oh yes? Like what?"

"Yourself, of course! A person as can stand against anything. Not many have your strength. Yo've proved yo can do whatever yo sets your mind to."

The feeling in Emily's voice made Mary's presence even more of an intrusion.

"Well said!" Mary patted Emily's shoulder.

They were side by side on a sofa in the smaller sitting room of the house in Holland Park, home of Louise's aunt, and the place where she and Peter had been living since their father died and their real home in Birmingham was shrouded in dust sheets. Louise, in a blue silk dress that folded loosely round her thin body, sat opposite in a basket chair. Between them a low table was set for afternoon tea – seed cake, buttered scones, strawberry jam, dainty sandwiches lying on fine bone china plates. In contrast, the lawn outside in the walled garden was parched and shrivelled. Even the big weeping willow had yellowed. It had been a long blistering summer.

"I'm glad we picked the same day to visit the invalid." Mary smiled primly at Emily. "I've not seen you since Mrs Pankhurst took our deputation to His Majesty. What a skirmish that was!" She transferred her smile to Louise. "I think it's right that Mrs Pankhurst has called off our campaign for the duration of the war. There are several of us who need to recuperate. You in particular, Louise. Three hunger strikes would bring anyone down. Plenty of rest and good food is what you need to make you fighting fit again."

Mary stood up. Louise held her breath.

"Now, I must go or Mother will worry." She buttoned her jacket. "I promised not to be long, but I did so want to see you at the first opportunity . . . and deliver this of course," she tapped the circular letter in Louise's lap as she bent to peck her cheek. "Goodbye, my dear. Don't try to do too much too soon. There's no need to ring for the maid. I can see myself out. Goodbye, Emily."

As the door closed Louise held out both hands. "I thought she'd be here for ever! Since she's become a Lady, she's more earnest than ever. Did you know her father had inherited the title? He's an earl now. I still can't think of her as 'Lady Mary'. She looks more like a schoolma'am with her hair scraped back and that dowdy hat! But I mustn't be catty. She's a good sort. It's just that I've been dying for a proper talk."

"And me!" Emily skirted the little table and took the outstretched hands, holding them tight. "It's grand to see yo up and dressed. We were that worried. I've never seen Pete so bothered. Mrs

Boston said your heart is a bit dicky. Is that true?"

"No, of course not! Aunt G will exaggerate so. The doctor says I've been suffering from exhaustion and malnutrition, which turned into a tiresome fever. But I don't want to talk about illness. I've had enough to last a lifetime. Tell me about you. What's been happening? How are things at work? How's your sister, May? Bring up that little chair and sit close. I want to hear everything." She watched Emily settle herself, observing with familiar pleasure the lopsided smile broaden until creases of humour almost hid the brown eyes.

"May's well enough if it wasn't for her hip playing up. But yo knows her . . . she won't let it get her down, just laughs and says what can yo expect with crippled legs! She's a corker! I dunno about work, though. We're both that worried."

"Why, what's wrong?"

"Folk ain't ordering new clothes. It's the war."

"But what about all those extra army uniforms? Somebody will have to make them."

"Not with fancy lace collars and embroidered flowers they won't!"

Louise burst out laughing. "Don't tell me you skilled people in Mrs Silver's workshop can't change from one sort of sewing to another. I won't believe it."

"That's what Pete says." Emily sighed. "We could make uniforms all right, but it ain't that simple. Mrs Silver has tried. She even wrote to some government bigwigs, but don't get no answers. If yo asks me, everything is in a right old muddle. Anyroad, she's not getting younger.

19

We reckon she'll close the business and retire."

Louise lost her smile. "And then?"

Emily shrugged. "Pete says I should set up me own workshop. He says I'd be sure to find enough sewing to keep May and me, and if I didn't he'd see what he could dig out for us – them's his very words!" She smiled.

"He's been offering a lot of advice! Is he becoming a pest? That brother of mine can be a real knowall. Don't let him boss you around, Emmie."

"Oh, he ain't been bossy. We've had lots of good talks. 'Course, I knows he likes a joke, but he can be serious too."

"Sounds to me as if you've been seeing a lot of each other," Louise said casually, surprised by a flicker of jealousy.

"Yes, I suppose we have. He's taken me out in the Maudslay several times. Mostly Sundays, because of work, but there were other days. We went for a nice walk in Kensington Gardens, just before they released yo. Lovely evening it was. Folk sitting in deckchairs, and youngsters floating boats on the pond," she began to giggle. "Yo'll never guess who we saw!"

Louise tried to be easy and natural. "Who?"

"One of them Holiday twins from Brum. Yo know, them as wore bloomers when we went on the bicycle parade. I dunno whether it was Una or Maude – I never could tell 'em apart. She weren't in bloomers this time. She had on ever such a smart muslin dress, cream over pink with cutwork all down the front – lovely! She saw Pete first, but she didn't recognize me straight off. When she did her eyes almost dropped out, she was that surprised! I thought she was going to come across the grass for a word, but she didn't, dunno why. I give her a wave though." Emily's smile was mischievous. "Small world, ain't it? D'yo think she's like us, left Brum to live in London?"

Louise's head was full of innocent memories – Peter's insistence on mending Emily's bike after the accident in Sandpits which had first thrown the three of them together; the way he contrived to be around whenever Emily had called; his sentimental nickname for her, "Our poppy from the cornfields"; his eagerness to take her up in his ridiculous hot air balloon. A new hard light seemed to blaze down on the memories, transforming them into something else. Something she had never before imagined. She felt furious. How dare Pete take over her friend! How dare he lead her on, fill her head with impossible fancies – heart too, probably!

Louise became aware that Emily was looking at her with some curiosity, and remembered she was still waiting for an answer. But what was the question? She said: "You *have* been seeing a lot of him!" and realized it sounded like an accusation. She began to pick at a loose bit of cane on the arm of her chair.

Emily looked away towards the window where a fly was buzzing uselessly against the glass. "Yo knows how he is. Always on the go – up in that balloon of his, or speeding in his motorcar. Now it's aeroplanes! Anything that moves . . . and he likes company."

Louise was astounded. "You haven't been flying?"

"My stars, no!" Emily laughed. "One trip in that balloon was enough to last me for ever – remember how we nearly came to grief? Throwing out them leaflets used up whatever nerve I had. I ain't got none left."

There was an awkward pause while they avoided looking at each other.

Suddenly very tired and queasy, Louise picked up the letter.

"What d'you think of this instruction to give up campaigning while the war's on? All our demonstrations, our hard work, the risks . . . those awful pipes forced up our noses . . . women have *died* – and all for nothing!" She felt tears rise and shook her head impatiently. Disgust at herself, at Peter, the war, everything, invaded her.

"It'll be over by Christmas – that's what they says."

"D'you believe it?"

"Guessing's a daft game, but yo're wrong to say that what we did was all for nothing. We've got together – all sorts of women, *together*. Yo and me." The restraint, there a moment ago, had gone. Emily's brown eyes were very clear and serious, looking directly at her now. "Can yo see it from my side? Someone like me from the backstreets of Brum becoming the pal of a woman like yo. That could never have happened before. The campaign brought us together. Gave us power."

"Brought you and Peter together as well," the words were out before Louise could stop them and she felt instant regret, yet was curiously relieved.

22

She glanced swiftly at Emily, trying to gauge her reaction, conscious of a sense of distance between them. Emily's face was wiped clean of expression.

"That's right," no expression in her voice either.

Louise felt dispirited. Everything was rapidly becoming far too much effort. She stared down at the thick pile of the carpet, shoulders drooping.

"Yo looks proper washed out, and here's me keeping yo talking," Emily said with sudden concern. "Mary was right, what yo needs is plenty of rest. I'll be off." She got up.

Seized by unreasoning anxiety, Louise sat forward in her chair. "No . . . please don't go. We've hardly scratched the surface. You can't imagine how starved I am of talk," she laughed rather shrilly. "What a joke – everyone worrying about me being so skinny, when it's being cut off from friends, talk, everything important, that's doing the real damage." She was facing the door, and over Emily's shoulder saw Peter come in. He looked windswept. His hair, usually slicked down with coconut oil, had sprung into wild sandy curls. He came towards them, throwing motoring-cap and goggles into a chair, reaching for a scone.

"I'm starved. Glad you've left some grub," he looked from one to the other. "I say, have I gatecrashed on a tiff?"

"No, of course not," Louise said peevishly.

"I was just going." Emily put on her hat. "Louise is tired."

"No I'm not."

"There you are, she's not. Sit down, Emmie!" Peter pushed her into the buttonback chair. "You

23

can't rush off. We're having that spin in the Maudslay, remember? Anyway, Lou's been begging for company. She's got all the time in the world to sleep and eat and idle away her days. You see, she'll plump up nicely for Christmas!" He leaned across and patted his sister's cheek.

Louise shook him off irritably. She saw Emily struggle not to grin.

"Yo makes her sound like a turkey."

"How could I? She hasn't any wattles," Peter said through his scone. "Now if you were talking about Auntie Gertie, that would be different."

Both had their backs to the door. Peter, helping himself to another scone, had obscured Louise's view, but as he moved, she caught a glimpse of Aunt Gertrude bristling in the open doorway. Always a formidable sight – ramrod back, jutting bosom loaded with jet ornaments, iron grey hair drilled into submission – now she looked a picture of outrage. The stout cheeks were crimson. Even the wattles caged inside the high lace collar were mottled.

Louise waited for the wrath to break over them, but instead, her aunt closed the door firmly and looked directly at Emily as if she was the only person in the room.

"Ah, Miss Palmer!" It was the voice kept for servants and tradesmen. "You've brought my skirt? Mrs Silver can always be relied upon to be prompt."

Emily would have stood up, but Peter's hand was firmly on her shoulder. "I'm . . . afraid it ain't finished yet, ma'am."

24

Louise saw her aunt register satisfaction at having put Emily firmly back into her place as Trade.

"The order has been in a full three weeks. I hope I'm not going to be let down?"

"Oh no, ma'am."

Against her will, Louise felt drawn to help Emily fend off this unfair attack, but Peter slipped in first.

"This isn't a work visit, Auntie. Mrs Silver gave Emily the afternoon off, and . . ."

"She kindly came to see how I was," Louise interrupted.

"And after tea I'm taking her for a spin in the Maudslay," Peter concluded. He seemed blithely unaware of the stunning impact of his words. Going to the mantelpiece he twitched the bell pull. "We just need some fresh tea – the food will do splendidly. Lou, you need fattening up, you can start all over again."

"No I can't," Louise said baldly. "I seem to have lost the art of eating."

Three pairs of eyes turned to her, but it was Emily who reached out to touch her as if there had been no discord between them.

"I knows how yo feels. Every bloomin' crumb chokes till yo wants to heave up your insides. I saw yo didn't take nothing when Mary was here, but yo have to try." She pressed the thin arm. "If yo don't stoke the fire the engine won't work – that's what my mam used to tell me."

"Take heed," Peter said. "You're lucky to have a friend with so much sense. I shall feel easier knowing you'll be here to keep an eye on Lou,

Emmie, now I shan't be able to do so myself."

What he had said didn't sink in straight away. Louise said: "I can keep an eye on myself, thank you!" and then, as understanding began to trickle in: "What have you been up to?"

He was lounging against the mantelpiece. "Went for a medical this morning, and an interview. What a laugh! Had to match coloured strands of wool! Then they gave me an eye test and . . . this is the funny bit . . . they wanted to know who was my favourite poet! I said poetry wasn't my line, but I liked a good yarn like Raffles. That seemed to go down all right, because after the doc had prodded me about, I was passed A1"

Shaken, Louise sat straight. "Pete, an interview for *what*?"

"The Royal Flying Corps – what else? It seemed obvious, having got my Aero Club ticket. All I need now is a machine. Then I'll be off for a spot of small arms training."

A small sound of distress came from Emily and withered into silence.

That's the first she's heard, Louise thought.

"I've been looking at a Sopwith Tabloid, a real little cracker," Peter went on, apparently not sensing trouble brewing. "I've decided to buy her."

"Why do you have to buy your own aeroplane?" Louise asked quickly. "Doesn't the army supply them?"

"Shortage." Peter took a ginger snap and bit it. "Pilots are asked to lend their own machines where possible, and this kite's a bargain. She's called

Flossie. Ah, here's tea. Good!" His charming smile was offered to all the women, including the maid with the teatray. "Emmie, why don't you pour? Lou is still liable to drop things." He pulled up a chair and sat beside her.

Louise's unsteady emotions swung again. She wanted to burst into a peal of laughter at this piece of colossal cheek. What a rap on Aunt G's knuckles! Pete never minded what he said, but this was playing with fire. After all, Holland Park wasn't home. Fancy making Aunt G look on while her dressmaker . . . no, worse than that, her dressmaker's *assistant* . . . played hostess. He was a monster! Louise's earlier resentment towards Emily switched to concern. They were two of a kind, aunt and nephew, using poor Emily like a pawn, without a thought for her feelings.

In the crackling silence, Emily, scarlet with embarrassment, picked up the milk jug.

"A cup for you, Auntie?" Peter asked affably.

Aunt Gertrude's mouth set in a grim line. Ignoring him, she turned and swept from the room with a protest of rustling skirts.

"You elephant!" Louise couldn't contain her exasperation any longer. "You great blundering hippopotamus!" She was so incensed that her breath stuck in her throat, making her cough.

"Steady on, old thing." Peter picked up the nearest cup. "Here, drink this."

Louise could have happily thrown the tea in his face. "She'll never forgive or forget. You know that, don't you?"

27

"Frankly, I don't much care what she thinks about me," Peter helped himself to another scone.

It was on the tip of Louise's tongue to say, "Not you. Emily," but at the last minute veered away from being so blunt. She felt awkward and unwilling to side with Emily. "I think it's ridiculous having to supply your own machine," she said, not thinking this at all. Secretly, she both envied and was proud of him.

"Why? I'm luckier than most. I can afford it, which means I can do the thing I love – flying."

The pride mixed with a feeling of alarm for his safety and bewildered outrage at the way he was playing with Emily. "You've rushed in without a thought, haven't you? Typical!" she snapped. "Have you applied even a tiny bit of your mind to what will happen if you are in Belgium and the solicitors want you to sign things? I'm in no state to go rushing up to Birmingham. I can just imagine them looking down their thin legal noses if *I* was to turn up . . ." she stopped, furious with herself now.

"You're getting upset over nothing, Lou," he said soothingly. "There aren't any problems with Father's Will. The solicitors are satisfied," he tailed away, glancing at Emily.

"That's not my point." Louise was goaded on by the volcano inside.

"What is, then? For goodness' sake, hundreds of fellows are volunteering every day! It's the patriotic thing to do."

But how could she say with Emily there, "She isn't the right girl to be your wife. Her background hasn't fitted her for your kind of life. She would be desperately unhappy" – no, it was impossible.

"There are ways of saying things – right moments to pick," Louise chose to be deliberately vague.

"Very mysterious." Peter cut a slice of seed cake and held out the plate to Emily who shook her head.

"Trampling over everyone's feelings with your great size tens," Louise went on. "*Everyone*."

Peter began delicately to pick seeds from his own slice of cake. "Sometimes trampling is the only way. If people get huffy, it's just too bad." He gave her a long hard look.

She realized he understood. "You can't do it."

"It's already done."

Shock waves ran through her body. Was he saying he had *proposed* to Emily? She held on to the arms of her chair, head pushed forward.

Peter leaned towards her in unconscious imitation. He lost his mild manner. "And if you can't approve, then at least don't interfere."

They were both glaring now. Frowning and glaring. At last Peter's mouth relaxed into a wry grin.

"Oh Lou, what are we quarrelling about?"

"Me!" Emily said, standing up and surprising them both. "And don't say yo ain't, because I knows better. I shouldn't have let yo talk me into coming here, Mr Marshall."

"Peter," he said, shocked.

"Peter," she repeated, as if it were a lesson.

Louise tried to gather her scattered wits. "You've been here before, Emmie."

"Not to tea. Only to deliver Mrs Boston's blouse that time. And yo don't have to fight my battles neither, Louise, though I'm ever so grateful for the thought." Her glance held more warning than gratitude. She picked up the little netted purse earlier tucked down the side of her chair. "I ought to be going, anyroad. Our May'll be waiting." She moved to the door. "Goodbye, then. I hopes you don't go on feeling poorly, Louise."

"But what about our spin?" Peter hurried after Emily into the hall. Louise heard him say: "You can't just walk away. At least let me drive you back. We've a lot to settle . . ."

In a turmoil, she got to her feet. Taking the tea she had earlier spurned, she raised the cup as if it held wine, and with bitter sarcasm said aloud: "Here's to *friends*!"

She drank, then collapsing back into the chair, burst into tears.

~CHAPTER 3~

September, and the streets of London had begun to grow a patchwork of posters calling for volunteers to join His Majesty's Armed Forces. Coming out of the London Opera House into Kingsway, Louise didn't notice them – her mind burning inwards on the impassioned speech she had just heard. The power of Christabel Pankhurst's personality had seemed to reach out from the stage to embrace them all. Nothing else mattered.

"Why, I do believe it's Louise Marshall!"

Louise was jolted back to earth. A woman in an elegant plum-coloured jacket and skirt was being pushed against her by the crowd flowing from the theatre doors. Under a large straw hat, grey eyes set

31

too close for good looks stared out from a pale face. A smile hovered round the small mouth, waiting for recognition.

"Una! I'd heard you were in London. I should have guessed you'd come to Christabel's meeting. Wasn't she wonderful?"

Una's smile blossomed, revealing two little rabbit teeth that sat on her bottom lip. "Very stirring. And so right – we women have long been ready 'to do what it is best in the interests of the state to do'. We're only waiting for our marching orders."

"You remember her exact words!"

"They aren't easy to forget."

The genteel voice that had always sounded slightly false brought back the old Birmingham days with a vividness edged by melancholy. As if the fight for the Vote had slipped unawares into the past and become nothing more than an old suitcase of memories to be carried around. Louise felt disturbed.

She asked hurriedly: "Have you moved to London permanently?"

"No. I'm visiting Maude. She's married – did you know? She and her husband live in Maida Vale."

"I hadn't heard. I'm rather out of touch."

Standing outside the Opera House, the crowd of women swirled round them, with here and there a man looking oddly out of place.

"Look at all these women!" Louise stared about her fiercely. "Just *look* . . . all that bottled-up skill and intelligence. So much energy walking away down the street, and it's the same throughout

Britain. Thousands of us. An army. We're all yearning to help – don't you feel like this, Una? Doesn't it drive you mad that when we offer to take over men's jobs so they are free to fight, we get nothing but rejection?"

Una slipped a hand under Louise's elbow. "We can't have a proper conversation in the middle of this crowd. Let's walk and talk as we go."

Louise was faintly surprised to find herself being capably steered between groups of people on their way towards the Strand.

"That's better. Now then, tell me what you have in mind. You were never one to sit down under adversity." Una beamed expectantly.

Louise gave a short laugh. "You're going to be disappointed. Since I came out of prison I've been idling away my time, living with my aunt. A hibernating social butterfly."

"Don't be so hard on yourself. I know you've been ill."

"Yes. I still get tired easily, but I'm on my feet again. My brother suggests I keep myself busy by returning to Birmingham and opening up The Tower House again. But what's the point? It's been shut up for so long – the place is a white elephant."

Una looked remorseful. "I was so sorry to hear that Mr Marshall had passed away. Such a gallant gentleman."

Louise was amused by this astonishing view of her irascible father, but managed not to smile. "I miss him, but I'm glad he didn't linger. He would have hated having to depend on other people to wash and feed him. Of course the house *had* to be shut up," she shrugged, as if trying to throw off a weight. "I want to sell, but Peter is being pigheaded. I've tried to make him see that to run it would be like managing a hotel. Impossible in wartime without enough staff. He just says, 'It'll tick over all right with you seeing to things' . . . isn't that just like a man? Housekeeping is a thorough bore. I told him, but all he did was laugh! Now he's in France I suppose the argument will drag on or get shelved."

"In France? Why, I saw him in Kensington Gardens not so long ago. He was strolling along with Emily Palmer." Una shot Louise a sly look; hesitated . . . and when she didn't respond, tried again: "I wonder if Emily came to Christabel's meeting? Did she mention it to you?"

"I haven't seen her for some time," Louise said coolly.

But Una was like a small terrier, worrying away. "I thought you two were so close. All that campaigning together. Remember that Music Hall act – what was it? 'Emmie and Lou, Plenty of Patter with Songs at the Piano'. How we all laughed! You really pulled the wool over the eyes of the police that time."

Louise hunted for safer ground. "Peter flew across the Channel last week."

"Flew across?" Una's little eyes rounded with astonishment.

"Yes. By aeroplane. He got his Aero Club licence last June and now has his own machine, so the RFC seemed obvious. They sent him to Oxford first, on a small arms course. Then he was posted. I had a letter yesterday. He sounds quite chirpy."

They had been walking freely side by side past tall dingy London buildings, with the strip of sky growing darker and the gas lamps unlit. A hansom cab glided past like a shadow in the twilight. Una halted suddenly and put a gloved hand on Louise's arm.

"Men have all the luck, all the action, don't they? If we were two men now, we'd go to the nearest public house and have a long chat over a glass of beer. There's so much I want to hear about your experiences in prison – what it's like to be forcibly fed, how you coped, how you went back *again*. You're famous, you know! We are all so proud of you." Una's real self seemed to have burst through layers of well-schooled reserve. "I know exactly what you mean about being rejected, but there *is* something you could do."

"Don't suggest First Aid. The time I went to a lecture, they had a mock patient – a Boy Scout swathed in bandages like a mummy. Nothing to do with war – just like playing! And it was all I could do not to laugh. Besides, I'm hopeless about blood. Makes me faint."

"Nothing like First Aid. I don't mean to be pushy, but you do seem in need of some direction. If that sounds impertinent, forgive me, but I've always admired your gifts and can't bear to see them going to waste. The government is crying out for people like you."

Louise wished she would come to the point. "What are you talking about?"

"Rousing speeches! Christabel is a genius on a platform – such intellect, but you have a way of appealing to the heart that is all your own. If anyone could persuade men to volunteer, it's you."

She means every word, Louise thought, touched but a little uneasy. "That's very flattering."

"Flattery hasn't anything to do with it. I'm speaking the truth. Don't forget that if I can coax you to make enlistment speeches I shall be doing my bit for the war too!" She peered into Louise's face. "Are you willing? We could begin this Saturday. Maude is helping to run a church fête and there should be plenty of people – a lot of them men. What do you say? I'll arrange everything."

The evening, starting with Christabel's stirring call, and continuing into the blacked-out street with this voice from the past, began to take on a strange atmosphere of unreality. Powers outside herself had moved in, guiding her fate.

"All right. As you seem so sure I could do it. Though it's ages since I was on a platform."

"I'm positive."

They walked on, Louise silent, Una chattering about arrangements. At a cab rank they kissed goodbye.

Louise climbed into a taxicab, glad to be on her own. Her thoughts were all over the place – the drive would allow her time to calm down. She gave the address to the cabdriver – he looked old, too old to enlist. But what would happen if all the *young* cabbies and tram drivers, carters, postmen and the rest, became soldiers? She examined her thin

36

hands, turning them over. They looked capable enough.

"You could drive an omnibus," she told them. "You . . . and you," hitching up her skirt and speaking to her feet in their grey suede shoes. "Maybe even an ambulance!"

She rejected the last idea. No, she couldn't face the sickening sight and smell of gaping wounds and severed limbs. She shuddered – but her spirits refused to stay crushed. At least she had *something* to do now. A direction at last. Satisfaction stole over her. Relaxing back against the seat, she looked out at the people on the pavements with a feeling of good will.

The vicarage garden looked tired and dispirited. Dust coated the leaves of the laurels, and the regimented rows of stocks were wilting from lack of rain. But the stalls were festive, and there was a small crowd standing on the thirsty yellow lawn.

Louise smiled at them across the table that was spread with a Union Jack, feeling a thrill of intense anticipation. A flower-decked photograph of King George and Queen Mary sat solemnly next to a carafe of water. Everything, everyone was waiting. She took a deep breath to steady her voice.

"Ladies and gentlemen, I don't intend to keep you away from the White Elephant stall and those delicious cakes for too long, but may I steal just a few moments . . . no more, I promise. I'm as eager as you are to try my luck at the Hoop-La! Have you seen that star prize!"

The little ripple of laughter was encouraging. As it died away she let her smile fade.

"I have something to share with you . . . something of great importance that cannot wait. This is such a lovely day, isn't it? – the sun shining down on us at this fête as we enjoy ourselves with our friends and our families – it breaks my heart to have to remind you that all this," opening her arms to them, to the dusty garden, trees, road, London rolling away beyond under the shining sky, "everything we hold so dear, is being threatened. A storm seems to be gathering, indeed has already broken, over Europe. We all know how our gallant allies in Belgium and France are fighting to overcome the might of Germany – and let's not make any mistake about how powerful that is – the Belgians and French are fighting for freedom! Imperial Germany intends to roll across their two countries, across the Channel, across our England, crushing every spark of resistance. We are to be taken over. Our towns and villages, our fair meadows and woods, our very selves will be owned by foreigners who won't hesitate to turn us into slaves. That is the plan. It isn't idle gossip or a scrap of rumour that has grown with the telling. It is the plain truth."

She paused, gripping the edge of the table, making the water in the carafe tremble. The people listening were perfectly still. She leaned towards them, studying face after face until the silence was absolute. Then, in a quiet voice, she asked:

"Do you know how far it is from Dover to Calais?"

There was a shiver of movement; a shaking of heads.

"Twenty-one miles. Travel another twenty and you will be at the battle front. Forty-one miles, my friends, less far than from this garden to Salisbury. Imagine – Salisbury has been taken by the Germans . . . and at what cost. Hundreds of people are dead or imprisoned. The lovely cathedral is a burnt, empty shell. Many of the beautiful old buildings lie in ruins. From its boundaries, wave after wave of troops, fully armed with rifles, cannon, and all the latest machinery of war, are marching and riding out along the road to London – crack troops – Uhlans, Prussians – men trained to despise ordinary feelings of humanity and kindliness. This army is rolling forward, murdering, pillaging, destroying everyone and everything that dares to oppose it as it travels nearer and nearer to us, here in this garden. Is this fantasy? It sounds like it, doesn't it? Impossible! But, my friends, in Belgium and France *this has already happened*! Is happening as I speak now!"

She paused again, feeling the tension between herself and the listeners like a live thing. As the silence reached breaking point, she said:

"I am a woman. I cannot take up arms and go to war, join our brave men who have already gone overseas to help their comrades and save our beloved country. But I can and will do whatever is in my power to prevent this horror from destroying all I hold dear. I plead with all of you to do the same, no matter how small a thing it may be. If enough grains of sand come together, a mountain will grow. A mighty mountain, capable of withstanding every evil. And you men – I beg you to give yourselves to the service of your king and country. We, your wives and children, your sisters and sweethearts . . . we urge you to fight for us and this beautiful land of ours. We will support you in every way. We will work for you, care for you, nurse you, keep everything shining and ready to welcome you home as heroes when the task is done. Don't let time trickle away. Every second counts. If any of you here have the courage and are able to enlist now, our recruiting sergeant will be happy to give you the king's shilling and sign you into the company of gallant men who have already gone to swell His Majesty's forces overseas. Who is going to be the first brave man? Don't delay . . . who will answer the call?"

Her words were drowned in a spontaneous cheer and loud clapping as a young man began to push through the crowd which parted to let him pass. Another older man followed, then another and another . . .

Louise joined in the clapping, beaming at them. "Thank you, thank you." Nobody could hear, but she didn't care, watching the men gathering in front of the recruiting sergeant's table.

The crowd was applauding Louise now. She smiled back at the sun-hot faces and, as the clapping began to die down, added: "I'm grateful to you for giving me your time, and my special thanks to those men so courageously answering their country's call." The hovering sense of triumph that had been gathering strength as she spoke now wrapped round her. She was back in harness! She saw Aunt Gertrude glowing with approval under her parasol. Maude, a plumper version of sister Una, was coming towards her.

"You were marvellous, Louise, simply marvellous. You had them eating out of your hand."

"I was hoping they would enlist," Louise said dryly.

"Well, you've succeeded! You always did know how to sway a crowd." Maude looked at her with admiration. "I remember saying so to Emily Palmer that very first time she came to one of our gatherings. By the way, did you know she's working for Sylvia Pankhurst now? At her place in the Old Ford Road. Some sort of clinic, I believe."

Louise saw Maude's carefully pruned eyebrows twitch up and heard the unspoken disapproval. A little of the sense of triumph receded. She said: "Emily and Sylvia are well matched. Both are full of human kindness and mistaken ideas."

"Emily always was rather an oddity, don't you think? Not exactly one of us." Maude seemed determined to have her say. "But I would have thought she'd stick with Mrs Pankhurst and Christabel when Sylvia broke away. After all, she's worked so closely with you, and I know you aren't a backslider."

The sun was very hot. Louise took a handkerchief from her Dorothy bag and dabbed at the perspiration on her face, then opened her parasol. "I'd love some lemonade if there is any left." She was not going to talk about Emily.

"Of course. Over here." Maude led her to one of the little tables spread with a red-checked cloth. She fetched two glasses and sat down with Louise. "Tell me your plans. You will naturally be carrying on with this splendid work?"

"Naturally!" Louise tucked some straying hairs back under her hat. "Una's already forging ahead with plans. She's a wonder, your sister."

"Oh I know. So organized. She puts me to shame." Maude sighed. "Tell me, where is the meeting to be?"

"Hyde Park."

Maude was impressed. "At Speakers' Corner?" Her little eyes widened.

Louise nodded. "Yes, but shhh . . ." she jerked her head towards Aunt G who was homing in, parasol held like a sceptre. She arrived with Una, both of them overflowing with congratulations and the urgent request for Louise to come and present the prize for the best home-made cake.

"I don't know what has got into you, Louise. You walk in, cool as a cucumber, and insist you will make an exhibition of yourself . . . *in public*! You are quite shameless. Hyde Park – Speakers' Corner indeed! A bunch of rabble-raisers, that's what those dreadful people are, standing and shouting at respectable people out for a quiet stroll. It's disgraceful! To think that a niece of mine should even consider such a thing, let alone do it, well . . ." Aunt G's wattles quivered. If Louise had suggested joining the Tiller Girls and going on the stage, she couldn't have been more shocked.

42

"I don't see why you object. I shan't be campaigning for the Vote." Louise sat down at the breakfast table. "I thought you approved. You did at the fête."

"That was Church," Aunt G said stiffly. "Hyde Park is different." Her tone marked down the green open space with its shady trees as a den of vice. "And on a *Sunday*," she repeated. "I simply can't think what has got into you, Louise."

"Men get killed on Sundays just the same as any other day," Louise said tartly. The conversation was becoming ridiculous! She felt her temper rising.

"It isn't as if I'm not aware of the importance of urging men to enlist," Aunt Gertrude went on, hands trembling. "But you do seem peculiarly gifted with the most unfortunate way of picking wrong methods, Louise. If only you had mentioned this earlier, I could have asked Mrs Winthrop to let you speak at her bring-and-buy sale in aid of the War Effort next Tuesday . . ."

"I'll do that too," Louise interrupted.

"You mean you still intend . . ."

"Yes."

Aunt Gertrude's restraint shattered. "I forbid it! I'm sorry, but I have a duty to you since your poor father died. He left you in my care. Until you are of age I cannot allow you to go on making an exhibition of yourself. First that shocking Vote nonsense, now this *public* speaking."

"Oh for God's sake!"

"Lou*ise*!"

"Well, what d'you expect? You talk as if I've spent my life wrapped in cotton wool. I'm not a child. I've been out in that jungle," she pointed at the window towards the street. "I've been jeered at, imprisoned, had tubes stuffed down my throat . . ."

"I will not listen to this . . . this brazen talk. While you are in my house you will behave like a lady. You object to being treated like a child, but if you insist on acting like a rude little girl, you bring it on yourself. You seem to think that the world revolves round you. What *you* want; what *you* decide. There are other people, Louise. I have standards and *you* will respect them."

It was a battle of wills. For a moment there was a loaded silence. The scent of fresh coffee filled the morning room. A dish of orange preserve was dappled with sunlight shining through trees and window. The honeypot sat between toastrack and glass butter-shell. Royal Worcester porcelain, silver knives, starched napkins. Across this civilized table the two women glared at each other.

"It's clear you've never been on a platform that was invaded by police," Louise said, voice low and passionate. "Maybe when you've been seized, thrown about, had your breasts twisted till you could scream with pain, it will change you. I can tell you, childhood is left behind. You grow up *fast*."

She saw Aunt Gertrude's jaw drop, face ablaze, but there was no joy in making her speechless. The burst of smoking temper cooled and dwindled almost as quickly as it had come. Louise stood up quickly and had to grip the back of her chair to steady herself. Her whole Suffragette experience concentrated in her head, jamming the wheels of her mind. She could scarcely think. The walk to the door seemed like a hundred miles. As she closed it, a great flood of envy swept through her.

It wasn't fair! Pete was out there, flying free. *Involved*. While she was trapped. Just because she was a woman . . . oh damn him . . . damn Aunt G . . . damn everything!

Going out of the house, she plodded to the mews where the Maudslay was parked alone in the stables. No horses now. Even they were allowed to go to the war!

Opening the bonnet without caring about grease on sleeves or bodice, Louise set about checking the plug leads, hose, and the fan belt.

~CHAPTER 4~

Belgium – 24 October 1914

Dear Lou,

I hang my head in shame. Can you ever forgive me for forgetting your birthday – your *twenty-first* birthday, which makes it all the worse? I don't know what to say, except that I forgot, which is no proper excuse but is the truth. We have been exceptionally busy for the past few weeks. I'm not allowed to say more – I hope you understand? The bottle of scent is the best present I could find at the nearest shops, which are at some distance from the airfield. I'll make it up to you when we meet.

Thanks for your parcel (coals of fire on my head!). That splendid Dundee cake didn't last long. Bob Jupe, another mad pilot, would have wolfed the lot if I had not kept an eye on him! He says did you make it? I suspect it is one of Mrs Meery's, but if I'm wrong, look out for Bob as a prospective suitor – he's on the hunt for a wife who can cook. (I'm only joking!)

Seriously, I've slotted into life out here. We have plenty of opportunities for flying, and my billet is comfortable enough. I wonder how things are with you? Auntie Gertie's letter said you are making recruiting speeches now. Well, well, little sister, you are full of enterprise! Is Emily in on this? She didn't mention it in her last letter. I hope you two have made up your differences.

Look, Lou, I've been going over all we said about The Tower House. See your point about size, work, so on. But out here is different. The old place is Home. Born there. Can't face parting with home. Something to hang on to. Stupid! Bear with me till this madhouse is over – Christmas they say.

Love, P.

Louise folded the letter which had arrived by yesterday's post, with the little crystal bottle of lilac perfume. She had read the letter several times with mixed feelings – part irritation caused by guilt over the unhealed rift between herself and Emily, but the greater part was anxiety for him. A typical Peter letter, to begin with. Breezy. Bold scrawl. Then lapsing into a jerky scribble at the end with smudges of ink. Something about the last paragraph (more than just the messy writing) left her uneasy. Nothing she could put her finger on, but it just wasn't the Pete she knew.

The crisp sunny day wouldn't let her brood too long. She went round to the mews. Her unease about Peter sank into the back of her mind as she wound the Maudslay into life, and climbing in, swung out into Holland Park Avenue. The Sunday road was wide and inviting – almost free of traffic. Exhilarated, she changed gear, driving up to Notting Hill Gate and skimming towards Marble Arch, then down Park Lane. After days of armed truce with Aunt G, Louise felt free as a bird. There was nowhere she could not fly! Dutifully she landed in Park Lane, turning off into a side street to leave the car, then, crossing to Hyde Park Corner, began to walk through the park.

Una was already there, wooden platform in place, recruiting sergeant at his table, and a small ready-made audience waiting.

"A few listeners always attract others," Una said briskly. "People are so nosy, I find."

"Thanks so much," Louise smiled at her. "You've thought of everything."

"I do my best." Una's little rabbit teeth held on to her bottom lip as she patted her bag. "I've got a final touch tucked away, just in case."

"What's that?"

Una beamed, ignoring the question. "The best of luck, my dear. I know you'll be a success."

Other speakers were in full flow. Under a nearby plane tree a one-armed man proclaimed the end of the world on Saturday week. Another was preaching some kind of revolution.

There were no women speakers and Louise was glad she had taken trouble with her appearance. As she stepped on to the platform, Emily, as often these days, walked uninvited into her thoughts. For an instant Louise thought she saw her amongst the crowd, her solid figure was so clear in her mind. She shook off the unwelcome fancy, smiling with studied warmth at the waiting people.

"Good morning, my friends . . . I want to ask you some questions. Who of you here wish to see German troops drilling in this park, who of you here wish to be slaves . . .?"

Her voice rang out, clear, cultured, full of emotion, words flowing with such practised ease and confidence that passers-by paused casually for a second look. Some were drawn into the crowd, pulled by her compelling presence. Others stood back on the grass, and on the edge of these a young man, propped on a shooting stick, stared intently.

She was a curiosity. Young, good-looking, beautifully turned out in peach silk and fine straw hat that set off her coppery hair . . . not at all the usual Sunday speaker. "The way you look matters," she had once told Emily. "Clothes are part of the trade if you intend climbing on platforms. We're like actors. Have you noticed how Mrs Pankhurst and Christabel are always superbly dressed?" Emily could only nod, mouth full of pins as she had fitted Louise's new spring suit.

The memory intruded, and Louise spread out her hands, forcing herself to think only of her appeal: "England needs you as never before, men and women alike. But it is to you men here now, I say with a full heart – answer General Kitchener's call! Give yourselves generously . . ." Scanning her audience, seeking eye contact, she noticed the intent, still gaze. It was this stillness rather than the smart grey suit or shooting stick that caught her attention. She glanced back, and at that instant he lifted his jaunty bowler with a small bow.

She inclined her head, including him in the smile she was giving away to everyone, then began to build up to a rousing finale, which was greeted by a burst of applause. Nodding and smiling, she waited until the first men moved towards the recruiting table before stepping down.

"You were splendid, Louise. Had them hanging on every word, didn't she, Grace?" Una's sharp gaze darted round the lingering crowd, came back to Louise and darted away again.

"Indeed, yes." A stout middle-aged woman with a St John Ambulance brassard round her plump arm shook Louise's hand warmly. "I'm so pleased to meet you at last. Una has talked about you a lot, and I want to hear much more. But may I ask a favour first?"

"Of course." Louise was watching Una walk away.

"Una said you came by car."

"Yes, I did." The crowd had thinned and she saw Una again, in front of the man on the shooting stick, holding out something that looked like a leaf.

Grace was looking round. "I had hoped for a word with her before I went. Where's she gone?"

Louise pointed, observing several other people look in the same direction. She heard Grace suck in her breath. An elderly man in a cloth cap called out:

"'Ere, that's a bit quick off the mark, miss! Give the bloke a chance."

Somebody shouted: "Mind yer own business, Alf, she's only doing what's right."

"Oh dear!" Grace said. "A white feather! Una always is too hasty. If it was me I'd want to know more before calling a man a coward in public."

An argument broke out as people paused to see what was going on.

"Look at 'im – dressed like a toff, and no guts."

"Let the bloke speak for himself. You can't condemn him out of hand."

"Well, *I* can tell a coward when I see one, even if you can't. My boy was killed out at Mons. *He* didn't hang back."

Louise became aware of curious glances coming her way. She thought: of course, they are associating me with Una . . . making me part of this white feather business! Indignation swept through her. She saw the feather accepted and twirled between finger and thumb. Heard Una say:

"Where is your sense of honour?" as it was tucked neatly into the grey breast pocket.

The young man tipped his bowler gravely.

"Oh, I've no patience!" Una turned away, and opening her bag, took out another badge of cowardice.

Getting to his feet the young man clipped the handles of his shooting stick together and limped towards Louise, passing her without any sign of recognition, though she was close enough to see the intense blue of his eyes. Child's eyes, she thought, but no child ever had eyes set in such a fretwork of ageing lines.

"I'd like to give Una a piece of my mind!" Grace glanced at her watch. "I'm sorry to bother you, but could you give me a lift to Charing Cross station? I got so interested listening to you, I quite forgot the time. I'm supposed to be at the canteen in fifteen minutes, before the hospital train arrives."

"Of course!" Louise was glad to move away.

Grace proved a talker and Louise was grateful not to have to make conversation as they drove towards the station. The white feather incident had called up disturbing memories of her campaigning days – mindless injustices caused by people forgetting to think before acting. White feathers for cowards were all right, but Una had jumped to conclusions that had been all wrong.

At Charing Cross she listened with half an ear to Grace's profuse thanks, waiting until she had disappeared before discreetly following her into the station.

Inside, she paused and took stock. Anxious relatives crowded as close as they could to the barriers. She went nearer, but kept apart from them, gazing at the ordered chaos.

Bearers carrying empty stretchers hurried to the platform. Porters towed trucks loaded with boxes or urns of tea and food. Ambulance cars were lining up. Drivers and orderlies stood beside their vehicles. Several of the new VAD nurses in uniforms of grey or blue, red crosses bright on caps and aprons, were pushing wheelchairs towards the platform where the hospital train was due any minute.

The full brassy sound of a bugle blared suddenly, cutting through the hum and clatter. Whistles shrilled. Louise felt the tightening of expectancy. Saw drivers, stretcher-bearers, orderlies, nurses, canteen staff position themselves like well-drilled troops. All sense of chaos vanished. On the platform were other trucks spread with white cloths holding tea urns, mugs, buns, sandwiches, cigarettes. Each wheelchair had its attendant VAD. Porters spread out. The train's whistle screeched. Pressed back against the wall, Louise felt the rumble of the approaching locomotive pulse through her body, and saw the train at last, carriage after carriage, a long grey snake with red crosses painted on its sides.

A hush cocooned the waiting people as the engine rolled slowly towards the buffers and, wheezing, came to a halt. Doors began to open and as the first soldiers stepped on to the platform a cheer rose towards the pigeons roosting on the roof girders. People began clapping spontaneously, Louise with them. She couldn't help it, stirred to her roots at the sight of these tired men, some in stained khaki, some in a strange muddle of clothes that were nothing to do with uniform. They came with arms in slings, heads bandaged, leaning on sticks, on orderlies, on nurses, but it was true what she had heard. They were all cheery. More than that, she decided, they seemed *jubilant*. They grinned and joked with the women behind the urns, accepting mugs of steaming tea, food, cigarettes, and being gently persuaded towards waiting ambulance cars, or tumbling into the open arms of their families.

Louise envied them. They had gone willingly to the battle front, been wounded for a glorious cause, and duty done, were home again to be fêted and nursed back to health. Heroes!

Now the wheelchairs were passing, and a steady stream of ambulance cars began to leave the station. Replacements drove in for the stretcher cases – some still smiling, others, motionless shapes under their red blankets, with grey faces and closed eyes, or masked by bandages with only peepholes to look out at the world. Louise heard groans, and once a muffled scream when a stretcher slipped as it was being loaded. Oh poor boys, she thought, poor poor boys!

Gradually the crowds lessened and disappeared. Nearly all the ambulances had gone. Louise would have gone as well, but she noticed one last ambulance car backing closer to the platform. She lingered in the shadow between a newspaper kiosk and a wall, watching a single stretcher emerge from the far end of the train. The stretcher-bearers handled it with great care. As it came closer she saw the usual red blanket, which twitched a little, as if the man beneath was lying on pins. His partly bandaged face seemed to be in shadow. But there was something wrong. She could see the bandage clearly which meant there was no shadow. And then, almost at the last minute as the stretcher was taken into the ambulance, she knew.

It wasn't a shadow, *it was a hole*. Where cheek, nose and mouth should have been, there was nothing but a cavern.

The shock was overwhelming. Her stomach clenched and her brain shrank. She had to lean against the kiosk for support, closing her eyes as she fought to stay conscious. The ambulance engine started up. She heard the rumble of its wheels as it began to move away. How long she stayed there, she didn't know, but at last, feeling able to trust her legs, she walked haltingly, like an old woman, out into the forecourt and across to the waiting Maudslay. A policeman offered to swing the starting handle. Louise was grateful. Trembling, she began to drive back to Holland Park.

~CHAPTER 5~

Corporal Mechanic Gordon Box, hands covered in engine oil, climbed down from the fuselage of the Sopwith Tabloid and eased the crick in his back. He was cold and starving hungry, but felt a glow of satisfaction. He knew he'd done a good job on the old girl. Wiping his hands on a piece of grimy rag, he glanced across briefly at yesterday's shattered Farman, with only its tail and wheels recognizable; the rest was matchwood. Crushed to death like its pilot.

Four kites gone in the last fortnight, Gordon thought dismally. Gathering his tools, he began to walk back towards a huddle of sheds on the far side of the airfield. Smells of frying bacon wafted downwind from the canteen kitchen, but he resolutely swerved away towards the officers' mess. Outside the door he swapped his tool kit from one hand to the other and knocked.

No reply.

Pushing open the door, he peered inside. As he did so, the pudgy duty orderly came through the doorway leading from the kitchen beyond.

Gordon eased himself out of the biting wind. "Seen Cap'n Marshall about, Nobby?"

"Went to his billet half an hour back." Nobby Clarke slyly winked a small pale eye. "With a couple of pals!" He jerked his head towards a crate standing in the middle of a trestle table against the wall. "Haig's best. Two full bottles. Weren't his only snifter neither."

"Bloody 'ell!" Gordon said profoundly.

Nobby sniggered and began to clatter knives and forks on to a tray as he prepared to set places for the next officers needing a meal. The sight of a green and white checked cloth switched Gordon back to his home in Coventry where a similar cloth was spread on the kitchen table. His ma was bending to open the range oven, and the remembered smell of faggots cooking was so potent, so delicious, that his longing for home and a good blow-out almost knocked him over.

"Looking for someone, Box?"

Gordon came back to the borders of Flanders and France, bitter cold and an empty stomach, with a jolt. "Cap'n Marshall, sir. Clarke tells me he's in his quarters, sir." He moved aside to let Major Hartwell pass, watching him unwind the long red scarf from his bull-like neck and take off leather gauntlets.

"When you find him, tell him to come *directly* to the mess. *Directly*, mind you. Any problems with Flossie?"

"She's dandy, sir."

"Good. She's needed *directly*," he stressed the word for the third time.

Something's up, Gordon thought. With a silent regretful goodbye to the bacon wad and cuppa he had promised himself, he saluted smartly and began to tramp back along the muddy path. He aimed this time for a group of huts nestling behind a clump of stunted trees. The trunks showed clearly the direction of the prevailing winds as they leaned like old hunched men towards the east, giving up last leaves to the strong southwesterly whining through their gnarled branches. From the south, Ypres way, came the rumble of heavy artillery. Some poor bastards are getting it, Gordon thought. A sudden gust of bitter wind cut through his clothing and he felt his flesh begin to shrivel. Christ, this place could freeze the tits off a marble statue! He shivered and wished fervently he had put on the bodywarmer Ma had knitted, even though it was several sizes too big.

Clustered together as if for protection, the huts had gravelled paths in between. Someone had painted street names in green on their grey sides: Walnut St, Acacia Ave . . . Halting at the third door along in Paradise Row, Gordon knocked. There was silence for several seconds.

He was about to knock again when a voice, slightly thickened round the edges, called:

"Who is it?"

"Me, sir. Box, sir. Come to report that Flossie is as good as new and real skittish. Raring to go, sir."

"Right. Thanks." The door remained closed.

Gordon, perished by now, fingers nerveless with cold, began to say: "There's something else, sir . . ." when he dropped the bag of tools painfully on one icy foot. The bag yawned, spewing spanners, screwdrivers and spare nuts and bolts in all directions. "Jesus!" Gordon lurched about, easing his foot, then crouched to pick up his scattered belongings. On a level with the bottom of the door, he saw it open, revealing a pair of down-at-heel leather slippers, khaki socks and the hem of a shabby blue dressing gown.

"You all right?" asked the voice belonging to the slippers and khaki legs.

"Yessir," Gordon retrieved the last of his tools and fumbled with the strap.

"You'd better come in. Give me that bag before you drop it again."

Gordon stood up, reluctantly handing over the bag, but hesitating on the threshold.

"Well, come in, man!"

He still hesitated.

"Come in, dammit! I'm freezing if you aren't." The note of command brought Gordon inside. "Shut the door!"

He shut it and stood awkwardly trying to flick some life back into his numbed hands. Then he recalled the message. "Major Hartwell says to tell you to go to the mess straight away, sir." For the first time Gordon looked directly at Captain Marshall, pilot of Flossie and veteran of four months' flying time, and saw bloodshot eyes swimming in pouches of red patchy skin. His glance slid sideways to the half empty whisky bottle and empty tumbler on the floor beside the army cot.

A small primitive coke stove crackled and glowed, giving off pleasant warmth and unpleasant fumes. Peter Marshall nodded towards it.

"You'd better thaw yourself out. And get this down you." He splashed whisky into the tumbler and held it out. "I suppose you've been working since God knows when. That hangar's like an icebox."

"Been on the field mostly, sir. Thanks!" Gordon took the whisky gratefully, noticing with some misgiving how much Peter's hand shook. "Bartlett helped me push her out." The whisky burrowed into his stomach, leaving a glowing trail that soothed away some of the unease at being in an officer's billet, drinking officer's grog, warming himself at an officer's stove. He could not imagine this happening with any other officer in the Wing. But then, Captain Marshall wasn't like other officers. An oddball. Nobby said he was a bit touched up top, but you could say the same of a lot. Some pilots crumbled after only a few weeks. He didn't envy them their flights into hell.

Gordon took another drink, feeling his finger ends pulse into painful life, and saw the captain sit down rather too suddenly on the edge of his cot. A letter carelessly left on the blanket rose with the sudden air pressure and fluttered to the wooden floorboards. As Peter leaned down to pick it up, Gordon had a close-up view of his bloodshot eyes and saw how the trembling of his hand was so great he had difficulty in grasping the cheap paper. "Emily", he read, as the captain strove to control his muscles by clenching his fists and tucking his elbows into his sides. Nothing seemed to help, and time was slipping away. Recognizing the signs, Gordon tried to weigh up whether or not to get back and try some delaying tactics on the major, who wasn't called the Hornet for nothing . . . he'd be buzzing soon! The thought died almost as it was born, but Gordon felt he had to do something. He put the tumbler back on the floor.

"Thanks for the warm and the drink, sir. I'd best be off." He tried to make his tone light. "Should I say you're on your way?"

The spasms had increased, running from arms into body. Peter did not answer, but raised his head and met the anxious eyes of the corporal who over the past four strenuous months had stepped from his position of being merely a capable mechanic and had become almost a friend – without the imprisoning strings that friendship usually demanded. His gaze travelled on to the whisky bottle. Gordon, understanding, retrieved the tumbler and poured out a generous measure. Taking it, spilling some but gulping down most, Peter closed his eyes and let out a gasp. Slowly his mutinous nerves began to give in and obey. When he opened them again, Gordon was looking at him with the familiar half-frozen smile always there in moments of tension.

"Get going, Corporal!" Peter looked down at his twitching arms. "I'll spruce up and be along in a brace of shakes." He burst into a tense laugh. "Hear that? *A brace of shakes*!"

"Sir!" Gordon saluted briskly and collected his tool kit.

Each was well aware that the other knew this was not the first attack by the demon that lay in wait, biding its time, testing its power every now and again.

"A brace of shakes," Peter repeated, his laugh dissolving into a giggle. He did not get up.

Gordon, understanding everything, dared to put out his free hand and let it brush Peter's shoulder on his way to the door. Then he went out, quietly closing it behind him.

In the bitter dawn of the following morning an early March sun nibbled at the horizon, breaking away small pieces of darkness, revealing a glaze of iced primrose light. The blustery wind of the night had dropped a little and a light frost tipped grass blades and the struts of the three aeroplanes lined up and ready for take off. Flossie, the Sopwith Tabloid, her sturdy little frame with the double wing span laced with a tracery of fine wires, was leader. Next to her was a Bristol Scout, and then a much-repaired Farman.

Gordon, wearing most of the clothes he possessed, including his ma's bodywarmer, was preparing to swing Flossie's propeller, waiting only for Captain

Marshall to climb into the cockpit and give him the order. Two other mechanics waited, blowing on their cold fingers and stamping their feet. Gordon eyed the captain over carefully and felt a trickle of relief. No sign of the demon!

Peter finished buckling the chinstrap of his leather helmet but let his goggles rest on the top of his head. Tucking his gauntlets under an armpit, he felt inside his sheepskin over-jacket.

"Keep this for me, Corporal." He pulled out an envelope. "If I turn up, you can let me have it back again . . . till the next time. If I don't . . . just see that she gets it." He didn't say who, and turned away as if to prevent any questions.

Gordon glanced at the address. "Miss Emily Palmer, The Mother's Arms, Old Ford Road, Whitechapel, London". A barmaid! So that was it! The cheap paper fell into place along with the request to "See that she gets it". Emily was no next-of-kin who would receive a letter of condolence from the CO if the worst came to the worst. But she must matter. Gordon smiled and slid the envelope into his pocket, looking up towards the cockpit.

Settling himself, Peter began the routine check of instruments and controls after first touching the point of each elbow then the tip of his nose before adjusting his goggles. The habit was absurd and he knew it. A superstition born out of his first flight over Flanders when he had pretended to cross himself as a joke, laughing with FitzGerald, in the cockpit of the plane alongside. FitzGerald had not returned from that op. He had. From that moment he could not have omitted this farcical ritual even if he had wanted to. Satisfied that everything was in order, he switched on the ignition, looking down at Gordon. He shouted:

"Switch's on. Contact!"

Gordon put all his strength into swinging the propeller, timing precisely when to nip out of reach of the whistling blades.

Peter's stomach nerves tightened with the onset of a fearful exhilaration as the engine roared into life. Sweet as a nut, he thought, but then it would be. Box knew his job. He waved to Gordon to take away the chocks, his hand on the throttle increased the revs, and he felt the first pull from Flossie as she began to taxi into position for take-off into the wind. He glanced at the Scout, then the Farman, seeing the goggled helmeted heads rising from their cockpits, scarcely recognizable now as Bradley and Jupe. Only Jupe's curling carroty moustache was individual, marking him out as a known person. An intense irritation scrubbed at Peter's mind.

"I'll bloody tell him to shave the thing off before next time," he muttered, hating the intrusion which had pushed uninvited into this clean other world of sky and cloud. He wanted to keep it like that – unsullied by the rotten everyday mess of war and death.

The irritation passed almost as quickly as it had appeared. He smiled a trifle grimly, then gave his attention to co-ordinating feet and hands, giving more throttle, and more, until the little craft could no longer resist the urge to be airborne and lifted her nose, leaving the frosted ground, sailing up into the cool pale blue of space.

The cold increased, but Peter, fortified with hot coffee generously laced with Haig's best, was warm enough to be able to ignore the wind searing round the screen and slicing through the scarf he had wound over mouth and nose. Sooner or later he knew the warmth would vanish. Cold was part of the price. For the present he dismissed it, and adjusting the throttle, put Flossie into a gentle cruise, looking over her side and down at the patchwork of fields and farms spreading innocently into the more sinister arms of a darker area on the horizon. A little winding muddy river, gilded by the rising sun, was alive with sunshine stars. The sight brought a shock. He had more than sixty operational flights under his belt, many of them from the present airfield. The scene should be unremarkable, but today was different. The sunshine stars pitchforked him back into another time, another world, when, floating above English fields, he had seen similar stars sparkling on the Thames below the wicker basket of the balloon that carried himself and Emmie towards Camber Sands for a picnic. Today was no picnic and Emmie was far away in London, but he felt the sense of her presence so strongly she might have been crushed up beside him in the cockpit. He could *smell* her. That mixture of sweet skin, Wright's coaltar soap and fresh-ironed linen. Another intrusion, and worse than the silly annoyance of Jupe's moustache, because it raised yearnings far more distracting and deadly.

He forced away the visions . . . Emmie pulling Suffragette leaflets out of her bloomers as they floated airborne over London; Emmie red-cheeked and sweaty as she cycled up the drive of The Tower House; Emmie painfully bumping noses with him at their first kiss; Emmie spread out temptingly on summer grass.

With considerable mental effort, Peter concentrated on altering Flossie's course enough to get a better sight of the landscape. The engine repaid him with a squirt of oil that sprayed his face and goggles. He wiped them clean with a rag kept tucked down by the pistol wedged against his leg, and focused on the dark area which was beginning to divide into the uneven shapes of the streets and houses of Ypres. The town looked different from his last flight. Less defined. Shells from both armies had done their work, smashing many of the buildings. Even the Cloth Hall, the grand central landmark, lay ruined, and at the foot of a chain of hills running along the east side of the savaged town was a sea of frozen mud. Blasted trees added to the desolation. A pattern of trenches and pitted roads this side looked deserted. Peter felt his gut tighten, knowing they were not deserted. An hour ago, before daybreak, they would have been alive with marching men, lorries, carts, horses, ambulance cars – all the paraphernalia of war. He searched for signs of enemy guns, enemy troops, and saw small puffs of white smoke coming in bursts from a ridge away to the left. The sound of Flossie's engine and the rush of air blocked out other sounds, but he knew the smoke meant gunfire. Artillery. He made a mental note of the position, categorizing the relation of trenches (new) to roads (old) in his head so he could draw them accurately on return to base. Aware of courting danger, he flew on towards the town, trying to seek out any hint of further new gun emplacements.

Suddenly, from the corner of his eye he saw the Farman pitch, then begin to roll. A stream of smoke fanned out from the tail and almost immediately the body of the aircraft burst into a wall of flame. With horror he knew exactly what had happened, though the reason was unclear. It was every pilot's nightmare. The fuel tank located just behind the cockpit had exploded, hit by a shell or bullet. The Farman, a ball of fire now, spun wildly, plummeting towards the ground, shooting out great licking tongues of orange and green, and something else. He saw the grotesque burning doll that was Bradley fall away and be hidden from sight by the wing tip of a plane flying directly below. He had just enough time to register that the Scout was wheeling away above when he felt Flossie lurch. A hail of flak came bursting up from what had seemed like desert land, and he forced the stick over hard to swing the little aircraft into a tight arc, his short-term aim to get her out of harm's way, meaning to reroute her back to the airfield if God was on his side. Only then did he see the German Taube properly, flown in apparently from nowhere. Flossie juddered and seemed to writhe like an animal in pain, the ragged movement passing into his own body and bringing with it bitter resentment. He was trying to gauge the extent of the damage done to her when the Taube swooped. He saw the eyes of the German pilot; saw him raise his arm and take aim with the pistol in his hand.

No time now for fine judgements. Forcing Flossie into a steep dive, Peter pulled her out of it hard so that every shaft and strut, every joint, every atom of her wounded frame screamed in protest. He sweated. The wind made discordant music through her wires as he was pressured back against the seat, cheeks and mouth remodelled into gargoyle shape. Blood drummed and throbbed in his ears, seeming to double in volume until he thought his head would burst. He knew he was taking dangerous chances. Experience warned him he was a hair's breadth from blacking out. And there was Flossie. Wounded protesting Flossie . . .

"You can do it, my beauty. You can . . . you can . . ." he didn't know what he was saying and, by instinct rather than careful thought, eased her into quieter flight. Every now and again she hicupped and the fuselage shook as if with fever, turning his resentment into wild bursting anger. Flossie was his, part of him like his arms and legs were part of him. How dare they cripple her! The Taube was still visible, and still chasing, though further away. But near enough for a pot shot, Peter calculated. He reached for the pistol.

It was then that the demon chose to strike. Awful uncontrollable shaking gripped his arms and forced the muscles to take instructions that were nothing to do with him. Peter swore, using every foul word he could dredge up, then abandoned even that release in the battle to tame the rebellious nerves that threatened to get between him and the control of the aircraft. He knew that already he had asked a lot of poor sick Flossie. Knew also that the Taube was gaining. There was really no choice and somehow he did the impossible, circling and climbing higher and higher. Two thousand feet; another five hundred. He brought the aeroplane back into straight flight, the effort costing him almost every last ounce of energy and bringing fresh sweat that iced along the rim of his helmet. He could taste frost crisping on the scarf where his breath had moistened it. An icicle formed on his nose. His eyebrows were rimmed, eyelashes stiffening, but these discomforts were lost in the greater pain of the mining that had begun again inside his skull. Hammer blows of a giant that blurred his vision. He could no longer feel his feet nor fingers and did not know whether or not his arms still shook.

"Keep awake, keep awake, keep awake . . ." he talked aloud, not hearing the words, but feeling them with clumsy enormous rubbery lips. "Keep awake, keep awake . . ."

The chain of words was the last conscious thing he remembered.

Nobby was the first to spot the little aircraft as he came out of the latrines. He saw its lurching flight and bellowed:

"TROUBLE!"

in case anyone was near enough to hear, then began to run in the direction of the hangar where Gordon and a couple of mates were working. An engine was roaring and he had to reach up and clout Gordon to get his attention – jabbing his finger skywards and yelling:

"FLOSSIE! TROUBLE!"

"Jesus!" Gordon bounded outside in time to see Flossie's sturdy shape still airborne, but losing height too fast as she lurched and yawed towards the airfield.

"Keep her up, keep her up," he prayed, beginning to run. He was vaguely aware of boots thudding behind him on the frozen grass, and heard a shout, but took no notice, pouring all his concentration into willing the little kite to make it to the safety of open ground. She skimmed the tops of the stunted trees beyond Paradise Row, missed the huts by inches and came bouncing in almost sideways on. The wheels churned at the hard ground as the shuddering aircraft slewed round and keeled over on to one wing, dislocating it. The wheels were lifted clean off the ground as the fuselage tipped, broke off at the tail, then fell back heavily, buckling the undercarriage, leaving a mess of splintered wood, torn fabric and tangled wires.

The engine was still idling when Gordon got there, the propeller slowly whipping the air. At first glance the cockpit seemed unharmed – but what was inside brought him up short.

"Christ Almighty!" Nobby breathed, coming up behind.

For an instant they stood, staring at the pilot.

Peter sat stiffly upright, fists in their gauntlets fiercely gripping the joystick, eyes wide open behind his goggles. A perfect unbroken icicle of frozen saliva hung from his chin.

Gordon reached forward suddenly and pulled off the goggles, but the eyes did not move.

"Christ Almighty!" Nobby repeated. "What's the matter with him? Is he still alive?"

Gordon didn't answer directly, but began wrenching at the harness. "Don't stand there like a bloody stone! Give us a hand before this whole soddin' lot goes up and we all get cooked!"

~CHAPTER 6~

As Christmas passed into a cold wet spring without any sign of the war ending, Louise could not get rid of the haunting memory of the faceless soldier. Feelings of horror conflicted with patriotism and she gave up the recruiting speeches. How could *anyone* go on living with half a face? How could she go on encouraging *anyone* to suffer such a fate? Explaining her feelings to Una produced a flood of words and no understanding. She tried in vain to shut the questions away, but the dreadful image kept springing to the forefront of her mind, always at the most inconvenient moments . . . in the middle of dinner; talking to Maude over the phone; as she walked into Lady Grant's sitting room crowded with Red Cross knitters. Each time she thrust it away unanswered because always there was a rush to do other things. For the moment she would escape, as now, waiting for the hospital train to arrive at Charing Cross.

"Aunt G says I'm getting dreadfully absent-minded," she told Mary as they spread margarine on bread for sandwiches.

Mary looked up briefly. "Does that worry you?"

"Not specially."

"Well, then!" Mary raised her precise eyebrows, and Louise grinned ruefully.

But later that night as she lay sleepless in the dark – always a time when stark truth rose up and confronted her – it all came back, and with twice the impact, ruining her efforts to follow Aunt G's instructions and "pull herself together".

"You are a dithering mess," she told herself. "What's gone wrong? You were always the one to push the ditherers, stir them, kindle their enthusiasm. Remember Emily; Vera . . . remember *Una*! It's as well she's gone back to Birmingham. She wouldn't have time for such feebleness."

In her most private thoughts, Louise admitted she found Una a sharp conscience-pricking thorn. Una wouldn't question, probe, have endless doubts. She would take a decision, have her plans worked out in a trice and get on and do whatever it was . . . but then Una was always so hasty!

Cutting sandwiches didn't come into the category of a decision at all. It had been a consequence of Grace and several other helpers going down with influenza, leaving the canteen desperately short-handed. Mary had been roped in at the same time.

73

But it was different for Mary, now a fully-fledged VAD with an office job.

Louise longed to sleep.

If only she could get rid of the feeling that everything she had fought for over the past years had turned to failure. She felt hollow. Futile. Yet Mrs Pankhurst had a point. What use was a vote if there was no country to vote *for*? So, war effort first. Sign on with the new War Service Register and wait . . . and wait. Even jobs in the munitions factories had evaded her. "Health not up to it", they had said when she applied. But was it really health? Wasn't she rejected because of her prison history? She was one of *them*. A wicked woman! A revolutionary!

The thoughts revolved and sleep would not come. Instead, Emily walked into her head along with Peter's words: "I hope you two have made up your differences . . ." pricking at her conscience. Since his departure for Flanders she had put off trying to get in touch with her old friend.

"But why should I take all the blame?" Louise looked at the glimmer of ceiling revealed by the moon. "She hasn't been in touch either. It isn't all my fault." What was Emily doing now? Was she still with Sylvia? Or had she gone into a factory? Maybe she was a nurse. She would do that splendidly. A little snort of sour laughter escaped. How ironic that it should be *Emily* with the easy choices. The girl from the backstreets of Brum, not the girl born with a silver spoon in her mouth.

The circling feelings began again. Affection, resentment, irritation, hurt . . . round and round.

She rolled over on one side . . . the other side . . . curled up . . . stretched out . . . At last in the small hours she dropped into a restless sleep.

What seemed like only moments later she was being shaken into wakefulness.

"Louise, you've overslept. You'll be late. Louise!"

She opened bleary eyes and saw Aunt Gertrude's expression of distress that didn't tie up with merely being late for the canteen. There was a letter in her hand.

"What is it?" Louise was immediately wide awake, heart hammering.

"Peter," an extraordinary sob escaped and a single tear trickled down one flabby cheek.

"Dead?" The word shot out before she had time to take in that it wasn't the buff-coloured telegram.

The old woman shook her head, and unable to speak, handed her the letter.

It was from the commanding officer of Peter's wing. Louise scanned the thin sheet.

Dear Madam,

I regret having to inform you that your nephew, Captain Peter Marshall, is at present in base hospital, receiving treatment after a difficult flight operation left him in a state of some nervous collapse. I am glad to be able to reassure you that he is physically unharmed, though at present unable to resume his duties.

I am, Madam, your obedient servant,
James Hartwell (Major)

Eight weeks later on a chilly Friday at the beginning

of May, a grey train marked with red crosses chugged away from Southampton docks and began the journey back to London. Several carriages had been modified into wards – compartments removed and replaced with lines of bunks. Other carriages, still unaltered, carried Tommies able to walk or at least sit out the miles to Charing Cross. Officers had their own compartments. In one of these were six men dressed in a motley collection of khaki uniform and pyjamas, wound round with woolly scarves, feet in seaboot socks, or in one case an enormous trench slipper. Four were playing cards, chatting and joking across a makeshift table of cardboard propped on their knees. The remaining two sat by the window – a dapper little man with clipped military moustache, a bandage round his head, and Peter. Both were gazing out as factories, houses and streets swept by and became meadows and woods.

Peter stared fixedly at the changing blur of scenery. Except for an intermittent shaking of his whole body, he attempted to sit stiffly still, hands tucked into the sleeves of his British Warm and gripping his wrists. For all the notice he took of them, the other passengers might not have existed. Only by detaching himself from contact with strangers could he resist the persistent sensation that he was about to disintegrate. At all costs he had to hold himself together. During the weeks at the base hospital in Rouen when he could scarcely move a muscle and the ward seemed peopled by leering hallucinations, he had discovered one lifeline. He used it now, muttering the absurd chant that conjured up the old carefree days and was his sole defence against attack.

"Sandbags, statometer, trowel, barometer, trail rope, grapnel, hamper, ripcord, map, Emily, Emily, Emily . . ."

The dapper man looked at him with concern and then smiled. "So you're in this ballooning game too, friend! Real ballooning by the sound of it, not just the old tethered kites."

Startled, Peter shot one glance at the man, then stared at the floor. The trembling began again in his arms and he was unable to speak.

"I'm an observer myself," the man went on easily. "Spent the last three months watching Jerry lines from one of those Drachens – bloody unwieldy things, aren't they? No wonder they nickname us the Nuts!" He paused as if to give Peter a chance to chip in, then added, pointing at his bandage: "Got a Blighty one a thousand feet up. Bloody lucky as things turned out. Given me my first home leave since I went over." His smile widened and he proffered his hand. "Nice to meet a fellow Ballunatic! The name's Wynn-Davies."

Peter stared in dismay at the stubby fingers with their fur of black hairs. The effort of clasping the hand even briefly was colossal, but he did it to prove that he had been right in asking to travel like any other man going home on sick leave – that he really could manage alone – then dropped the fingers as if they were red hot, shoving his hand back into the safety of his sleeve. He did not give his own name in return.

Wynn-Davies felt the trembling and said

77

sympathetically: "You've had it tough too, I can see. I expect you're glad of a breather."

Peter felt the words were an assault. He knew they were kindly meant, but there was no way he could join in any friendly exchange. His head squealed for silence so he could recapture order and make it through to the journey's end.

The look of concern returned to the other man's face. "Sorry, pal. Always did talk too much. I can see you've had it up to here!" The hairy fingers rose to bandage level. "I'll leave you in peace . . . Nature calls anyway!" He smiled, getting to his feet.

By exerting all his energy, Peter managed a slight nod as Wynn-Davies squeezed past the card players and out into the corridor, then left to himself, returned to the window, letting his eyes be mesmerized by the streaking lines of scrub and grass on the railway banks as he listened almost feverishly to the clack of wheels and heaving breath of the locomotive. From time to time his body jerked involuntarily, as if trying to break bonds, but gradually the spasms quietened. He did not notice that the dapper man failed to return, and he was able to channel any wandering edges of concentration into plans for surprising Emily. How astonished she would be to see him! Apple cheeks bunching into that warm smile . . . brown eyes sparkling . . . those strong hands held out in a wonder of delighted welcome . . . For the first time a small smile eased the new lines round his mouth, and as London's sprawl took over from the countryside, he felt a different tension that was tinged with pale pleasure. He had held the demon at bay and managed to travel home alone and unannounced.

"I don't believe it," Louise murmured.

"What's that?" Grace asked.

"Just seen an old . . . friend." From her place behind the tea trolley, Louise pointed to the crowd at the platform barrier. She muttered: "All of London and she has to be here!"

"You'll have to speak up, dear, I'm a bit deaf and you're on my wrong side."

"It doesn't matter." Louise saw Emily waving excitedly, delighted to see her in the old way. She felt a rush of pleasure, quickly followed by embarrassment as Emily beckoned. Her arm felt as heavy as a ton of bricks as she waved back. She mimed serving out food and drink from the trolley, shrugging.

Grace's eyes were sharper than her ears. She turned to the commandant. "She's time for a word with her friend, hasn't she?"

"If you look slippy." The commandant's bun under her black cap bounced as she nodded.

Reluctantly Louise threaded between the waiting wheelchairs and stretchers. Emily had pushed close to the barrier.

"I'm that pleased to see yo," she said eagerly. "It's been much too long. I never knew yo were working here. How are yo keeping?"

"Much better thanks. And you?"

Emily glanced down at her stocky self with a half-mocking laugh: "Fit as a flea. As usual. Got some news though."

79

"What's that? I can't stay more than a moment."

"Just that I've got another job – with Sylvia."

"I heard. Doing what?"

Emily looked faintly surprised. "Helping her down the East End with a welfare centre she's started. For mams and their kiddies. There's a clinic and a day nursery, but . . ."

Two blasts from a train whistle cut short what she was about to say. Other whistles followed, one of which Louise knew came from the canteen commandant.

"I'll have to go." Already the station was humming with activity. People scurrying. She turned away. Then sudden intense curiosity made her turn back. "Why are you here?"

"It's our Vic, he's copped a Blighty one."

"Nothing bad, I hope?" Louise recalled clearly how fond Emily was of this particular brother.

"Shot in the leg, but not that bad. Can't walk for now." Emily was grinning ear to ear, so it couldn't be very serious.

With a sudden rush of warmth for her, Louise caught her hand and squeezed it briefly. "I hope all goes well for you both," then hurried away.

The train was steaming slowly up the platform. As always, Louise was moved almost to tears by the sight of the heads peering from open carriage windows. Strained haggard faces brightening with smiles, arms stretched out, waving to the waiting wives, mothers, children, lovers.

"Real British tea . . . not tasted the like since I left . . ."

"Ham sandwiches, darlin' . . . *ham* sandwiches . . .

Charlie, d'y'see that . . . *ham sandwiches* . . ."

"Thanks, love – and ten Woodbines."

"Got any coffee, princess?"

"Here, they've got fruit cake, Jock . . ."

Requests, thanks, jokes, everywhere. Louise felt as if her arm was about to drop off from the number of mugs of tea she had poured and food she had handed out. In the sea of faces, individuals were hardly distinguishable. She was glad to be busy, not wanting time to think about the stretcher cases.

"There!" Grace eased her aching back. "That's the last of the cheese and pickle."

"Got any lemonade, miss?"

"I'm sorry," Louise looked up and saw, beyond the shoulder of the Tommy, Peter making his way slowly along the platform. The shock was so great, so joyful, she whisked from behind the trolley with no thought of asking permission, dodging between the mass of wounded being disgorged from the train. Desperate not to lose sight of him, she looked down the platform. For one brief moment the idea that he was heading towards Emily – that she had lied and was here to meet him, not her brother Vic – brought sudden outrage, which died almost immediately when she saw he was not alone. An orderly carrying a small suitcase was walking with him.

She caught up with them just before the barrier. No sign of Emily, but already there was no room in her thoughts for anyone but Peter. She came up behind him, touching him and calling his name at the same instant.

He sprang round and away from her, terror in his eyes as he stared at her apparently without recognition. He was shaking from head to foot, the spasm continuing even after she overcame her first fright and the natural reticence always between them, and threw her arms round his neck kissing his cheek. The shaking ran into her body.

"Pete, it's Lou," she murmured, pulling back a little to examine his face. "I'd no idea you were coming home. I was helping dish out tea and things . . . and there you were! Marvellous!" She hugged him again. "Where are you going now? To Holland Park?" She saw the orderly give a slight shake of his head, and words from the CO's letter "a state of some nervous collapse" came into her head.

Peter licked his lips and at last seemed to focus. "I'm . . . sorry, Lou." Speaking seemed a tremendous effort. "Was going . . . to . . . telephone. Surprise you."

She felt frightened again. Was this shell shock? She had caught glimpses of Tommies suffering from it. Knew it took many different forms. She pulled her scattered wits together. Smiled and somehow managed to start them all walking again as if nothing was wrong.

"Are you going by ambulance? I've a marvellous idea – why don't I be your ambulance? I've got the Maudslay parked close by. I could drive you wherever you are supposed to go."

They were through the barrier now and when Peter didn't answer, Louise put the question directly to the orderly. "Would that be helpful?"

"It would, miss, if Captain Marshall don't mind. We're that pushed for vehicles. You can see."

Peter seemed neither to hear nor care, but looked

at the packed courtyard, his head moving from side to side in a slow arc as if his eyes could not understand what they saw. He was still trembling as if with fever, though not so violently. Louise realized that he was incapable of making any decision. Immediately she made it for him, with a curious little internal leap of joy and the strong feeling that this was a moment of importance. She had no time to work out why, but went on carrying the sense that something significant had happened to her almost disconnected from Peter, even while asking directions.

"Which hospital is he going to?"

"Westerbrooks, miss – out Chertsey way," the orderly guided Peter towards an ambulance near the head of the queue. "I'll just have a word with Joe, miss. He's taking the others . . . tell him what you suggest." He let go of Peter's elbow, going to the driver.

Peter muttered: "Got to get out. Must go," licking his lips again, eyes darting. He seemed frantic and very pale. Sweat was standing out on his forehead.

"Come on, then," she said soothingly, and took his arm.

The orderly came back.

"Does he have to report to anyone in particular, Corporal?" she asked.

"I'll see to that, miss. If you'd just sign here," he held out a crumpled form and pencil stub. "Joe says he's got one more patient to load up, then he'll be off. He says to follow him. Left turn a mile along the road between Addlestone and Chobham. Westerbrooks is up a long drive."

"Thanks." She signed, raised her free hand to Joe to let him know she understood, then took the suitcase. Keeping a firm grip on Peter's arm, she walked with him across the station courtyard to where the Maudslay was parked.

The journey was almost silent. In the old days with the old Peter, they would have chatted all the way. But the new Peter was withdrawn, staring fixedly through the windscreen. Now and again she glanced at him, longing to ask what had happened, how he felt, how long his sick leave would be, but his face was a mask she didn't know. His hands gripped each other as if for comfort. The sight upset her so much she didn't look again.

Once, Peter said: "You won't tell Aunt Gertrude I'm back?"

"Not if you don't wish it . . . though she'll have to hear sometime." She changed gear, thinking how strange it was to be driving him like this. He had sat in the passenger seat only when teaching her how to drive, never as a passive unspeaking traveller. Impulsively she began again: "Pete, I . . ." but the cold unhappy mask dried the words.

Westerbrooks was a surprise, because it reminded Louise instantly of The Tower House. The crust of turrets and absurd flights of brickwork fancy, with Gothic arched windows, which now confronted them, gave out a feeling of home. She glanced at Peter and saw that the mask had relaxed a little. Perhaps he too had a sense of homecoming?

They parked beside Joe's ambulance car and went in through heavy double doors to a stately panelled hall transformed to a reception area. Blue carpet, easy chairs, a desk with large ledger, neat pens, and a stone jar filled with dried grasses made it very welcoming. A smaller bowl of primroses stood on a side table like a signal of new life and hope. The matron, in starched cap and immaculate dark dress, came to meet the new batch of patients, allotting each man to a waiting VAD nurse. It was a good place. Louise said so quietly in Peter's ear.

"Civilized," he agreed, and this ordinary answer was like a breath of the old Peter. He pecked her cheek too, when she kissed him goodbye. It was on the tip of her tongue to say she would be along tomorrow and would tell him all about an idea forming in her mind. But he had begun to shake again so she postponed it, asking instead:

"Would you like me to come again soon?"

"Monday." Peter picked up his suitcase.

At least he's in touch with the days of the week, she thought, and some of the grinding anxiety for him lessened. As she steered the Maudslay back under the long arch of elms that edged the drive, the earlier sense of this being a time of significance came back, bringing with it the germ of the idea. Without any agonizing, any self doubt, any indecision, she had organized the delivery of her first patient to hospital. Like all good ideas it was so simple, she wondered why she hadn't thought of it before – or perhaps why she had dismissed the possibility without thinking it through.

"I'm a woman of independent means now. Twenty-one. I can do as I please," she patted the steering wheel: "*We* can do as *we* please. You and me together, old girl. We'll make a first-rate

85

ambulance team. We might even get to France. What do you think about that?"

Talking to the Maudslay seemed perfectly natural, and the car purred sweetly as if in tune with her being. Louise thought she detected a surge of power in the engine that was better than any human reply, and smiled at the absurdity, but the satisfaction remained.

At the end of the driveway she turned out into the road heading back to London. Only then did she remember the commandant and Grace. Grace might understand her reasons for abandoning her post. The commandant never would.

She patted the steering wheel again. "Who cares! Any fool can cut sandwiches. Not everyone can drive."

~CHAPTER 7~

Louise closed the front door of the Holland Park house, and listened. The grandfather clock ticked reassuringly. There was no other sound and she stood revelling in the peace of the quiet hall, realizing that even Peter was not there. His presence in the house over the last ten days had not been easy, and after a hectic day driving wounded between Charing Cross station and various London hospitals, this near silence was a joy.

Her dishevelled reflection stared back from the wall mirror – streak of oil down one cheek, grubby hands, wisps of hair escaping from pins and sensible hat. Nothing that tea and a steaming leisurely bath wouldn't put right – the thought had scarcely arrived when the mirror showed her the front door opening. With a sinking heart she turned, bracing herself to listen to the hundred and one little grumbles Aunt G would want to pour into her unwilling ears . . . and saw Peter come in. She smiled, finding that after all she was glad to see him.

"Been for a walk?"

"Not exactly." He threw his baton on to the hall chest with a clatter. He was wearing full uniform, buttons polished, shoes gleaming.

"Oh? Where then?"

"For an interview. Medical Board."

"Already? I didn't know. What did they say?"

"In their wisdom they have decided I'm what they call fighting fit."

He spoke with a briskness that surprised her. She frowned, examining the lines of strain etched round his eyes and mouth. "*Fighting* fit? Are you telling me they intend to post you back to France already?"

"I've been holidaying since May. We're well into July now. Can't wag it indefinitely."

Her frown deepened. "I wouldn't have labelled your stretch in hospital any kind of truancy. After all you've been through . . ." but what had he been through? She didn't know.

"Don't start lecturing," he snapped, and spun away from her. "I can't stand lectures." His fingers drummed on the wooden chest.

Louise sighed irritably. "Sorry. I'm all in. I was at the station at seven and haven't stopped since. I was about to make myself some tea before sprucing up. Do you fancy a cup?"

As he followed her down the passage and into the kitchen where the kettle simmered on the range, she gave herself silent instructions. This time be firm. Don't let him put you off. For heaven's sake, he's your brother isn't he? You *love* him! For his own good you need to know more about his illness. It's your plain *duty* to find out.

Feeling virtuous, she made the tea and settled on a quiet inoffensive question: "Have they told you which day you will be leaving?"

"The seventeenth. Saturday week."

All her plans and good intentions were blown sky high. "Oh no . . . what time's the train?"

"Eleven thirty in the morning. Why?"

"It's the day of the march. We shall just be setting out!"

"What march?"

His mind was obviously elsewhere, and she looked at him with exasperation. "Women's Right to Serve march. I told you the other day. You know – Mrs Pankhurst has planned it. Blackfriars Bridge to Whitehall, then a deputation to see Mr Lloyd George." With an effort she managed to speak lightly.

"Oh that!" Peter flicked a hand as if brushing off troublesome flies. "Don't bother me with Suffragette business now."

"It's not just 'Suffragette business' as you call it," Louise tried not to let him rile her. "Granted Mrs Pankhurst's running it, but the matter is of vital importance to winning the war. Women can't be ignored."

"There's no need to stuff those old arguments down my ears. Where's that tea?"

She lifted the teapot and her hand shook slightly with the effort of staying calm. "The government must take notice. They need our labour to keep things ticking over. Women are strong, capable, willing . . . *we are here!*"

Peter went and looked out through the barred kitchen window, his back to her. Only the knowledge he had suffered deeply – was still passionately unhappy, she suspected – kept her from throwing the cup at him as she might have done in the old days. She took a deep breath and poured.

"How will you get to the station if I'm not around to drive you?" The notion of having to choose between the march and seeing him off was a dilemma of enormous proportions.

"Taxi . . . hitch a lift . . . something. What does it matter? Anyway, you hate goodbyes, and I'm quite capable of getting myself to the station, you know. I'm not a child." He hesitated, then came back to the table and sat down.

She pushed the cup and saucer across the scrubbed wood, then the sugar basin. He took two spoonfuls and stirred them into the tea, round and round and round . . . "Sorry," he said gruffly.

She poured her own tea and sat down opposite. "That's all right. This wretched war winds everybody up. I'm the same. And you're absolutely right, I do hate goodbyes, but I'd hate even more to think of you alone on that platform, or with only

Aunt G for company. Waiting to go back to . . ." she broke off.

He drank deeply, then lowering his cup, sat nursing it. "You go to your march. Much better not to have goodbyes. Got any biscuits?"

"There's some cake." Willingly she fetched a tin from the larder and cut him a large slice from the Dundee, with a sliver for herself, watching him bite and gobble between more gulps of tea as if in an enormous hurry.

She nibbled, sipped, looked at him speculatively, gathered herself. "Pete, I know you don't like questions, but can't you tell me what happened to you in France that made you so ill? It must have been terrible." His fingers began to drum again – staccato taps. He seemed visibly to shrink. "All I could get out of that doctor at Westerbrooks was that you'd been suffering from neurasthenia. I know that means nerve trouble, but it's so clinical. Says nothing about how things were for you – how you felt . . . what happened."

Silence came down like a stifling fog.

Louise leaned forward. "I'm not meaning to pry. Don't think that. I ask because . . . well, because I care about you."

For the first time he looked directly at her. A hunted, haunted appeal in his eyes that she had never seen before and which wrung her heart. What he said knocked her sideways.

"Emily didn't mention any march to me. I would have thought she'd want to join in. Hasn't she been told about it?"

Stunned, Louise tried to pick through all her

visits to Westerbrooks, but couldn't remember a single instance when Emily had been mentioned. Words fell out of her mouth: "You mean she's been *visiting* you?"

"Yes, of course." He laced his fingers together, elbows on the table, fixing her with a changed hard stare. "Why shouldn't she? Are you and your crowd deliberately shutting her out?"

"*No* . . . and what crowd?"

"Your Suffragette bunch."

"Don't talk rubbish!"

"Then it's more personal after all. *You* have kept it from her. You are avoiding her because in your opinion she's not good enough for our family."

"Pete!" her brain was reeling. "Look, I've had a hard day. I'm not going to get into a silly squabble."

"Is that all you think it is, a squabble? Use your imagination. How do you think Emmie feels, knowing you consider she's not off the right shelf?"

Louise was appalled. "Did she say that?"

"Not in so many words, but I know. You've always been a self-willed donkey, Lou, but I've never thought you were a real snob before."

She couldn't quell her temper any longer. "If I'm a snob, at least I'm not blind."

"Meaning?"

She made a last effort to steer away from what promised to be a full-blown quarrel. "You talk about using imagination – well, *you* just put *your*self into her shoes. When the war is over you'll be taking Father's position as owner of the

Brass Foundry, with a way of life Emmie would never feel easy with, if she was expected to be part of it . . . oh, have another cup of tea. Let's talk about this some other time when we're both feeling stronger. It's you I want to hear about."

Peter became very still. "Brass Foundry," he muttered – then crashed to his feet overturning the chair: "BRASS FOUNDRY!" His staring gaze seemed to bore into her. "LOU . . . TOMORROWS DON'T EXIST ANY MORE!" He shook his head. "There are no tomorrows!" Swaying, he gripped the edge of the table, while from the hall the grandfather clock solemnly recorded the passing of another hour. Then as if all his joints were stiff with age, he slowly bent and put the chair back on its feet.

Overcome with pity, Louise stretched out her hand across the table, meaning to touch his arm and comfort, but couldn't reach. He was too far away.

July the seventeenth was going to be a pig of a day. Louise peered through the rain streaming down the taxi window and thought of Peter climbing into that other taxi that was to whirl him away to Victoria station and France.

The trees lining the north London street swayed in the unseasonal wind. Water sloshed and sprayed from the taxi wheels. The sky lowered.

Would she ever see him again? Louise snapped off the thought, throwing it away before it could add her tears to the watery day. But oughtn't she to have gone to the station; seen him off; stood waving like all the other families?

"A pig of a day," Una echoed her thoughts. Una had come to London from Birmingham yesterday specially to take part in the march, staying overnight with Maude. The twins were very committed.

"We'll all be drowned at this rate," Maude grumbled. "Everything will be ruined."

"Don't be such a Jeremiah!" Una said briskly. "Have you remembered to bring those flags we made? That's much more to the point."

"It's you who can't remember. They've been delivered already. One of the marshalls took them, and Lottie's bringing the banner – I *told* you. Satisfied now?" Maude sounded waspish, and Louise wondered if this scratchiness between the united twins was an omen, just as Emily's absence seemed like another omen? Peter had brought her message saying she would be with them in spirit – much use that was when physical presence was everything.

The taxi drew up in a side street a little way from Blackfriars Bridge. "Can't take you no further, ladies. Road's blocked." The driver grinned and glanced up at the weeping sky. "Enjoy yourselves!"

"We will," Una got out and handed over the fare.

"Yes, we *will*!" Louise had caught a glimpse of the crowd filling the Embankment. As they went in search of the board with their section number, rain and wind ceased to matter and her spirits rose. Some of the nagging doubts faded. After all, the weather had not kept the marchers away. Women as far as the eye could see. Everyone from old grannies with market bags and mothers carrying babies, to working girls in off-the-peg macintoshes jostling smart ladies in expensive tailored suits. It was going to be all right!

"Ninety bands – how's that for a stirring display?" Maude said, dodging a dripping umbrella. "And national costumes from all over the world. You have to take off your hat to Mrs Pankhurst. She really understands how to put on a show. Did you know we're being led by a barefoot Belgian in rags? There's an eyecatcher for the press if you like!"

Louise did know, but was more concerned with the many familiar faces that brought a feeling of warmth. "Isn't that Lottie over there?" she waved vigorously at a large woman doing battle with a wind-blown banner. Skirting a cornet player and a bass drum, Louise went to her. "Lottie! And Clara . . . *Elsie* . . ." So many old friends! She was caught up in handshakes and hugs. "I'll take those," she said to a marshall who had come round with hand-flags for each section. She wanted the chance to say hello to all these old comrades.

"Red, white *and* blue for your lot. Aren't you the lucky ones!" the marshall handed over a damp pile. "Next block is all red. Then all blue – very spectacular!" She moved away.

"Leave me out," Lottie said. "This bloomin' banner's like a dozen live eels . . . Gawd strewth!" as a sudden gust of wind ballooned the purple green and white cloth.

For a moment Louise gazed up at the Suffragette colours, then began to pass round the flags, chatting and laughing. The sense of belonging was like a homecoming. Rain trickled down her neck, dripping off the brim of her hat, but she didn't care. She had done the right thing in choosing the march.

"I'm going to sign up first registration table we come to," Lottie flexed her arm and almost lost control of the banner again. "It'd better have more muscle than that bloody useless Women's Register! Oh, how much longer before we get started?"

As if she had triggered a signal, a bugle sounded in the distance towards Whitehall. It cut through the babble of voices. The buzz of the crowd, the little blasts of brass band tuning, died away and were replaced by a cacophony of clashing tunes. The nearest band had struck up "Rule Britannia", the brassy sound mingled with cheers as the long tail of women began to inch forward. Through the sea of faces Louise noticed spectators were lining the pavement, backed by an occasional barge mast and glimpses of the wind-ruffled river. For an instant the clouds thinned and a pale washed sun shone briefly on the banners and cheerful flags. Surrounded by women, shoulder to shoulder with women from all walks of life, a sisterhood – and she was part of it. Humbled by the honour, swelling with pride, Louise raised her flag high, and began to sing with the band:

". . . Britons never never never shall be slaves . . ."

Peter could not stop looking at her. If only he could freeze the passing of time and hold on to this moment! Extraordinary how obsessed he was

96

with this girl. He couldn't explain it to Lou, not in a thousand years – nor even to himself. She was totally unlike any girl he might have fallen for in the past. Certainly she didn't fit into the category of a possible wife. Yet he dreamed of that.

He examined her face. The familiar landscape of rosy cheeks, brown eyes flecked with black, straight brows tailing into little rebellious hairs that grew at different angles, uneven line of short nose, round determined chin – all seemed new; yet to be explored. A great desolation gripped him. No time left. Would there ever be any time again?

The waiting locomotive belched a cloud of steam under the canopy of Victoria station.

"I'll have to go in a minute."

"Yes." Emily returned his intense gaze without shyness. He had the impression that she, too, was reading every line, every mark, every tremor and pulse in his face, as if this was a last chance.

A last chance.

He blurted out: "I'm being posted to the Kite Balloon Corps. I didn't tell you before because . . ." he shrugged. Gooseflesh ran along his arms and his stomach knotted but he managed a smile.

"Flying – in a balloon?" Emily was visibly startled.

"Not exactly flying. Kites are tethered to the ground."

"Oh!"

He recognized a measure of relief in her voice and repressed a shiver. "This chap I met on the way back to Blighty set me thinking. And there

97

was another chap in Westerbrooks had a brother who's a Ballunatic . . ."

"A *what*?"

"Only a joke. 'Kite Balloon Observer', if you want the proper name. Anyway, the brother made enquiries for me, and it's all fixed. Apparently they're crying out for volunteers."

"Oh!" Less relief this time.

"Don't worry," he said, but secretly felt glad she was worried because that confirmed she really did care for him. Suddenly, violently, he wished he was in the moving train with this harrowing business of saying goodbye cut short.

"You will keep on writing to me, won't you?" he asked. "Letters mean a lot. Keep me going."

"Of course, if yo wants."

"I *do*," he said firmly. "I'll write back."

"All them rules," she burst out. "What yo're allowed to write and what yo ain't. Don't leave much elbow room for anything real," she hesitated, as if waiting for a reaction. "I ain't prying, but it bothers me not knowing about how it was for yo out there in France . . . how it will be. It's like a wall between. Us over here. All yo boys over there. Like two separate worlds."

He smiled in wonder. "That's exactly it, Emmie. You've gone plumb to the middle as usual – two separate worlds – and if I could explain I would, but it's impossible. You need to go out, *be* there, to understand what it's like. I don't want to go, yet I'm pulled back. It's where the war *is*, the real war . . . and all the chaps. I can't let them down. Nobody at home knows what the war is

98

really like – *nobody*!" He looked deeply into her eyes, trying to fathom her thoughts, but could not and smiled hopelessly. "I feel I'm living a dream over here and I have to get back . . . be where it's real."

"Yo saying home ain't?"

"In a way." Knowing she could not understand was an intolerable ache.

Her face flushed and she rubbed a finger under her nose, giving her head a brisk little shake. "They really only ever gave yo aspirins as treatment?" she asked incredulously.

The switch to practicalities was so like her he had to smile again. "I had one or two injections in the base hospital – to shut me up when I got rowdy."

"Seeing things not there," she nodded. "They'd give yo morphine."

He stared in amazement. "How did you *know*?"

"Our Vic said about the nerve cases. He told me a lot when I visited him in hospital – treatments an' that." She dug in her pocket and brought out a small brown paper parcel which somehow tangled with her fingers, slipped and fell amongst the dust and feet on the platform.

They both bent down, reaching for it, bumping shoulders. Peter gathered up the little package and they came up together with unsteady laughter.

"We often do that," he said.

"Bashing each other, yo mean?" Emily's voice was husky; eyes too bright.

"I wouldn't say that precisely."

"How then?"

99

"Oh, never quite saying . . . doing, what we really wish."

"Is that how yo sees us?"

"It's how I see *me*!" He went to take her hand and realized he was still clutching her parcel.

"No – yours," she said as he pushed it at her. "A goodbye present, to be opened on the train. Nothing grand, so don't get excited."

He could not speak. His throat felt closed. Around them other soldiers, their families, friends, lovers, were converging on the open carriage doors. A small boy, cap on back to front, was clinging to a khaki leg. His mother, clutching a baby, was wrapped in khaki arms. Behind them a dark girl was trying to push through to a soldier yelling: "Bella!" from an open window.

No time left.

Peter swung his new kitbag on to his shoulder, desperate to reveal to Emmie everything in his head – his whole wartime experience, every last horror, so that the barrier that kept them apart would break and the burden of memory be lightened by sharing. But the sick leave was over. He had wasted his chances.

Emily was scrubbing her nose with a handkerchief. "Glad Louise can't see me acting so daft. Did she . . . say anything about seeing yo off?"

"No," he tried to soften the stark word. "I didn't . . . tell her that bit, but I gave her your message about the march." All these words and not one saying what was really in his mind. He put his free hand on Emily's shoulder, propelling her towards an open first class compartment door.

"Stay there!" Climbing in, he dumped the kitbag on the luggage rack; left his baton and cap on a windowseat. The package he had already stowed in one of his tunic pockets. He felt very cold.

Behind Emily's head, framing it, Lord Kitchener's poster portrait with outstretched finger said: YOUR COUNTRY NEEDS YOU!

An upsurge of bitterness almost toppled Peter's carefully prepared scheme to make sure these last minutes stayed calm. He could not believe that England needed him. He was about as useful as a punctured tyre. On the platform again, he asked her:

"Tell me what you will do when the train leaves. I want to be able to picture you."

"Have a good bawl I expects." Emily blew her nose. "I'm halfway there now. After that I'll go back and scrub the kitchen floor. Somebody dropped a bottle of castor oil last night. Glass and stink everywhere. Yo wouldn't believe how the pong of it clings!" She pinched her nose between finger and thumb, rolling her eyes. She looked so comic he was forced to smile.

Porters were beginning to slam doors. The guard's green flag was ready; whistle between his lips. No time left!

"Emmie?"

"Yes?"

Words tumbled from him: "It's because of you I joined the Kite Ballunatics. I'm borrowing a piece of your courage so I can go up in the air again. I'm scared to death, just like you were when we flew to Camber Sands. You didn't let fear stand in your way. That's how I'm going back."

He saw her hand go to her mouth as the whistle shrilled.

Turning away he wormed into the corridor, making sure he stayed by the door, only to discover when it was shut that the window refused to open more than half-way, no matter how he tugged the leather strap. At that moment he realized there had been no last kiss. Not once while they had been standing on the platform had he put his arms around her.

The train jerked and began to crawl forward.

"Emmie . . ."

She was walking alongside. Awkwardly he dangled an arm through the beastly half-open window. She seized his hand and pressed it against her mouth, but had to let go because too many people barred the way.

He tried for the last time. "Emmie, there's something I've been meaning to say . . ." but it was useless. Noise of people, engine, clacking wheels, drowned his voice. A hundred other things he had meant to tell her and now never could, swarmed into his brain and tormented his tongue. He craned his head round the window-frame, seeking a last sight of her; thought he saw her waving, but could not be sure because she was one amongst hundreds on the packed platform.

Fruitless though it was, he found he had to shout after all. Had to try, because trying was all that was left to him: "If I ever get out of this mess we'll be married, I promise . . ."

As the carriage passed the end of the platform his confession was lost in a ragged chorus of singing that spilled out from the station into the smoky open air.

"Rule Britannia, Britannia rules the waves
Britons never never never shall be slaves . . ."

Cut to the heart by such trusting innocent blindness which grated painfully against the loss of his dear girl and this journey back into fear, Peter left the window, stumbling over legs until he reached his seat. For a long while he stared at the soot-blackened bricks of London, and was still staring as green parks changed into fields. At last he remembered the parcel and felt in his pocket. Untying the string, he opened it and found a small leather wallet containing a little notepad, envelopes and ready sharpened pencil. On the first page of the pad she had written:

Good Luck – now and wherever you go.
Always your true friend,
Emily

He stared at the words for several minutes as if seeking something missing. Then, closing the wallet, he stroked it with his finger before slipping it into his pocket again, and went back to studying the passing of England.

~CHAPTER 8~

The idea was hazy at first. Louise couldn't be sure how long it had been nestling at the back of her mind.

Easing the Maudslay into a small space in the station yard, she went to find the chief ambulance officer to let him know she was there.

As usual the hospital train disgorged just as many wounded – more, if that were possible. Arriving at a hospital with her first consignment, she overheard one harassed orderly saying:

"What d'they think we're playing at – bleedin' sardines?" It was then the hazy idea took on crystal clear outlines. *The Tower House must be turned into a hospital.* Why ever hadn't she realized that before? All the problems solved in one go.

The house wouldn't have to be sold – which would please Peter – and she wouldn't be saddled with housekeeping on her own. There would be trained staff under her. Everyone who could was opening their doors. The most unlikely places such as schools and church halls had been cleaned up and filled with wounded. She had even heard of a library exchanging books for beds.

"Thanks for the ride, miss." The soldier hitched his crutches more comfortably under his armpits. He winked. "Yer smile's like a dose of sunshine."

He lurched away, and after seeing the other patients safely inside, she drove back with a stream of plans going through her mind. She felt exhilarated. Even the thought of what Aunt G would have to say couldn't dampen her excitement.

She shelved the idea for the rest of that day to give it time to grow into proper shape with practical details nailed down and ready for discussion . . . and went on shelving it for another six weeks because that selfsame night Aunt G slipped going downstairs and broke her leg.

They have sent her back too soon if you ask me, (Louise wrote to Peter two weeks later). She suggested today I give up the ambulance work and stay home to nurse her all day! Some hope! We'd be at each other's throats in no time. I still haven't told her about the hospital plan for our old house, but I can't put it off much longer. Una is in the Birmingham branch of the St John Ambulance Brigade now, and you know what she's like. I told her my idea, and she's already getting beds and medical supplies earmarked. I shall have to cool her down a bit, or she'll be in there herself and taking over the reins. I'm not having that. I want to do my bit, though I can't be a nurse – you know what a ninny I am about blood! By the way, thanks for the separate letter. I managed to whisk it away without Aunt G reading your reactions to the plan. Though perhaps if I'd shown her, everything would be cut and dried now. Anyway, it was thoughtful of you.

How trivial this must seem to you, facing guns and death. I'm glad you were accepted as a Kite Ballunatic – what a comical nickname, but on the nail if you ask me. Why anyone would want to go up in a basket tied to a bit of blown up silk is beyond me, but you always did have strange hobbies! Yes, I know it isn't a hobby any more, and I'm proud of you. Take care of yourself, and if you can let me have any real news I'll be grateful. We're so out of touch over here.

I've packed a parcel which I sent off to you yesterday. One of those Peek Frean Dundee cakes you say keep so well, and some of Mrs Meery's Shrewsbury biscuits. Also a box of Velma chocs and the pack of cards you asked for. I'll write again soon. Perhaps I'll have things sorted out by then. Who knows!

Affectionately,
Lou

She yawned and stretched. The clock on the mantelpiece in the morning room chimed seven, but she felt as tired as if it were three in the morning. Another long day stretched ahead. I'll have it out with Aunt G tonight, she promised herself. I'll take up some cocoa and tell her the hospital plan. Then I'll add a postscript and put this in the letterbox first thing tomorrow morning. It seemed suddenly important to let Peter know that the plans were going ahead. In that way at least, she could support him. She wondered where exactly he was, and what he was doing . . .

A wicker basket sat on the ground below the Drachen balloon. The blunt nose and plump tail fins made Peter think of a curious fat fish. After six weeks of training he was still not at ease. In a strong wind these balloons were unstable. Could even tip on end. Not encouraging.

He climbed in.

The basket shifted, although the steel cable that tethered the Drachen was taut and men were hanging on to the several guy-ropes, steadying it. Peter wished fervently that old Box had been there. He missed old Box. A fine sweat drenched his forehead and round his mouth.

"Should be first-rate viewing weather," Second Lieutenant Tubby Carter said – already aboard and hitching his harness to the fixed parachute at the rear of the basket.

"Yes." Peter didn't add that it would be good viewing for Fritz as well. He began the routine check of the Drachen's luggage – aneroid barometer, hand-telephone, binoculars, map-rest, ballast, his own parachute, valve line . . . and the vital red ripcord. He hoped to God there wouldn't be any need to use *that*!

Tubby, as cameraman, was fiddling with the Thornton Pickard, sliding in the first photographic plate.

They were in a small wood, conveniently placed on a slope overlooking the village of Vermelles, where a balloon bed had been prepared and the winch lorry was in place. Aloft, the balloon would give a clear view of the Hohenzollern trench-fortress where the Germans were well dug in. Rumours of a plan to attack this intricate enemy stronghold were buzzing. But there were always rumours – Peter secured his parachute – fact was what counted.

At Tubby's request a special little platform had been constructed to take the camera on the lip of the basket. He was leaning forward, frowning and peering through the sights. Whistling out of tune under his breath.

"Problems?" Peter asked.

Tubby shook his head – still whistling, still out of key.

Peter could feel the silver flask Lou had given him pressing hard against his leg. It went with him everywhere. He took it out, wondering what she was doing this minute. Probably still in bed, lucky blighter! Tucked by his feet were sandwiches in a mess tin – bully beef slapped between hunks of bread. He drank. The spirit raised his spirit. There was a flask of tea as well, but the whisky was the life saver. Good old Lou!

He glanced at Tubby. "Ready then?" and saw him nod. The secretive breathy piping coming between Tubby's teeth was just recognizable as "Three Blind Mice". Peter knew better than to expect spoken answers until they were airborne. He had his own superstitions, and touched elbows and nose quickly before signalling to the sergeant in the winch lorry. Then stared skywards.

A hawk hung high in the air. Wing span and body like a black cross against clean blue. First sunrays spiked the horizon.

The winch creaked.

Slowly, swaying, the strange tethered fish began to rise. Its underbelly scoop, not yet fully inflated, flapped, then tightened as the air pressure increased.

The free hawk quivered and hung motionless again.

Looking away and down with sun dazzle still in his eyes, Peter gradually focused on the men below. Slowly they reduced in size until they were no bigger than lead soldiers. Fifty feet, a hundred, two hundred, one thousand and on. Cold began to bite. No sounds except sighing creaks as a light wind played through ropes and basket. The illusion of peace wrapped round Peter; relaxing; soothing the gnawing fear. The war lay asleep on the ruined land. Low September mists made milky pools. Collecting over natural dips on the ground, over shell holes and mine craters, gradually vaporizing as the sun broke free above the wood. The haze cleared and a network of trenches came into focus. Beyond and more remote in enemy territory was the little mining village of Loos.

"Oh, damn this thing!" Tubby wrestled with his parachute that was getting in the way as he leaned forward to angle the camera.

Through binoculars, Peter methodically scanned the landscape. A new gun emplacement came into view, the muzzle of a howitzer visible above ground level.

"Look . . . beyond the railway," Peter held the binoculars out to Tubby. "Middle distance – two o'clock. See?"

Tubby took them and beginning another flat rendering of "Three Blind Mice", turned to the camera and shot his first picture.

There was a sudden rumble of gunfire. puffs of smoke rose in the east. The old fear grasped at Peter's stomach, but this time he refused to let it take hold. Giving it all his attention, he began to check the map.

"Louise, wake up! Lou*ise*!"

Dragged from a sweaty tug-o-war on a bright green field splattered with blood, where she was dressed in Peter's old rugger kit, Louise crawled back into dazed consciousness. Her aunt, stick in hand, was leaning over the bed shaking her.

"What's the matter?" Her sticky eyes took in the gaping wrapper, scraggy plait of hair, quivering jowls, the expression of real fear.

"They're here. We shall all be blown to pieces . . . OH . . ." a near scream as distant thunder rolled.

Even in her sleepy state, Louise knew that Aunt G wasn't afraid of thunderstorms. Reluctantly she got out of bed and went to part the curtains. Through the window she saw a glow above the rooftops, somewhere in the direction of the city. Flashes of light glittered like distant fireworks, and as the glow brightened, two searchlight beams met high in the night sky, illuminating what looked for all the world like a thin silver pencil. The roar came again – not thunder, she realized, but bombs exploding. It was an air raid!

"Come away – you'll be killed!" Aunt G shrieked.

"No need to panic," Louise said, exasperation quickly overtaken by pity because the old girl really was shaking. She put a coaxing arm round the stout waist. "Come downstairs, we'll make a cup of tea. The Zeppelins are nowhere near here, the bombs are miles away. We'll be safe enough in the kitchen." She hoped this was true, but couldn't stir up much concern. The Zeppelin had looked so frail and faraway. Enchanting, rather than any kind of threat.

In the kitchen, the kettle was already simmering on a gas ring and Mrs Meery, the housekeeper, was puffing the bellows at embers in the range grate – a daunting sight, her head bristling with curling rags, enormous purple shawl shrouding a flannel nightgown, pink bed-socks peeping from unlaced boots.

"If our time's come, ma'am, we might as well go comfortable, that's what I says."

Louise wanted to giggle. What a pair! – she stifled a yawn – a music hall comedy act . . . Emmie and

111

Lou, Plenty of Patter with . . . Oh God! She remembered that Emily lived in the Old Ford Road, perhaps underneath those Jerry bombs!

The last webs of sleep vanished and a cold chill settled as the booming roar increased and was followed by faint but distinct bursts of gunfire. Germans were up there in the English sky! Zeppelins with their load of bombs could fly anywhere . . . Holland Park . . . *anywhere*. She felt trapped; helpless – and for an instant thought of Peter having to endure this not once, but again and again. Perhaps these were the last moments of her life?

Louise pulled herself up. This was ridiculous! She began to busy herself, finding comfort in the routine of opening the cupboard door, fetching milk, sugar, tea-cosy, biscuit barrel.

"Tea, ma'am," Mrs Meery passed a cup, but Aunt Gertrude's hand trembled and the cup dropped. Tea and shards of china spread across the floor quarries.

"Oh dear . . . oh dear, oh dear!"

"Never you mind, ma'am. A bucket and cloth'll see to that before you can turn round."

"It's all right, Auntie," Louise put a soothing hand under her elbow.

"It's not all right!" The old woman seemed to get her second wind, mouth tightening. She pulled away and sat down. "Don't talk such nonsense. I'm not going to stay here and be turned into mincemeat. If we live through this dreadful night, we pack first thing tomorrow and go to Birmingham. Meery, you can get out the dustsheets as soon as you've drunk your tea. Louise – get the Bradshaw. I want to check the train times."

Louise and the housekeeper stared at her, then at each other.

"Birmingham!" The name burst from Mrs Meery as if she had been directed to leave for Australia.

Louise, who had been preparing herself to deal with a case of hysteria, now had to do a complete mental turnabout. After weeks of frustration, everything had dropped into her lap! But it was too easy. She felt suspicious.

"The Bradshaw, Louise!"

Birmingham, but with Aunt G in tow – she hadn't bargained for that! With an effort Louise got herself together.

"We can go by car, Auntie."

"Travel in that machine of the devil? Never! We go by train."

Louise recognized the signals – small pulse in wrinkled forehead; flaring nostrils; pursed lips. She gave in.

So did Mrs Meery as she finished mopping the floor. "Very well, ma'am."

It took two days to pack, close down the Holland Park house, arrange for post to be sent on, tell friends and neighbours where they were going, and inform the London Ambulance Column that there would be no Maudslay to help swell their numbers.

"We'll miss you," Joe said.

Since the first drive in convoy, when she had taken Peter to convalesce at Westerbrooks, Louise had become friendly with this ambulance driver.

"I feel like a deserter," she said.

"That's daft, miss. You know from your own experience we're desperate for hospital places. Why, last night they had to put up beds in the canteen at Number four General." He nudged her. "We'll be sending you our overspill before you can blink twice! So you'd better get up north quick."

She smiled, amused and partly reassured. She had never thought of Birmingham as "up north" before. "Goodbye, Joe."

"Goodbye, miss."

This wartime life is full of goodbyes, she reflected as she got into the Maudslay. There was one last hurdle – to break the news to Aunt G that The Tower House was to be transformed into a hospital. Bracing herself, and with a final wave to Joe, Louise drove under the archway of Charing Cross station for the last time.

~CHAPTER 9~

The Tower House rambled in more directions than
Louise remembered. She had carried in her mind
a picture of "home" as a substantial overdecorated
house that only just failed to be a mansion, which
stood back in large gardens approached by a shady
tree-lined drive. Reality was shabby paintwork,
dirty windows, a rioting garden, piles of dust
and endless passages! She felt flickering pity for
the servants who had cleaned them. Outside,
steady rain pattered against the windows. There
was a smell of mice and damp wallpaper. She
had removed the dust sheets from the morning-
room furniture before sitting down to make her
list, but the little room she recalled as cheery
– fire crackling in well-blacked grate, polished

fire-irons, flowers on the chiffonier – now had a dejected look.

Memories had hounded her from the moment she began to drive back through Hardwick Village – a village no longer, but firmly tacked to the skirts of Birmingham. So many landmarks! The chestnut tree under whose shade she had picnicked and quarrelled with Peter after the Suffragette bicycle parade. Gates to the golf club where Father had been a member and where she and Emily had painted slogans on the greens. The corner of Dial Lane and High Street where she had made her first stand for the Cause, on an orange box!

In the house, memories swarmed – Emily sitting bolt upright and red-faced on the morning-room sofa, beside prim Vera as they waited for the parade to begin; and reaching further back, her wild descent down the stairs on a teatray; and further back still, the lavender scent, sweet smile and swish of silk petticoat that was all she remembered of her mother.

She pushed the memories away, but Emily insisted on sitting firmly on the sofa opposite.

"How I *wish* you were here, Emmie. You're always so . . . practical!" Louise bit the end of her pencil hard, leaving a circle of teeth marks. She frowned at the list.

"17 rooms, usable as wards. 2 bathrooms. 3 lavatories. Kitchen. Scullery. Back scullery. Housekeeper's room (could be staff canteen). Useful stabling and outhouses for storage . . ."

There was so much to do . . . packing away excess furniture, cleaning, seeing town councillors,

Red Cross officials, organizing medical supplies, beds, bedding, rounding up butchers, milkmen, bakers, a plumber to mend a leaking pipe – the prospect was daunting.

And Aunt G with Mrs Meery were due in New Street station on the twelve-fifteen train tomorrow! By then there must be at least one bedroom ready, this room cleaned, and an orderly kitchen. Aunt G was a stickler for food hygiene.

Fires were priority. Oh heavens . . . coal!

She trudged back along the passages and out into the courtyard paved with blue brick, where a row of out-houses stood at right angles to the old stables. Stepping over puddles, she selected a key from the heavy ring of house keys, and opened the coalhouse door. A small heap of coal was piled at the back. Two hundredweight, she judged. It would be gone in no time, with all those hungry fires. A few damp sticks sat in an old cardboard box. For a second she felt defeated, then squared her shoulders. Coal could be ordered, sticks dried out, rooms swept and dusted. Thank goodness Father had always insisted on the best of everything which included a huge new gas stove . . . and thank goodness again for Peter's forethought in insisting she learn how to turn on the gas main.

There were little bubbles of rust round the burners, she discovered, going back into the kitchen, but they lit obligingly. The sight of the blue flames made her absurdly happy. Even the gassy smell of the oven was a pleasure. Turning the flames low, she arranged the sticks to dry on the oven rack. Filling a coal scuttle, she brought it in to sit by the drying warmth.

The morning-room fire proved sulky, but at last she persuaded it to burn up. She felt triumphant.

Washing in cold water at the scullery sink she went upstairs to the blue bedroom with its westerly view across garden to boundary poplars and hills beyond. Less damp and coldly vast than the master bedroom opposite, but the feather mattress felt clammy. Collecting bed linen that smelled of mushrooms, she went back to the kitchen. A long clothes airer hung from the ceiling by a system of ropes and pulleys. Letting it down was easy. Pulling it up again, loaded with bedclothes, was hard work but she managed, securing the rope round the wall hooks. Her shoulders ached. An hour gone already and she'd done almost nothing! She filled the kettle and put it on the gas stove.

The stone hotwater bottles were sly and hid. She had to go through cupboard after cupboard because never before had she needed to find such everyday comforts for herself. The kettle began to sing as she ran them to earth on the top shelf of the larder. Climbing on a chair she reached for the first bottle.

Out in the passage a bell rang.

Louise sighed heavily. Got off the chair. Checked the row of bells and found it was the front door, then ran along the passages and across the hall with a growing sense of sympathy for those childhood servants she had taken for granted. Sleeves rolled to the elbow, unaware of the coal dust streaking her face, she opened the heavy oak door.

118

"Una!" she put out welcoming hands, then pulled them back. "I'm filthy! Do come in. I'm *so* pleased to see you!" surprised to find she was speaking the truth.

"I'm rather wet." Removing cap and cape, Una shook them, wiped her shoes, then came indoors. She was in uniform with a VAD brassard round the sleeve of her grey St John Ambulance Brigade frock. "I was on duty in the ward till two, then cycled straight over from Richmond Hill. I reckoned you would be here by now. Sister Withers – she's our ward sister – is very interested in your plan to turn The Tower House into a hospital. Our Hill Crest used to be a private house, did you know?"

Louise didn't but wasn't given a chance to say so.

Una swept on: "Hill Crest was the very first hospital in Birmingham to be run solely by the Brigade. We're so proud of it. Oh, by the way, Sister said she's seeing our chief commandant this afternoon, and she'll mention that you've arrived . . . so he can start things moving. And I dropped off at Locksley's as well. Mrs Locksley said her husband would call round this evening – if that's all right?"

"Who's Mr Locksley?" Louise was bewildered by this barrage of words.

"A plumber. You did say over the telephone you had a leaking pipe, didn't you ?"

"Yes. Una, you are a brick!" Secretly Louise felt pleased that her little scheme had worked, relying on Una's bossy ways to get results. "Come into the kitchen . . . do you mind? I was just about to fill hotwater bottles to air Aunt Gertrude's bed."

"She's never here already?" Una sounded scandalized.

"No. Tomorrow. I want to sleep in the bed tonight, to make sure it's bone dry. She's so fussy about everything being well aired."

"I don't suppose she took too kindly to the idea of living in a hospital," Una said.

Louise grinned. "Took it like a lamb . . . no – like a true British lion!"

"Are you telling me she doesn't mind?"

"More than that, she approves wholeheartedly – it's one of the few times we've seen eye to eye," Louise added candidly. "And now let's have a cup of tea – I'm gasping."

"Bottles first," Una said firmly.

Louise gave in. For once she was almost glad to be bossed about and told exactly what to do. She found herself making a fire in the bedroom, then cleaning the washstand bowl, jug and chamberpots, while Una took over the airing of the mattress, sweeping and dusting, running everywhere – even into the garden wilderness, and coming back with a handful of grasses and late cornflowers. "To brighten the place up," she said, arranging them in vases for dressing table and chiffonier downstairs.

When she came back into the kitchen, Louise was about to make the tea.

"Why don't we have a grand wash up first? We need clean cups anyway." Una put the question as if it was accepted fact. "We can wash enough crocks and pans to keep you going tomorrow at least – save time," and she whisked the kettle from the stove.

Louise watched her tea-water bubble into the enamel sink basin with resignation, and went to fetch a teatowel from Mrs Meery's carefully prepared hamper.

Later, as they sat either side of the brightly burning fire in the morning room, she thought: this is more like home! They were tucking into Mrs Meery's chicken legs and plum cake. A huge blue willow pattern teapot was on the hearth. Steaming cups sat on the little table between them. The teapot gleamed. The cups sparkled. The fender shone.

Louise eased her shoulders.

"I don't think I've ever worked so hard. Physical work, I mean. I had to scrub down my cell in prison, but that was nothing to all this," she spread her arms.

Una laughed, little rabbit teeth resting on her bottom lip. "If you think that's hard, you've a surprise coming!"

Aunt Gertrude ran her finger along the top of the hall settle and looked at the result. "I can see there is plenty of work waiting for you, Meery!" She looked at Louise: "I thought you said you had dealt with the cleaning?"

"I have. I missed that bit." She's not been here two minutes and she starts grousing, Louise thought, but wasn't going to be drawn into an argument. There was still far too much to do. "Leave your hand luggage, I'll take it up in a minute. Come into the morning room. That *is* clean! I'll find someone to take your trunks upstairs. I'm sure you'd like some tea?" Her mind was on the mountain of jobs clamouring for attention.

"*I'll* make the tea, miss," Mrs Meery was hanging on to her carpet bag as if it threatened to run away, "if you don't mind showing me the way to the kitchen." She gave a short sniff, as if Birmingham air was suspect.

"Oh, thank you." Louise was truly grateful. Any offer of help was a bonus. She hoped the old battleaxe would settle. To have capable help in the kitchen would be a wonderful relief.

The next two days were packed to the brim and overflowing. Everything seemed to happen. Not smoothly – each operation fitting with the next – but in jerks, with jobs left undone, too many things arriving at the same time, moments of panic as when the lavatory cistern overflowed and Mr Locksley, so helpful the night before, had that very day joined the army and gone to camp with the Birmingham Pals Brigade. Louise careered between Tower House and town centre, making calls at the Town Hall, St John Ambulance HQ, the main police station, even the local vicarage – in snatched moments listening to her aunt's complaints about the number of cobwebs, impertinence of the baker's boy, and why wouldn't Louise stop behaving like a scalded cat!

On the second day, hospital beds arrived in the middle of breakfast, brought by a removals van. The elderly driver and a boy made up the team. Louise looked at them in dismay.

"I was hoping for some help with shifting two wardrobes and some boxes," she said. Neither looked as if they had muscle power.

"Don't you worry, miss. It's knowing how to lift, see?" The driver shouldered a weighty trunk and piled it on top of another in the box room which was to be Louise's bedroom. "Just a knack. That's all y'needs."

He was right. Before lunchtime, he had six of the upstairs rooms, the drawing room and dining room cleared enough to take the hospital beds.

People began to arrive. Mrs Croft, the vicar's wife, came with her daughter, Marion, and a basket of home-grown apples and pears. They were full of praise.

"Such a wonderful idea. Truly patriotic work, Miss Marshall. Now what can we do for you?"

"If you know anyone who would come and clean, I'd be grateful."

"I'll find out. You can rely on me."

Mrs Croft was as good as her word. The same afternoon two women arrived to start work straight away. More surprisingly, Marion came back.

"Mother says I can have every afternoon free to help, if you think I can be useful," she told Louise.

"Wonderful! It'll be mostly running errands, if you don't mind that . . . until things have settled a bit and we get ourselves organized."

"Oh yes! Anything." Marion's pale cheeks flushed. "I've always wanted to work in a hospital. All those poor Tommies, Miss Marshall. I was at Snow Hill station when a hospital train stopped for a while the other day. I saw two boys who used to sing in our church choir. Poor Charlie had lost his leg. It was terrible." Her eyes grew moist. "You can be sure I'll be happy to do whatever you ask."

That evening Louise watched her go down the steps on the way home with a spring in her step not there before. She felt a spark of satisfaction. This was doing something valuable at last. She wondered if she too would be confronted by someone she knew amongst the wounded. She hoped it wouldn't be Peter.

It wasn't Peter, and the meeting took place sooner than she would have expected – on her very first trip to Snow Hill in the Maudslay, ten days after the Tower House Hospital opened its doors.

But before that Aunt G had a row with the carter who delivered a load of medical supplies, because he ignored the tradesmen's entrance and brought horse and cart to the front door!

Before *that*, Sister Muriel Withers arrived with the chief commandant, to take up her duties as matron.

"Pleased to meet you, Miss Marshall," Sister Withers, faded fair hair screwed into a tight bun under starched white cap, prim unsmiling thin lips, held out a hand that felt like a limp damp sponge.

Louise was instantly put off, and suspected the feeling was mutual. She introduced her aunt, and they all went on a tour of inspection which brought compliments from the chief commandant and probing questions from Sister Withers. Louise learned a lot about Hill Crest, its high standards, how Sister Withers was reluctant to leave but felt duty bound to get this new hospital on its feet. She also learned something of Aunt G's reaction to the newcomer, seeing her nod with queenly approval when this professional nurse explained she would be bringing one other professional nurse with her to oversee the band of VAD helpers she expected to be supplied.

Louise decided to make her own position clear before getting swept into this band. "As I can drive, I have already arranged to help with the ambulance service."

"Miss Marshall has had experience driving for the London Ambulance Column," the chief commandant confirmed.

"I see," Sister Withers was plainly not impressed.

Louise was annoyed. But not half as annoyed as she was when she discovered that The Tower House was to be a convalescent home for officers.

"I really cannot imagine why you are making so much childish fuss," Aunt Gertrude's hard grey eyebrows showed her surprise. "You surely don't mind?"

They were at breakfast. We always row at breakfast time, Louise thought, and this was an added irritation because today she was beginning her new ambulance duties, and liked to start a working day calmly.

"Of course I mind," she attacked the butter with her knife. "Why didn't you talk it over with me?"

"I didn't imagine there was anything to talk about. You wouldn't expect me to allow my brother's old home to take in the ranks?" She sounded scandalized.

"I don't see why not. But that isn't the point."

"Well, if you are happy to entertain the officers, what is the trouble?"

Entertain? A row of broken arms, shattered legs, bandaged bodies and a faceless head, passed before Louise's eyes. She wanted to yell out, but instead said tightly:

"This happens to be my house. I am entitled to take part in decision making."

"Your brother's house, and he isn't here, Louise. I am only looking after your interests." Aunt G polished her knife with her napkin. "I do wish people would dry cutlery properly. Everything should be polished with a second cloth before being returned to the drawer."

Louise gasped. A war on; men being massacred – and here was this crazy old hen bothering about the niceties of drying knives! She said icily:

"Peter and I are part owners, as you well know." This was true. She was still amazed that her old-fashioned father had written this clause into his will. Equal shares. He had never approved of equal sharing of the Vote. "In future you will come to me before taking it on yourself to make any more such sweeping arrangements." Picking up her toast, she left the table and the room, not trusting herself to say more.

Outside, the late September day was really too warm for her new uniform jacket, but nothing was going to persuade her to take it off and so hide the gleaming white armband with its scarlet cross. She felt proud of it, and proud of being a VAD helper. She had been proud for two whole days now.

Driving, as always, soothed her. She headed towards Snow Hill station, passing along the dingy familiar streets, by factories and sturdy grimed houses, turning into Livery Street and steering between yellow-brown tiled walls into the station yard. Several assorted vehicles were lined up, some custom built, others adaptations of vans or private cars like the Maudslay.

Inside the station she found the familiar bustle. Trolleys piled with food, urns, cigarettes, stationery. Stretchers. Wheelchairs. Grey uniforms like her own were everywhere.

The train approached. The platform was swiftly cleared of outsiders and, after making enquiries, Louise went to wait with her car. Eventually three soldiers were brought – "walking" cases with bandaged arms and cheerful faces. Making them as comfortable as she could in the back of the car, she started the engine and was about to leave when a medical officer, in Brigade uniform, waved to her: "Have you room for another, miss?" his other hand was under the elbow of an officer leaning on a stick. The left arm of the officer's tunic swung free, but the arm itself was still there, slung loosely against his chest. Part of his face and head was thickly bandaged.

"Yes . . . in the front," Louise got down and opened the passenger door. The officer limped towards her and as he was helped inside, she saw his one visible eye, bright blue and deep-set under a strongly marked eye-brow. The eye looked at her for rather longer than necessary, and he smiled with one side of his mouth, a strange twisted little movement, before he sat down with care.

"Thanks."

"Are you comfortable?" she asked.

The strange smile came again. "Near enough."

"Three in the back to Hill Crest, miss. This gentleman to the Tower House Hospital," the MO checked his list. "That's your place isn't it, miss?"

Louise nodded and released the brake.

"Your place?" the bandaged officer eased his arm.

"Where I live," she explained. "The Tower House Hospital used to be my home – still is, I suppose."

"You don't sound too sure."

Louise smiled. "You could hardly call it home now – it's full of hospital beds." Realizing this sounded unwelcoming, she tried to put things right: "I hope you will find it comfortable."

"Any place in Blighty is paradise by comparison," the eye kept scrutinizing her.

"Have you come from Flanders?" she asked uneasily.

"Gallipoli. Forgive me saying this, but I believe we have met before."

She said stupidly: "I've never been to Gallipoli," and shot him a quick glance, feeling foolish.

The smile twitched again. "This was in London. Hyde Park. You were making a speech, and I received a white feather."

"Oh!" Colour flooded up her neck into her face. His unconcerned candour and her own cringing memory of that day, mixed together into acute embarrassment. It was on the tip of her tongue to deny having anything to do with the feather, but it wouldn't be true. She was involved, if only second hand. In the end she said:

"It was a rotten speech."

"On the contrary, I thought you very fluent and convincing."

"I've given up making speeches," she said. "That was my last. I'm better at driving a car," and to prove it she swung the Maudslay smoothly into the flow of traffic on the main road. She half expected him to go on talking, and when after several minutes he remained silent, she gave him another quick glance. His upper lip was beaded with sweat, all visible skin ashen and his undamaged hand was clenched.

Alarmed, she asked: "Are you in pain? Do you want me to stop?"

He gave a slight shake of his head. "Keep going. It will . . . pass."

One of the Tommies said from behind: "You deliver the officer first, miss. We don't mind a joy ride, do we, lads?"

But Louise had already taken the decision and was heading for home.

~CHAPTER 10~

Peter put his note to Louise in an envelope, took a fresh sheet of paper, a swig of whisky, and began the important letter.

1 December 1915

Dear Emmie,
Your letter and parcel arrived today. I can't tell you how welcome both were – you cheered me up as always. Thanks for the chocolates and those knitted gloves. You have a good eye for size. They fit well and will keep me warm aloft. I am enjoying what I do now, isn't it amazing?

He paused and stared at this deliberate untruth. Before every balloon ascent he was chilled to the marrow with fear, but part of his scheme was not to admit this to anyone, not even Emmie. Whisky helped. He took another drink.

I must tell you about a recent piece of luck. Remember old Box, the mechanic back at the airfield? The crafty blighter has wangled a transfer. He turned up here two days ago. I had the surprise of my life when I found him tinkering about with one of the winches.

Peter paused again, wondering if he was ever going to get to the real purpose of this letter. Paralysis seemed to have struck both mind and hand. He lifted the flask again, thinking: I'll have to break this habit – who wants a drunk for a husband? Not Emmie, that's for sure, after all the trouble with her father. The trouble with himself, he realized suddenly, was that nothing further away than the next couple of hours was believable. But the letter had to be written. For Christ's sake, he wanted to write it didn't he?

More whisky.

Now for the good news. There is a strong chance I shall be home for Christmas. If the leave comes off I will go straight to your digs as soon as I get to Blighty and wait there. I want you to come home with me, and every Brummie knows that can only be Birmingham! We must not waste this leave. I want us to spend *every minute together*.

He underlined the last three words and reread the letter. It seemed very unsatisfactory. Why hadn't he written: "We must get married"? He chewed his pen, unable to find the right words. It was all too easy to be misunderstood. Finally he gave up and dashed off the usual ending. Folding the letter, he pushed it into the envelope, licked the flap and sealed it, writing the address quickly before he could change his mind, then took both letters to be mailed.

The adjutant, a small man whose wide flexible mouth seemed constantly on the move, sat at a table in the only waterproof room of the ruined cottage that served as an office. He was working through a pile of letters. Those already censored lay in a cardboard box.

"Rotten job," the adjutant's mouth twisted and came to rest.

"Well, you won't have to vet these," Peter dropped his letters into the box.

"Thank God I'm nearly at the end. Have you finished for the day?"

"Yes."

"Fancy a decent meal?" the adjutant stretched and scratched. "There's a splendid little estaminet about two miles up the road. Madame cooks excellent omelettes and the wine isn't bad. Excellent daughter too!" He sketched curves in the air with both hands.

"I know," Peter said.

"Do you, by George!" the adjutant laughed. "Secretive devil, aren't you? Well, what do you say?"

"Why not!" Anything was better than moping about camp with bad thoughts for company.

"I'm off duty in an hour."

"Right." Peter turned rather too quickly, steadied himself and aimed for the door. Outside, in the dank December cold, an impulse to retrieve his letter to Emily swept over him. He would tear it up and write: "I am coming on leave. We will be married immediately, as we both want this more than anything in the world. We mustn't waste what luck has given us."

But he knew he would not do it . . . could not. Such effort was beyond him.

He shrugged. What would be . . . would *be*.

Louise waved Peter's note like a flag. "He's got leave for Christmas, Auntie. Peter's coming home. Isn't that marvellous?"

"Very good . . . news . . . indeed," the old woman spoke in jerks as she made her slow way down the stairs. "What . . . day exactly . . . does he . . . say he'll arrive?"

"He doesn't! He'll just turn up, you know Pete . . ." Before she could develop this, Matron Withers came out of the morning room, now her office, and put a supporting hand under Aunt Gertrude's elbow as she arrived at the last step.

"If you could spare me a moment, Mrs Boston," she murmured, steering her towards the office door.

Another time Louise might have been irritated at being left out of any consultation, as well as amazed at her aunt allowing herself to be swept

133

along by someone who in her opinion was only a shelf or two above a servant – but today was different. Peter was coming home, and everything was bathed in the sunlight of that fact. She beamed at Muriel Withers and received a startled twitch of the lips in response. Rob Cathcart, limping into the hall from the canteen, was drawn into the same warm glow.

"You seem in good spirits, Miss Marshall," he allowed a careful smile to stretch the new scar tissue that had grown across the burns on the right side of his face.

Louise wondered if he found smiling painful. Over the weeks he had never complained. "Yes, I am. My brother has written to say he's got leave from France – for Christmas."

"No wonder you're happy! I'm delighted for you."

He really means it, she thought, noticing the pinkness of the new skin deepen. She couldn't help being reminded of a freshly boiled peeled prawn, the eyelid puckered like a walnut. "Thank you . . . I feel like dancing!"

"Wish I could offer to take you," he patted his leg, "but this fellow here won't let me. Never go birds'-nesting!"

"You fell?" She had often wondered about his limp.

"I did. All forty feet. Trying for a rook's nest at the top of an elm."

"That sounds rather dangerous!" She was amazed to hear him talk about his past. Usually he was like a clam about his private life.

"It was – I was only eight at the time."

She looked at him curiously. What an odd chap he was. So reserved, yet when, weeks ago, she'd plucked up courage to apologize about the white feather, he had laughed. Said *she*, not the feather, had spurred him on to talking the medics into passing him fit for active service. But she couldn't take it in such a lighthearted way. The embarrassment stayed and she avoided him when she could.

She wanted to escape now, and glanced at her watch. "I hear Dr Beaumont is very pleased with you."

"So pleased he is sending me packing this afternoon." Rob flexed his arm as if testing how much it hurt. "It's been a long haul."

She realized he was dressed very smartly – blue hospital uniform well pressed, red tie neatly knotted, hair and shoes gleaming. "But that means you will be home for Christmas . . . marvellous! You will *be* at home? They can't mean to return you to the Front immediately?"

"Who knows what the army will do? I shall be in Blighty for a while at least. As a matter of fact I was thinking of staying on in Birmingham for a time," his blue eyes watched her boldly. "My father has a house in Edgbaston. He'll put me up."

Louise wondered why he didn't say "My home is in Edgbaston". He was full of little mysteries. She glanced at her watch again.

"Are you in a hurry? I was wondering . . . I can't take you dancing but would you like an evening out? To the pictures, or for a meal? I know you lead a very busy life, but . . ."

"Very," she said quickly, and felt a twinge of shame for being so sharp. "But I love moving pictures." From behind the closed morning-room door she heard her aunt's dictatorial tones, which meant she was laying down the law about something.

"They are showing a Charlie Chaplin at the church hall tomorrow," Rob said. "If I call for you then about seven, will that be all right?"

"Yes," she wished she could hear exactly what Aunt G was saying. Interfering, no doubt.

"Good," Rob said. "That's settled. Tomorrow at seven."

Louise's attention focused sharply. "Tomorrow? I'm not sure . . ." she realized she hadn't been listening properly and had agreed to something she didn't particularly want to do – and yet it might be fun. My bit of war effort, she thought.

"Make it half past. I can't be ready before then." She smiled at his casual salute, and this time walked away without bothering with excuses.

The wind was cruel and had been so for days. Huge protective canvas screens had been built round the inflated kite balloon strapped to its bed of canvas sheeting. The screens were supported by tall wooden poles set in the ground and braced by wires. A second screen of wire netting, supported and braced in the same way, surrounded the canvas with a gap of a few yards between. A fringe of trees round this clearing in the little wood gave extra protection. It was, Peter thought, jolly ingenious. Wire netting and trees acting as wind break for screens and balloon, preventing them from being torn from their moorings by the gale.

He studied the sky. Big white clouds, underbellies brushed with grey, were sweeping across in an easterly direction.

"Brass monkey weather," Tubby said, coming up behind him. "When does your leave start?"

"Tomorrow morning." Peter rubbed his arms, suddenly chilled.

"You'll be all right then. Nobody's going up in this wind. Blighty, is it? Or just a rest in Paris Plage?"

"Blighty."

"Jammy devil! Some buggers have all the luck." Tubby was envious. "Well, I'm off. Coming?"

Peter followed him through the trees, away from the trembling balloon, along the track towards Number Five section – a cluster of huts and tenting tucked into a small dip in the flat landscape. The tents billowed and flapped. The night before, one had collapsed, cracking the ribs of the man on his camp bed below.

Soon . . . soon he would leave it all behind. Only hours now.

"Christmas with your folks," Tubby seemed unable to tear himself away from this heart-warming prospect. "I've always fancied Christmas in London. Bright lights. Tinsel. Dressy shop windows. Lots going on."

"As a matter of fact I shall be spending Christmas in hospital in Birmingham," Peter grinned.

137

Tubby turned and stared. "Nothing wrong with you I don't know about, is there?"

"Shouldn't think so. Birmingham is my home town. My sister has turned our house into a hospital."

"I say, that's a bit hard! Enterprising, though. Is she a nurse?"

"Ambulance driver."

"A gel of some spirit," Tubby said. "I'd like to meet her."

Peter didn't think Lou would want to meet Tubby. He went back to wondering what sort of a Christmas it would turn out to be, and decided to start the process of turning dreams into hard fact.

"I'm going to get married," he said.

This time Tubby stopped and slapped him on the back. "Congratulations, chum! I never knew you were engaged."

"I'm not, exactly."

"Mean you haven't asked her yet?" Tubby burst into a roar of laughter, "Sweep her off her feet, y'mean. Never give a woman a chance to change her mind!"

"Oh she knows. Next leave was the arrangement," this was only a white lie, he told himself. Naming the day was a detail and in any case his responsibility. Date and time meant little. Devotion was all, and Emily *was* devoted.

"We ought to drink to the bride's health . . . and the bridegroom, what d'you say?" Tubby raised an imaginary glass.

He almost agreed, then said: "Later, perhaps,"

with a sense of triumph. It was a first step. "I've got to start packing."

Tubby shrugged. "I'll drink yours as well then."

They parted, Tubby heading for the mess and Peter to his hut, where he gave an extra twist to the cap of the whisky flask before starting to sort out his belongings.

Less than a quarter of an hour had gone by when the door swung open, letting in a blast of cold wind, and Tubby.

"Get your winter combinations on, chum. We've orders to go aloft."

"Christ, Tubby, you're not serious? I'm packing!" Peter looked at the clothes strewn over his bed. "I'm going on bloody leave!"

"No joke, chum. CO's orders are to get a move on. 'Immediately' he said, and we all know that means ten minutes ago."

"In this wind? The man's a lunatic!"

Tubby grunted. "He's also the CO. Emergency, he says. Report's just come through about Fritz planning some new push to celebrate Christmas. We've to get up there and look for new trenchwork, massing of troops and transport, in fact any bloody thing! The winch lorry is already on its way."

Peter slammed the hairbrush he was holding hard at his bed, then without a word began to pile on all his warmest clothes.

When he reached the balloon bed the wind had lessened, but not significantly. Gordon Box was there, and Peter handed him the special letter, watching him stow it somewhere under his oily working clothes.

"Bit breezy, sir," old Box said.

Peter exchanged glances and knew he understood. There was no need for an answer. He climbed into the basket. As the Drachen pitched and shook, inching upwards, he tried to keep his mind on routine instrument checks and away from icy fears. Through the bluster of the wind he could hear the men below as they hung on to the ropes, trying to control the balloon's slow ascent. The underbelly scoop inflated with air too rapidly and Tubby staggered, cursing. Peter almost lost his grip on his jangling nerves, but the Drachen steadied again and began to lift a little faster . . . rising, rising, until the cables tethering it to the winch were fully paid out and they hung high in the frosty air. Peter put the binoculars to his eyes, scanning the chilly landscape, picking out the enemy lines. It wasn't easy with the wind gusting through cables, whipping the canvas, making the balloon judder.

"Bad as being at sea," Tubby mumbled through his scarf. "Worse!"

"Don't puke over my feet, that's all!" Peter was trying to position himself for a steady view.

"Hope you remembered the whisky." Tubby was working on the camera. "We're going to need a bit of firewater before we finish, if we aren't to turn into bloody icicles."

They worked in silence for a while. Below, the land lay clearly defined. Trenchlines; hillocks and dips of scarred earth; the dead fingers of blasted tree trunks; clusters of ruined farmsteads, everything in miniature. Looking upwards, Peter saw a tiny aeroplane flying like a distant black moth, then two aeroplanes . . . *three*! He recognized them as German Fokkers.

Tubby, glancing up from his camera, also saw, and pointed: "Pete! Fokkers . . . see?"

Together they stared – mesmerized.

"The buggers are coming this way."

"They're coming for us!"

They both searched the sky.

"Where the bloody hell are our lot?" Tubby yelled.

As Peter reached for the hand-telephone, the slender shapes of the aircraft were close enough now for him to see the elegant black crosses on wings and sides. Closer and closer they came. He shouted into the phone: "Winch us down, winch us down!" Shook it. Shouted again. Waved it at Tubby. "Bloody thing's dead!" Down on the ground he saw telltale puffs of smoke, and heard bursts of ack-ack fire from the anti-aircraft guns. "What in God's name are they playing at? Fritz is too bloody close . . ."

The Fokkers were on them with a stutter of machine-gun fire.

"Sitting ducks . . . sitting bloody ducks!"

He heard Tubby's yell as he reached for the red ripcord too late. The Drachen shuddered, tail fins wrinkling and beginning to fold. A jet of flame roared upwards, billowing clouds of oily black smoke, then the whole balloon exploded into sheets of flame. Almost at the same moment he felt a tremendous blow in the back, as if he had been kicked by an elephant. He collapsed on the floor of the wildly staggering basket. Fire was everywhere. It was raining fire; spitting fire; roaring fire. Green and gold flames ran along ropes, licked at the wicker basket, grew wicked and hungry. Tubby screamed as blazing fabric fell on him. He beat at it with flailing arms. Peter, trying desperately to move towards him, found that his legs didn't seem to be there any more and cried out: "JUMP JUMP JUMP . . ." as the basket began to hurtle earthwards. Then the fire was on him. Intolerable pain scorched his skin. A stench of burning hair stung his nostrils. As the sky fell away and darkened, his ears roared. A last scream burst from his distorted mouth and was lost in the thundering rush of air.

If the snow settled, it was going to be a traditional white Christmas. After a difficult day of driving, Louise was now perched on a chair in the old drawing room, pinning up paper chains made by the patients. The easy chairs and Persian carpet had been replaced by six hospital cots and a square of lino, but the red velvet curtains were the same, framing a Christmas card garden.

Louise gave the drawing pin an extra push and her chair wobbled dangerously.

"Careful!" The officer known as Stork swung across on his crutches and put out a steadying hand. "No room for more invalids. Full house!"

She smiled. "I'm all right thanks," and, getting down, she carried the chair to the opposite side of the room and climbed up again. The picture rail was awkward and she had to stretch to reach it.

"Bit higher . . . more over to the right," Stork

instructed. "That's it. You do have the prettiest ankles."

"Don't be saucy!" she said, but she wasn't annoyed. She turned, laughing. It was Christmas Eve. "Come on, slowcoaches. Haven't you finished the next chain?"

"Two more rings to stick." Captain Lester, stumps of legs stuck out in front of him in the wheelchair, pasted quickly. "There. Leave 'em a minute for the paste to dry."

Outside, huge snowflakes whirled past the window, settling into smooth white drifts and curving up the glass. As she paused to admire, Louise saw Marion Croft come into view, skirts lifted as she picked her way along the snowy drive with Rob Cathcart. She felt the colour come into her face. Rob should be in France! But she was determined not to rush to the front door, and deliberately turned back to the chainmaker.

"Is it ready yet?" she asked.

Captain Lester shook his head. "Give it time. Don't be so impatient!"

"Oh, all right!" She got off the chair. "I'll be back in a minute to pin it up," and went into the hall, just as Marion came in with Rob. She smiled with feigned astonishment and genuine pleasure. "Rob! I thought you were in France? Have they sent you back? Are you all right?" she stopped, hearing herself grow too anxious. Snow was glistening on his greatcoat, turning to droplets of water on the officer's cap in his hand. He smiled at her, crinkling the scarred skin into papery lines without effort.

"We met at the bottom of the drive," Marion said. "Major Cathcart has leave over Christmas, isn't that good?"

"Stealing my thunder," Rob's smile included her.

Marion blushed, putting a hand to her mouth. "Oh I'm sorry! Was it to be a surprise?"

"It certainly is a surprise," Louise was thinking of Peter and wondering how she was going to manage to divide her time equally between the pair of them, while wanting to be with Peter all the time and Rob for a good deal.

"I'm sorry I'm a bit late," Marion said wiping her feet vigorously on the mat. "Mother wanted me to take round Mrs Brook's shopping because she can't get out in the bad weather. I'll just take off my coat and then I'll get started." She hurried away to the cloakroom down the passage, and for a moment Louise and Rob were alone. They smiled at each other.

"A changed woman," Louise said. "She's come out of her shell."

"Yes." Rob had taken off his greatcoat and put it over the back of a chair with his cap. Then he came and put his arms round her, saying: "May I?" and kissing her before she answered.

Louise found herself wishing to avoid being touched by the scarred skin, and felt ashamed. Rob's lips were cool and firm on her mouth, and he smelled pleasantly of clean damp wool and sweet flesh. His moustache tickled her nose in an intimate tender way. Her heartbeat increased. It wasn't their first kiss, but somehow it was much

144

more important. Disturbed, and more than a little flustered by her own uncertainties, she withdrew slightly, murmuring:

"A changed *man* . . . you weren't always so bold."

"No time to waste," he said simply, blue eyes looking at her with such open admiration, such a totally vulnerable look, that she was embarrassed. This declaration of love – and she felt sure it was a declaration – left her floundering. She didn't care for the feeling.

"You never answered my question."

"Why I'm here you mean?" he kept his arms round her. "Typical army confusion is the answer. You know I was sent to camp in Grantham . . . well, two days ago we were all set for France. Got as far as Dover, as a matter of fact, then the information came through that there was a delay. No reasons of course, at least none we discovered. Not that we pressed when we learned about the Christmas leave! And here I am!"

From being almost deserted, the hall suddenly began to fill with people. Marion had come back. Aunt Gertrude shuffled from the dining-room ward. One of the VAD helpers came running downstairs on the heels of a nurse.

Louise caught some of the surprised glances and disengaged herself, but not without squeezing Rob's arm.

"Major Cathcart, how good to see you again. How well you look." Aunt Gertrude's stick tapped across the hall. She held out her hand. "Welcome home. Are you here for Christmas? We are expecting my nephew any minute. The decorations are going up. What do you think of our Christmas tree?"

Rob shook hands, looked briefly at the decorated tree standing in its tub of red crinkly paper, said: "Very handsome. Yes, I do hope to be here for the festivities," and returned to looking at Louise. "I quite thought your brother would be home already?"

"Well, he must be in England by now – could be here any time." Louise felt heartened at the thought of Peter coming in, meeting Rob. She wanted that, she realized. They could all share Christmas together. An enchanting prospect. As she put her hand on Rob's arm, smiling at him, the bell rang. She went to the front door and opened it.

A telegraph boy, clothes powdery with snow, stood on the top step, his bicycle leaning against the bottom. A wheel-line and pattern of footsteps stretched back down the drive. He held out a buff-coloured telegram.

She took and tore the flimsy envelope. The message inside was brief and quite clear.

REGRET TO INFORM YOU CAPTAIN PETER MARSHALL KILLED IN ACTION FRANCE 20th DECEMBER . . .

For a lifetime Louise stood in the open doorway staring at the scrap of paper in her hand. Behind her the other people had become still and silent. She looked at the telegraph boy. How blue and pinched his nose was!

"You don't need to wait," she told him. "There isn't any answer," and turned away. Her body was heavy, her head floating as she walked back into the hall. She held out the telegram, feeling a flicker of concern because her aunt was so old and this would be a terrible shock. She saw the wrinkled hand shake as Aunt G distanced the paper in order to read.

"Oh my poor boy," the old woman's shoulders drooped; the telegram shook with her hand. With effort she straightened enough to look directly at Louise. "He died defending his country. We can always hold on to that. A truly honourable death . . . an *honourable* death." Her voice was husky and edged with tears, but the conviction was unmistakable.

Louise felt sick. The image of the faceless soldier sprang in front of her eyes and a heavy hopelessness settled. Faintness made her head buzz and she fought against it, aware of Rob's arms round her again. For a moment she leaned against him, glad of his support, then freeing herself, she went to her aunt and guided her through into the morning room, to give her the comfort of the nearest armchair.

~CHAPTER 11~

Gordon Box didn't want to be limping along the Old Ford Road. He would have given anything to be back in the Salvation Army hostel with a hot cuppa in front of him. Better still, in a warm pub with a waiting pint and some cheery conversation. He sighed. The February day reflected his gloomy mood as the setting sun struggled from behind a cloud, crawled halfway up an alley, showed up the grime on some shop windows, then vanished again. A woman, bike loaded with sweep's brushes, cycled wearily past, followed by a depressed-looking nag pulling a coster's cart.

Gordon hung his stick over his arm and took out the envelope to check the address for the third time.

Miss Emily Palmer
The Mother's Arms
Old Ford Road – London

Well, he was on the right road . . . get on with it!

Slipping the envelope back into his pocket, he hobbled on, making good use of his stick because his leg was hurting again. It was the first time he had ever had to break the news of a death to someone in Blighty and he wondered what sort of a woman she was and how she would take it. He hoped she wouldn't faint.

The light was growing poorer each moment, and with no gas lamps to help, he had difficulty in reading anything. Then at last he spotted the pub sign – The Mother's Arms. Crossing the street, he went to grasp the doorknob when the door swung back. A woman in a battered black hat, carrying a bundle of shawls, came out.

"'Scuse me," Gordon said.

She gave him a hard look which softened as she took in his hospital uniform and stick. "Hello, Tommy! Whatcher want?"

"Miss Palmer. She works here, don't she?"

The woman started to shake her head, then smiled, showing broken teeth. "Oh, yer means Emmie, her that calls in on the way home from work to clean nights?"

"She cleans, does she? I thought she'd be a barmaid."

The woman laughed. "Yer remember when the place was a pub! It's not the Gunmaker's Arms now, mate," she jerked a thumb up at the sign. "Miss Sylvia changed the place into a clinic. But yer luck's in. Come tomorrer and Emmie would've been at her Red Cross class." The bundle began to wail and she jigged it up and down. "Friend of hers, are yer?"

"No. Just delivering something from . . . a soldier friend of hers."

She nodded. "Go on in. It'll be all right. Cheerio then, Tommy."

He watched until she disappeared into the gloom before rapping on the door. When there was no reply, he opened it and stood uncertainly on the threshold, unthinkingly letting gaslight escape.

From the depths a voice called out: "Shut that door! Yo'll have the bobbies on us!" and a young woman in a sacking apron, bucket of soapy water in one hand, came through into the passage. "Looking for someone?"

"Miss Emily Palmer."

"That's me."

"Oh!" Any romantic picture of the captain's friend Gordon had nursed collapsed on the spot. Stocky; broad face; determined jaw; no-nonsense bun of thick brown hair; hands roughened with hard work – he tried to pair this Brummie lass with the well-spoken captain, and had to remind himself that the captain had been an odd sort of cove, so he oughtn't to be amazed. He fished for the letter.

"Cap'n Marshall asked me to come and see you personal like, miss . . . that's if anything happened to him. I'm . . . very sorry." He watched her anxiously and saw the round eyes darken as colour drained from her face. For a long moment she did nothing, then putting down her bucket she dried her hands carefully on the sacking before taking the envelope. The gaslight shone down on the bold handwriting. She turned the letter over and over, but didn't attempt to open it.

Gordon felt he ought to make an effort. He couldn't just say "T'ra then", and blunder out. But what to say?

Before he could decide, Emily said simply: "Thank yo," with such genuine sincerity, Gordon felt his throat thicken.

He coughed. "That's all right, miss. It's the least I could do," shifting his leg to ease it.

She noticed and said quickly: "There's so much I wants to ask yo – but not here – somewhere yo can sit down. Are yo in a hurry or can yo spare a bit of time?"

"I'd be glad to talk. That's if . . ." it seemed pointless to say "if it won't upset you".

She gave him a shrewd look. "I know Peter's been killed, but I don't know how, and I *need* to know. It's very important," she put a hand on his arm. "Look – wait here while I have a word. They won't mind if I leave early."

He didn't enquire who "they" were and leaned against the wall watching her gather up the bucket and walk back down the passage. Minutes later she reappeared in a shabby coat and hat. There was no sign of the letter.

"There's a pub down the road that does good hot pies," a sudden crooked smile lit her face. "Are yo hungry?"

151

"I could do with a drink," he said, and saw her smile again.

They went outside into the semi-darkness and thin rain. He found hobbling along next to this girl quite a novelty. He wasn't much of a one for girls as a rule. She walked with an easy swing, very upright, but matching her pace to his.

"Have yo been home long?" she asked.

"Eight weeks."

"*Eight* weeks?" Her head turned towards him, but under the shadow of the hat brim her expression was hidden. "All that time in London?"

"No. I come down yesterday. I was in base hospital for a while, then to Blighty and Coventry. That's me home town. They've only just let me out or I'd've been to see you before."

She didn't ask any further questions and he was relieved when they turned into the Bunch of Grapes, which was warm and blessedly full. As they entered the smoky saloon a soldier and his girl got up from a table.

Gordon went to it. "What'll you have?"

"Stout, if that's all right?" Emily was poised to fetch the drinks herself, but he said:

"I can manage. Honest! D'you want a pie?"

She shook her head. "No thanks, but yo have one. Another time . . ."

He understood and fetched beer for himself and Emily's stout. "The barmaid's bringing me pie. Being wounded pays off sometimes!" He eased himself into the chair and grinned.

"Cheers!" He took a long pull at his glass.

"Cheers!" she sipped the stout then put it down

on the marble-topped table. "Will yo tell me exactly what happened to Peter? Do yo know?"

The moment he had dreaded.

He said quietly: "Oh yes. I was there."

"So yo can tell me everything?"

He examined her face. "You really want to know? It wasn't . . . too good." He was glad of the cover of voices. "I try not to think about it meself."

"And I don't really want to force yo, only there's no one else as can tell me the truth. Nobody as *knows*."

He cupped his hands round his glass. "Cap'n Marshall was up in one of the kite balloons, on a spell of duty . . ." he glanced at her and she said almost impatiently:

"Yes, yes, I know what he did."

"Him and another officer were up together on an emergency observation when these Jerry Fokkers flew in. Three of 'em. Been waiting, if you ask me. A kite balloon hasn't much chance, being tethered, miss. 'Course we winch 'em down sharpish if there's trouble, but this time Fritz was too quick, and what with our guns potting at the Fokkers who were doing the same at the kite, well . . ." he realized he was tiptoeing round the edge of what had happened, trying to soften it for her, and didn't know how to go on. He licked his dry lips.

"I know it must be hard," Emily was turning her glass; turning it. "I'd like yo to tell me straight – it's the only way."

He knew she was right, and wetted his lips with the beer. "When there's an attack, miss, nothing is ever very clear. So much going on, see, and what with the kite being so far up, I can only tell you what I saw from below – three Fokkers going for our kite, our ack-ack guns firing, and then a great funnel of flame and smoke. In no time everything was on fire – balloon, ropes, basket . . . everything. We tried to winch down the kite but it was out of control and the basket was already falling. There was all hell let loose on the ground too, because Fritz was chucking bombs at us. What with everyone shouting different orders – well, it was chaos. I tell you, miss, no one could've lasted more than a couple of minutes in that furnace – the cap'n probably died straight off. He'd been shot, see. I know. I found him in what was left of the basket after it hit the ground." He hid his shaking hands under the table. The image of the fireball staggering against a grey-blue sky and the awful mess in the basket was more real than the marble-topped tables and pub mirrors.

"Is that . . . all?" she sat forward, very pale, staring at him.

All? What else did she want? The stink of cooked flesh? A description of burnt-out eyes and blackened teeth? Arms and legs twisted all over the shop?

He said: "More or less. Except when I was helping lift out the cap'n I copped it meself."

They sat on in a cocoon of silence, surrounded by the hum of voices and clink of glass. The pie remained untouched, but Gordon was grateful for the beer. He looked at the woman sitting so quietly opposite him, hands folded. Pallor had made great smudges of her eyes, but she seemed remarkably collected. No tears. No ring either, he noticed, and remembered overhearing the captain talk about getting married at Christmas. Not to this one, he felt sure, and looked at her curiously, trying to weigh up whether or not she'd been really head over heels for the captain. She seemed as cool as a cucumber.

"I'm ever so grateful." There was a tremor in her voice. "I know it must've cost yo something to go over it again."

Her concern seemed genuine and he was touched. "War's war, miss. You just have to get on with it." Wrapping up the pie and pocketing it, he said more lightly: "But it puts me off me food!"

A smile flickered as she stood up. "Can I buy yo another glass of beer before I goes?" she asked.

"No – thanks all the same." He got up stiffly. "Shall I walk you home?"

She seemed taken aback. "Don't it hurt to walk? Yo never told me what sort of wound it was."

"Shrapnel – thigh and chest. But exercise does me good. They told me to do plenty of walking . . . and breathing!" He had made her laugh a little. Nothing much, but he felt pleased. She didn't accept or refuse, so he went with her out of the pub and they continued along the street together.

Emily lit the candle stub and, wrapping her flannel nightgown closely round her stone hotwater bottle, pushed both down the bed. The letter crackled in her skirt pocket where it had been since old Box had handed it over. She laughed – a small stuttering sound. To call him "old" was daft. He looked not much more than a lad – all jug handle ears and spots! And his curiosity had stuck out a mile. Well, she thought, he can be as nosy as he likes, he'll not get a word out of me about Peter.

Peter!

Emily shut her eyes and clenched her fists as anguish took her by storm. But she would not cry. Not yet, anyroad. Not till she had read the letter.

She undressed at speed. The room was freezing. Already ice ferns were growing on the windowpane. Scrambling into the warm nightgown she pulled out her hairpins, gave a few token strokes with the hairbrush and, wrapping a shawl across her shoulders, whisked into bed.

Now was the moment.

She slit the envelope with a kitchen knife. Her heart beat thick in her throat as she saw the familiar hand-writing on the paper she had given him.

A letter from the dead.

My dearest,

You will never receive this letter unless I am no longer alive. I want to make that clear. If I live and beat this old war I shall tear it up. But I'm so afraid that if anything happens to me, you won't be told (you see I don't trust Lou in this one thing and to say that shames me but it is true). Next of kin get the telegrams, you see. So I am trusting old Box to deliver this letter personally if the worst happens.

That is enough of explanations. There is nothing much else left to say, except that I love you more than anyone else I have ever known. Since I was sick in the head I've come to realize how much I depend on you and your glorious common sense. You are a rock. Absolutely honest and trustworthy – you would never let me down, and you are such fun to be with. Any chap with you for a wife couldn't hope for a better. We both of us understood that we would be married after the war. No hope of that now, but I want you to promise me to go on living and loving and not be too sad about me. Remember the good times. The example of your courage gave me the courage to come back to France and face ballooning again. Since we flew together over London and down to Camber Sands there hasn't been a single day you haven't been with me – in my mind if not side by side, us together.

Have a happy life,
Lovingly,
Peter

I sent him to his death, she thought, and was appalled. All the emotions caged since Mam had sent the pitiful scrap of newspaper cutting burst out and swamped her in tears of guilt and grief that ran helplessly down her cheeks, and falling, hooked on to her shawl. She wept for what might have been. What could never have been. For her own dreams and his. He had been scrubbed out. All that remained were his letters and a bundle of memories. The bleak announcement in the Birmingham Mail: "Captain Peter Marshall, Royal

Warwicks, killed in action 20 December 1915," was meaningless. Peter was not here any more.

Memories tumbled through her head.

Never again would they go for long drives in the Maudslay together, or have those quiet talks, just the two of them sitting in the park holding hands. No more kisses in the shadows of the trees. No more fun either – how they'd laughed themselves silly that day he'd tried to sew on a shirt button!

"Us together," she said out loud, and fresh guilt added to the guilt already there because she hadn't been able to scrape up enough courage to face him and break away. All along she had known that what they had was nothing more than a romantic dream. All along!

Now she had begun to cry she found she couldn't stop. Tears poured. She felt hollow and drained – as if her insides had been sucked dry. Oh, the waste . . . the stupid useless waste! A life switched off, like turning out gaslight, before it had properly begun. Everything he had been, everything he might have been, burnt up.

Thoughts bombarded her, until spent with weeping, anger, and long hours of work, she drifted towards unconsciousness. In the small moment that hung between being awake and asleep, she thought: poor Louise – and slept, crying in her dreams.

~PART 2~

EMILY: 1917–1918

~CHAPTER 12~

From her driver's perch on the coal cart, Emily watched the trim figure in VAD uniform get out of the familiar car and stand on the running board for a better view of the traffic jam. Under the severe St John Ambulance Brigade cap the bones of the face were more sharply defined, lines where none had been before, but there was no mistaking Louise. Two long years since they had last met. Two long silent years!

Emily's first thought was how to get away. But there was no escape. Traffic stretched in front and behind down Snow Hill, cutting across into Livery Street. She saw Louise turn towards her, scanning the line of lorries, carts, vans, cars. There was a faint chance that with Dad's old cap clamping down her hair and her face covered with coaldust, she mightn't be recognized. The beautiful tawny eyes looked at and past her, and she was just letting out a breath of relief, when Louise suddenly turned back. Colour flamed up the slender neck and burned into her pale cheeks. Stepping down from the running board she came to the cart.

"Emily? Yes, it is . . . *Emmie!*"

"Don't wonder yo had doubts. I must look a proper sight!" Emily was acutely aware of the contrast in looks that had always divided them and was exaggerated now – bandbox and scarecrow!

"I'd no idea you were back in Birmingham. Last I heard you were working in an aero-engine factory down the east end of London somewhere."

Emily was surprised she knew that much. "I was. I came back to look after Mam and our Lena. Mam's been poorly and Lena's too young to manage on her own." It was part of the truth. Emily tightened her hold on the reins.

"Emmie, I . . ." Louise hesitated, glanced rather wildly at the traffic: "Oh this is hopeless! I'm supposed to be in the station yard meeting a hospital train – this is such an amazing chance . . . so much to say, to talk about . . . but they're waiting for me," she looked at Emily desperately: "Can you see what's going on?"

Emily thought: she's really embarrassed, yet she means it about talking. Her first spontaneous thrill of pleasure was replaced by wariness. "Some old nag's dropped dead just inside Livery Street.

They're dragging it into the gutter. We'll be moving in a minute."

"I must go and start up the car again then. Can't keep the patients waiting even longer. The Tower House is a hospital now – did you know?" Louise lingered. She seemed to be talking about everything except what she really wanted to say.

"A hospital! Yo've solved all your worries then about what to do with the place." Emily wasn't going to let on that she already knew but that it had slid into the back of her mind. Now a buzz of excitement filled her. The Tower House had become *Louise*'s hospital! As their eyes met, she guessed they were both thinking of Peter. His presence was suddenly and disturbingly real – the link between them which could never be broken; not by time; not by troubles.

There was a shuffle of movement amongst the crammed vehicles. Wheels creaked.

Louise said: "I'll have to go.

"Yes."

"But we must see each other again – we *must*."

"When do yo finish? We could meet after," Emily offered hastily, amazed to find herself seizing this chance. "I could come over to The Tower House Hospital." She enjoyed saying "hospital".

A dray, two vehicles beyond the Maudslay, had begun to inch forward.

"Yes, yes . . . any time after eight." With a sudden warm smile Louise hurried back to the car.

Emily watched her turn the starting handle. At the last minute Louise turned and waved.

Emily raised her blackened hand, marvelling at this twist of fate that seemed to have opened up hospital doors to her at last. Flicking the reins, she clucked her tongue at the old carthorse, and slowly the coal cart pulled away, rumbling on down Snow Hill.

The walk up the gravelled drive between laurels and rhododendrons was overwhelming. The trees had been autumn yellow on her last visit four years ago. Now they were feathered with a first budding of green. Everything else was unchanged. The big house was still like a Bath bun gone mad, all crusted with bits of decorative brick and little turrets. Then she glimpsed a woman in nurse's uniform at one of the bedroom windows, and nostalgia began to recede. That *was* different! Emily saw the heavy oak front door open and a young woman with piled wheat-coloured hair came out and down the steps.

"Miss Palmer? I'm Marion Croft," she smiled shyly, holding out her hand. "I work here part time. Miss Marshall asked me to look out for you. She's gone up to change and says she won't be long."

They shook hands, and Marion became suddenly eager and confidential. "Do come in. Don't you think Miss Marshall was *inspired* turning this great place into something so useful? I'm supposed to be office staff, but we all turn our hands to whatever is needed. I helped out in B ward with meals today. I had to help feed one of the patients. Such brave boys . . . men, I should say."

The hall had been changed into an office-reception area with a carpet, desk and two easy chairs. The old grandfather clock was the only piece of furniture Emily recognized. Other less tangible things spoke of change – the chink and clatter of plates and cutlery coming from what had been the drawing room; a babble of male voices; occasional laughter; feet tapping over lino.

"Won't you sit down?" Marion indicated one of the easy chairs, and Emily sat, only to stand again almost immediately because Louise was running down the stairs. She was still in uniform but without her cap, her burnished coppery hair falling as lovely as ever. Emily had the strong impression that only at the last minute had Louise stopped herself from hugging then kissing her. Instead, both her hands were seized and pressed.

"I saw you from my bedroom window. I'm so glad you've come."

Emily wanted to believe her, but a shadow of caution held her back. She said: "And me," feeling pressure on her hands again.

"Try and fend off anyone asking for me, please, Marion dear," Louise begged, blessing her with a smile.

Marion blushed with pleasure. "Of course, Miss Marshall."

"Thanks – half an hour at least. I haven't seen Emily for simply ages." She let go of Emily's hands, treating her to the same smile. "Come into the kitchen."

Emily followed her along the maze of passages, very conscious of the magic of personality that went with Louise wherever she was, but aware that her own reactions had changed. In the old days she would have blushed like Marion, and felt overwhelmed. Now she held back, waiting to see what would happen.

The range was crackling in the huge kitchen, and the biggest gas stove Emily had ever seen stood against the adjacent wall.

"Peace!" Louise blew out her cheeks, and going to the stove lit a burner, pushing the kettle over it. "We'll have a cup of tea in no time. Are you hungry?"

"Well . . . yes. I didn't get time to eat at home. Too busy washing!" she laughed ruefully, looking at her nails which were still grimy. "That coaldust gets everywhere."

"How do you come to be delivering coal?" Louise called from the larder.

"Mam got herself the job when me dad was conscripted. She took over from him."

"I thought he was boss of a brewery dray?"

"For a while – till he got the sack for drinking some of what he was supposed to deliver. Then he went back to the old job – the coal round."

It was an orderly kitchen – table scrubbed white, a row of scoured pans hanging from hooks, ironed linen draped over the airer against the ceiling, but through a doorway into the scullery Emily glimpsed a mountain of washing-up waiting to be done.

"And you gave up your factory job to come and take over when she became ill? That was very dutiful." Louise reappeared with half a mutton pie and a small dish of cold potatoes. "Will this do? I'll get some pickles and plates." She went to a cupboard.

"It looks a feast." Emily avoided any talk about the factory, and was able to go on avoiding it because a small woman with starched lace cap over salt and pepper hair, walked briskly into the room, skirts crackling.

"What's all this? Where's Cook?" her thin voice was razor sharp.

"I sent Mrs Meery to put her feet up half an hour ago. She wasn't feeling at all well." Louise was equally sharp. "This is Miss Palmer, a friend of mine. We were just about to have supper. Emily, this is Miss Muriel Withers, our matron."

No love lost between them two, Emily thought, acknowledging the curt nod with a brief smile.

"Not another on the sick list – that's the last straw! Washing-up not done, I'll be bound," the matron whisked through into the scullery and out again. "As I thought. It's too bad. We shall be needing those cups and saucers for the bedtime cocoa. I will not tolerate slovenly work. People give into their aches and pains far too easily." She stared at Emily.

"I'll wash up if yo likes," Emily offered, and saw the instant surprise. Narrowed eyes looked her up and down.

"Good for you, Emmie," Louise said with warmth. "You don't mind do you?"

"'Course not!" Emily was thinking it a bit of a laugh, finding herself a skivvy – considering she'd

167

put on her one and only good dress for the visit.

"Very obliging," the matron said briskly. "We could do with more willing hands every day."

The opening was too good to miss. Emily said: "If yo're serious, I'm looking for a job," and saw she had amazed them both. "It's true," she assured Louise. "Mam's going back to work tomorrow, so I was going to have to look round for something." She saw Louise hesitate and wondered if everything was moving too fast. They'd had no time for a real heart to heart to bridge the gap. It was a bit of a cheek forcing herself into Louise's hospital without a by-your-leave. But she met her questioning gaze with a firm smile and a nod.

"I can vouch for Miss Palmer," Louise said staunchly. "You couldn't find a better worker. When can you start, Emily?"

"Now."

"Splendid! That's settled, then. I'm sure Miss Withers has no objections. But you must finish your supper first. I insist. Sit down!" Louise put a plate in front of Emily then cut her a slice of pie. The breezy manner and quick decisive way she put down the knife and served the potatoes with a flourish were all signals Emily recognized. Lou was busy getting her own way. She wasn't going to lose at any price!

It had all been astonishingly easy. Both feet were in the door and the job had tumbled into her lap. All she had to do was eat up and get started at the sink. The temptation was great, but though she might have willingly fooled the matron, Emily couldn't bring herself to deceive Louise.

She took a deep breath. "There's something yo should know before yo takes me on. I ain't got that Leaving Certificate from the last job they says yo're supposed to have now the war's on."

The matron pounced on this. "Why is that?"

"When I left the factory the boss wasn't too pleased."

"She had to leave. Her mother was ill," Louise said quickly.

"I see – so your employer didn't consider nursing your sick mother an adequate reason for resigning your job."

Emily said nothing, hearing the hint of sympathy.

Muriel Withers smoothed her skirt and adjusted the collar of her dress. "I think," inclining her head, "in such . . . unfair circumstances the certificate can be overlooked – as the recommendation is so . . . er . . . reliable," she sniffed. "You will be required to work from seven thirty in the morning until seven at night. We can't offer full board because we're extremely short of space, but you will receive a midday meal and £20 a year – statutory pay for every VAD helper." She waited.

"I'm ever so grateful," Emily said diplomatically. "Yo won't regret taking me on – I'll make sure of that."

With a brisk nod, then a hard stare for Louise, the matron whisked out of the kitchen.

"And how exactly did you come to leave your last job?" Louise asked as they sat down to their supper. "Don't hedge. I know there's more to it than you said."

"I really *did* give in my notice and the boss was that furious. He'd wanted to sack me first."

"I don't believe it – whatever for?"

"Bella and me threatened him with a strike."

Louise went off into a peal of laughter.

"Emmie, you're priceless! What was the reason and who is Bella?"

"Wages – and treatment. D'yo know what they called us women workers? Dilution of labour – sounds like bloomin' washing-up water, don't it? They didn't like us taking over men's jobs, but they needed our hands to work the lathes an' that when the men went off to fight. Our boss had some fancy excuse about us not being able to do the same amount of work in the day as a man could, said the men that were there had families to keep, so we needn't think he was going to pay us the same wages. I wasn't having that! I was helping to keep our May and sending money home. Bella was the same. She worked at the factory on another lathe like me, and we got pally. Our Vic's a bit sweet on her too. She didn't give in her notice, but she got the push all the same. I came back to Brum and she's got a theatre job down the Elephant and Castle. We keep in touch."

Louise took some time cutting a piece of potato into small neat pieces. "How very . . . wise," she said hesitantly, keeping her eyes focused on her plate. "Something we ought to have done . . . *I* ought to have done," she pushed the food into a small pile.

Emily finished what she was eating, speared another piece of pie with her fork and put it in her mouth, deciding against saying anything. After a moment the conversation moved to other things, and it wasn't until they were washing up that Louise became hesitant again.

"I don't know how to put this . . ." she paused, still holding the saucer she had dried.

Such a confession from someone who could always find the exact words to say the most difficult things, made Emily look at her. "If yo means about keeping in touch – what is there to say? What's past is done and gone. Words can't alter nothing." She saw a spasm almost of pain pass across Louise's face and blank out, and wondered if she had been too hard.

"No, I suppose not," Louise said slowly. "In some ways I have been wrong," she paused again, then went on with a rush: "Emmie, I know we can't take up where we left off, but we've been through so much together – those things can never be wiped out."

The look she gave Emily was open and candid – no barriers, no defences. Stirred to her roots, Emily wanted to drop the dishmop, run and put her wet arms round her friend and hug her. In the old days she would have done so, but now a stubborn determination not to be beguiled or rushed kept her at the sink. "I know," she said. "I shan't ever forget neither."

"Well, my girl, and where have yo been? In and out like a whirlwind, no tea, too rushed for a civil word and off again," was the greeting Emily got when she came up the entry and opened the door into her home kitchen.

"I went over to Louise Marshall's place, Mam. Is there a cup of tea going? I'm about done."

Her mother picked up the teapot. "I should've thought yo'd had enough of her Ladyship!"

Tired though she was, Emily couldn't help a private smile at this back-handed support. "Louise is all right, Mam. Yo can't blame her."

A sniff and a disapproving jerk of the bony shoulders. "I always said no good would come of getting mixed up with them Marshalls. Your dad didn't like it neither. They ain't our class."

"Class ain't got nothing to do with it," Emily said irritably, knowing only too well that class had got between herself and Louise, herself and Peter, herself and her ambition to nurse in France. She pushed away the humiliating memory of the interview at Red Cross headquarters in London, asking: "Had a letter from Dad yet?"

"No. But yo knows him – never wrote so much as his name if he could help it." Her mother passed her the mug of tea. "Our Ernie come round when yo were out. He stayed on hoping to see yo and almost missed his lift back to camp. Lena was upset too. She wanted to stay up and show yo how I learned her to read a bit from the Bible. Whatever made yo stay so long? Shouldn't have thought yo'd have much to say to each other. Not now."

"Well, yo thought wrong." Emily was glad to have missed her eldest brother. They had never been friends. "Lena can read to me in the morning. I'll make sure, even if I have to wake her up."

"Why should yo have to wake her – she's always first to have her eyes open."

Emily sighed, too weary to try and hedge. "Because I've got a job at Louise's place and have to be there on the dot of half past seven. It's a hospital now. That's why I'm late. I stayed to lend 'em a hand." She thought of the washing-up, the fifty-eight cups of cocoa she had made and taken round, of yet more washing-up, the breakfast trolley she had prepared, the floor cleaning when a urine bottle had been dropped, the pile of dirty sheets and pillowslips she had sorted.

"Job?" Mam looked up from poking the fire. "What sort of job?"

"Dogsbody. But they'll take me without that certificate. It's a *hospital*, Mam. A way in." In spite of her tiredness she spoke eagerly.

Her mother gave her a sharp look. "How much is her Ladyship paying yo?"

"Not Louise, Mam. It's official – VAD rates. Twenty pounds for the year and free meals."

"Yo've gone silly. Twenty pounds a year? Why yo don't sign on at a proper hospital and make yourself into a real nurse, I don't know. Yo'd get all your keep and learn yourself a profession. If yo're so fired to look after wounded Tommies, the hospitals are full of 'em."

"Because I'd never get to France. I've *told* yo before. Three years' hospital experience before them professional nurses are let to go overseas. It's different for VAD nurses."

"Thought that snotty VAD lot had turned yo down? And where's the nursing in this new job?"

The questions were not new. They had been going round and round in her head. "I know how it looks, Mam, but this is Louise's hospital. She knows me. I'll get chances to learn, they're that short of staff, everybody mucks in. It's my only chance."

"I don't understand yo," her mother poked the fire again hard. "We keeps hearing how they're crying out for nurses to train in hospitals. Plenty of our boys sick and dying over here. Why must you go to France?"

To explain was too difficult. Her need to get there was unbelievably strong, yet the reasons were too private, too sensitive to put into words – talking about guilt and wanting to see real war, Peter's war, and the urge she felt to help in mending and giving back life . . . saying all that out loud would sound daft. She said doggedly: "I have to get to France, Mam. I'm not a child and I've made up my mind."

"Yo could go out like Dorrie Jackson down the street. She's gone out with that Women's Army Corps."

Emily warmed her hands round the mug. "*Nursing*, Mam. I'm not aiming for anything else. And I'll make sure I get up at five tomorrow. I'm not going to leave yo with all that ironing."

"Don't talk so silly. Yo needs all the sleep yo can get."

Emily finished her tea and went to the door at the bottom of the stairs, opening it.

"Yo needs sleep as much as I do. Yo're starting work tomorrow, same as me and I'm younger than yo. I'll do that ironing."

"Yo looking for a clout?" Mam asked.

"No, but . . ."

"Then get up them stairs quick or I'll give yo something yo won't forget in a hurry."

For a second, childhood experience made Emily think she meant it. But the tone was wrong, and the lined face strangely gentle. Surprising herself, Emily came back into the kitchen, quickly kissed the worn cheek, then ran away up to bed.

~CHAPTER 13~

"I want you to understand clearly that this is
a convalescent home for officers – gentlemen,"
the matron's gimlet eyes studied Emily's face to
see if the point had registered. "Hospital staff
may speak when spoken to, but otherwise you
will attend to your work and keep out of the
way. If you observe these rules, we shall be
satisfied. You can begin with the washing-up,
then go and help Edwards with the laundry in
the wash-house."

They were in the old morning room. Emily had
been swept inside with scarcely time to take off her
hat and coat.

"That is all!" the thin eyebrows twitched slightly
with a hint of impatience.

So that's the size of things, Emily thought, going out and back to the kitchen – keep to your station and don't get any fancy notions yo're as good as Them! . . . all right, ma'm, I'll do as yo say because it suits me!

In the scullery she found a plump girl with vivid orange hair, face and arms a mass of freckles, already washing up.

"If yo've other things waiting, I've had strict instructions to do that," Emily was unintentionally brusque.

The girl smiled broadly. "The Withers been at yo, laying down the law? Don't take it to heart – we all gets the same first day. She can be a proper tartar, but she ain't afraid of work, mind. Yo're Emily Palmer, ain't yo? I'm Winnie Mason, one of the ward maids. Here – start drying. We'll get this lot done the both of us before yo can say knife. A little bit of help is worth a deal of pity."

Emily took the wiping-up cloth. "Yo been here long?"

"Couple of months. I don't live in. I come in on me bike every day. I was in service till our Billy joined up. Mam can't do for herself, see – rheumatics. So I came back to be with her. Yo got anyone in the war?"

"Two brothers and my dad. Dad's the only one in France right now."

"So's our Billy. I can't help worrying."

"I know. It's awful when yo don't hear. My dad was never any good at writing letters." Emily found herself chatting and laughing with this girl, making the rest of the morning spent in the wash-house with the sharp-tongued Mrs Edwards easier to take. The copper boiled. Emily pounded sheets in the dolly-tub – turned the wheel of the huge wooden mangle. Cascades of water squeezed out of the linen and splashed into the tub below. Damp with sweat and steam, arms aching, Emily kept her temper by ignoring the older woman's carping, deciding the best plan was to hold her own tongue and keep eyes and ears open.

But sticking to plans and rules wasn't so easy. There were the patients.

After a hurried midday meal of stew with hunks of bread, and tea to wash it down, Emily was sent to collect the patients' used crockery, and happened to wheel the trolley into the old dining-room ward when no other staff were there.

"A new inmate, by Jove! How d'do, m'dear. Pass that book would you?" An officer with one leg in plaster, crutches propped against his chair, smiled and pointed.

Another leaned forward in his bed holding out a paper bag. "Have a toffee?"

Handing over the book Emily took a sweet and slipped it into her pocket. "Thanks."

"Open my locker . . . er . . . what's your name?" the man in the next bed looked at her enquiringly.

"Palmer – Emily."

"Well, Palmer Emily, see that bottle behind the box? Pass it over . . . that's the ticket! Now then, let's lace up the old lemonade."

"Don't play tricks on the girl, Kearnen. You know perfectly well whisky is forbidden," said the officer who had asked for his book.

178

"Rubbish. Palmer Emily's a good sort, aren't you? We're going to get on famously."

"Just fish that pen of mine from under the bed – can't reach the blasted thing!" A request from a bed near the fireplace.

Emily fished, passed, fetched, scrabbled on her knees, willingly – but when she bent over to retrieve a pair of slippers and felt a hand grasp her thigh and squeeze it through her skirt, she forgot about rules. She whipped round.

"I'll thank yo to keep your hands to yourself! I'll do whatever I can for yo, but I ain't having any hanky panky and that's flat!"

There was a burst of laughter. Kearnen waved his beaker of whisky lemonade. "That'll teach you, Jonah!"

Jonah scowled from his wheelchair, and Emily, seeing he had a leg missing, the other without a foot, wished she hadn't been so quick to flare up.

"She's extremely touchy for a ward maid," Jonah drawled, triggering another shout of laughter.

Even Emily, resenting his patronizing manner, had to grin. At least he can see the funny side, she thought as his scowl gave way to a reluctant twitch of the lips. She took hold of the trolley and the incident might have ended there.

"Why are you wasting time?" said an indignant voice. "What do you think you are supposed to be doing?"

Emily whipped round again and found herself confronted by Mrs Boston. The shock brought colour rushing into her face, but the old woman glared, showing no surprise. Her mouth was set in the same grim line Emily remembered so clearly from the terrible day in Holland Park when Peter had made her pour the tea. She hadn't seen the old battleaxe since, and facing her now stirred up unwelcome memories and feelings.

"Get back to your work in the kitchen, Palmer," the voice was like steel; glance like needles.

"Miss Palmer has been helping with all those awkward things we chaps can't manage yet, Mrs Boston," Jonah said smoothly. "Bending and stretching is beyond us. We were having a laugh about it. But of course, now *you* are here . . ." he spread his hands and smiled charmingly.

This support from such an unexpected quarter and done in a way so reminiscent of Peter made Emily gasp, then warm to him. As she wheeled the loaded trolley into the hall she saw him wink, and thought: he's a corker – meaning to have a laugh about it with Winnie, but a nurse bustled into the kitchen pushing a bucket of soiled dressings at her.

"Get rid of these for me. Mason'll show you where." She was away before Emily could open her mouth, then reappeared, craning her head round the door. "I suppose you're the dressmaker? Matron says to start mending in the storeroom – up two flights, end of the passage . . . and don't take longer than four o'clock because you've to peel the veggies for tomorrow." The head vanished.

Winnie dried her hands. "No peace for the wicked! Come outside and I'll show yo the bins and the sluice where yo can wash out the bucket. Don't bother about the crocks, I'll see to them."

"Thanks," Emily said gratefully.

Upstairs she lost her way, opening the far door not into the storeroom, but a small ward of three beds.

A nurse in VAD uniform, a pair of rubber gloves on her hands, was bending over the nearest bed which was hidden from the others by a folding screen. There was no screen between the door and bed, and Emily saw the patient lying almost naked. He looked a thin stripling, hipbones protruding from a starved abdomen where an ugly inflamed wound ran in a jagged line from ribs to thigh. The flesh was laced and puckered like a badly sewn seam, the stitches dark against fevered skin. The lad was frowning, eyes tight shut, his face almost as white as the pillow under his head. She felt shock and intense pity, but wasn't repulsed and wanted very much to stay and watch everything that had to be done, while feeling an intruder, stumbling in on a very private moment.

The nurse looked up: "Did you want something?"

"I was looking for the storeroom. Must have lost my way."

"You should have turned right at the top of the stairs. Door at the far end." The nurse picked up a swab of cotton wool and went on with her work. Reluctantly Emily closed the door.

Throughout the rest of the day, isolated with the mending, and in the company of Winnie and Mrs Meery, Emily could not stop thinking about the boy on the bed, her mind replacing him with Vic, then Dad, then after a moment with Peter's "old" Box . . . and before she could stop herself

181

she was seeing the charred basket and Pete himself, his lovely curly hair shrivelled, skin seared and peeling . . .

She gave herself a hard mental shake, but the lingering impressions remained and were with her when she met Louise coming into the hall as she was about to leave for home.

"Oh Emmie . . . I'm glad you haven't gone yet," Louise had a letter in her hand which she slid into her pocket as if she didn't want Emily to see. "How's the first day been?"

"All right, thanks. Did all sorts – and got me knuckles rapped. Yo didn't say as your auntie was here."

"Oh Lord! I should have warned you," Louise pulled a face. "She's rapped my knuckles as well, more than once, if that's any consolation. Don't be put off."

"I won't."

"Good. I feel sort of responsible for you."

"I don't see why. I was the one to push meself forward. I wanted to work in a hospital."

Louise looked relieved. "I'm so glad. Pete always said . . ." she broke off, darting a glance – then went on firmly: "Pete used to tell me he thought you'd make a splendid nurse."

"Chance'ud be a fine thing." Emily didn't want to be reminded again about Peter.

"Come on, Emmie, it's not like you to give up!" Louise was all encouragement. "You're so capable – I'd tell that to anybody. Go on – volunteer!"

Emily was too tired to explain about having applied at Devonshire House before, only to be turned down. She wished Lou would offer her a lift. Maybe she would tell her on the way home – or tomorrow.

But Louise didn't offer a lift, and many tomorrows went by with time only for a quick "Hello" or a wave. Weeks slid past . . . wet June, July, sultry August. Emily began to despair of ever being anything more than kitchen dogsbody. Then one hot August morning the telephone rang as she came into the hall on her way to empty a bucket of slops.

Marion picked up the receiver: "Tower House Hospital, good morning . . . yes?" and then with a note of alarm: "When did you say? A couple of hours? Oh my goodness! Yes . . . yes of course, I'll tell her. Goodbye!"

Emily slowed down. "What's happened?"

"We've to find at least twenty extra beds . . . *twenty*! And the train is arriving any time now." She unpinned her hat, dropping it on to the desk: "Matron will be beside herself," hurrying away to find her.

Emily went on down the passage, passing Betty Pritchard and Dot Best, two of the VAD nurses, and gave them the news.

"*Twenty?*" Dot gaped.

Betty fanned herself with a chubby hand. "Whatever will Matron say?"

They found out when Marion came scurrying to tell all staff to go immediately to the office. As they crowded in, Emily could sense the tension. She looked across at the thin ramrod matron. Apart from a spot of colour burning on each pale cheek, she seemed as unruffled and in command as ever, coming directly to the point:

"There is an emergency. The numbers of wounded returning from the Front has increased beyond expectation." She glanced at the watch pinned to her bodice. "We have to accommodate twenty extra patients who will be here within two hours. Which means some rearrangement." She turned to Marion: "Telephone HQ and see how many beds they can loan us with pillows and blankets – and don't let them make excuses, Miss Croft. Insist on speaking to the commandant in chief if they persist with difficulties . . . Pritchard, Mason, Palmer, Best – take the mattresses from all staff beds including mine and Miss Marshall's, and place them on tables and floor in the common room. Then you can close up the beds in the wards as much as possible to make space for extra beds. Nurse Campbell, take Morgan and Fisher with you to settle all of our patients possible in armchairs, then make up their beds for the incoming wounded. Has anyone any problems?" She scanned the room – a brisk hard gaze that dared anyone to complain. "Very well, go and get on with it."

Emily went with the three others to the top storey. They began to strip down the first beds.

Winnie took hold of one end of a mattress. "I'm that scared. A bloke in our street has just come back from Wipers . . . says it's like a slaughterhouse. He saw our Billy there, near a place called Pashunsomethingorother . . ."

"Passchendaele," Betty said.

"That's it. Like a slaughterhouse, he says. D'yo reckon this lot comes from there?" Her usual cheerful air had vanished. She looked drawn and anxious.

Emily lifted the other end of the mattress. "Could be. If yo ask me we aren't told the half of what's going on at the Front."

They struggled downstairs to the common room and went back for another. All of them were running with sweat, backs aching, by the time they had finished.

"Oh for a cup of tea!" Winnie stretched her arms, easing her shoulders.

"You can forget the tea," Dot had glanced through the window. "Here's the first ambulance!"

Emily went into the hall and seeing Marion, asked: "How many beds did yo manage?"

"Fifteen they said, but there's no sign of them yet. I don't know what we're going to do. Matron says to send anyone spare outside to her . . ."

Emily left before she finished, and found Muriel Withers listening to one of the harassed drivers.

"You'll be getting thirty, miss – everywhere's in the same boat, having more'n they bargained for. We've got orders to make sure each hospital takes what's sent. Word has come through from London another train-load is on the way. Snowed under at Snow Hill!" He smiled bleakly.

Muriel Withers didn't smile at all. "Very well, we'll manage . . . Palmer," giving Emily a shrewd look, "go with the first patient to the common room and stay there. I'll send Nurse Campbell along as soon as she's free. Meanwhile, do what you can for each patient."

Emily felt a thrill of excitement. A chance to do some real nursing! In the common room she pulled back the bedclothes, watching the stretcher-bearers gently lift then lower the wounded man. His chest and neck were swathed in grimy bandages and a rough stained dressing was bound to his forehead. He seemed dazed.

"Any walking cases for us?" Emily asked.

"Dunno, miss. A couple, if yo're lucky. Our lot are all flat on their backs, poor beggars." They went away.

There was nothing she could do about the man's wounds, but she sponged his face and helped him drink some water, then settled his pillows.

"Thanks, Nurse," his fingers brushed against her hand and took hold of it. He murmured: "Clean sheets . . ." eyelids drooping.

Emily felt a lump come into her throat, but she could not stay. The stretcher-bearers were back with another man, then another . . .

"It's like musical chairs out there!" Nurse Campbell had come in loaded with a basket of dressings, swabs and ointments in one hand and a basin of disinfectant in the other.

"Have the beds arrived yet?" Emily asked.

"No. Matron's got nearly all our officers up and in chairs for the time being . . . Palmer, you'll have to help me swab out the wounds or I'll never be done." She peeled back a stained bandage. "And don't forget to find yourself some rubber gloves. Can't have anyone off sick with septic fingers. Pass that basin, would you? Oh . . . look at this . . . I don't know . . ."

Emily saw something squirming along the seam of the unbuttoned pyjama jacket, and recognized lice.

"Supposed to be cleaned up before they got here," Nurse Campbell whispered in her ear as she turned away. "Go and get the poor chap a fresh pair would you – and you'd better bring some more Lysol while you're about it."

There was no time for a midday meal, and by the end of the day Emily was beginning to wonder how much longer she could go on putting one foot in front of the other. Plodding into the courtyard with yet another bucket of soiled dressings, she saw the Maudslay being garaged in one of the far stables. In spite of her exhaustion she went across, hoping for a word with Louise.

"Why, if it isn't Emily Palmer! What an age since we last met. Louise has told me all about you working here." Una Holiday showed her little rabbit teeth in a beaming smile as she sat in the car.

Emily's heart sank and she cast a despairing glance at Louise, who didn't seem to notice.

"I've managed a transfer from Hill Crest," Una went on. "I'm not supposed to be here until tomorrow but with things as they are I thought I'd come and lend a hand tonight. By the way, have you heard about Mary Grant?"

Emily shook her head, wondering how to get Louise alone.

"Promoted!" Una sounded as triumphant as if it was her own success. "A senior post at Devonshire House – a *really* senior post. I suppose being a Lady does have a certain pull."

"I suppose it does." Emily gave up the idea of talking to Louise and tried to ease away, but Una was out of the car.

"Are you going to dump that rubbish? I'll come along. Might as well learn the places I need to know about. What good-sized bins!"

Una bustled after Emily, and when she finally got away from her, Louise had disappeared. The whole of this extraordinary day seemed to have crystallized her impatience to get to France. Not sometime in the vague future, but right now. She had wanted to ask Louise's advice, but the opportunity had gone.

The urgency remained, pursuing her home, getting up with her and had become even more pressing when ten days later she got to work and found Winnie snivelling into a bowl of washing-up.

"What's the matter, love?" Emily put an arm round her shoulders.

"Our Billy's been posted missing. We heard this morning. Mam's sure he's dead. She's that upset. Oh, Emmie, what'll I do?"

"Yo ought to have stayed home with her."

Tears began to flow down the sides of Winnie's snub nose. "I know. I'm afraid she'll have one of her turns and I won't be there, but the job . . ." she broke off.

Emily pushed her from the sink. "Blow the job. I'll finish this, and stand in for yo. Get off home."

188

"I can't do that! Matron'll never let me. She's been going on about how short-handed we are."

"Don't ask then – just go."

"Emmie, I couldn't. She'd throw a fit!"

"Let her." Emily grasped Winnie by each of her plump shoulders and turned her round. "And don't fret about losing your job. I'll tell her what's happened. Yo may get a flea in your ear, but yo won't get the sack if we're short-handed. I'll be the one on the carpet anyroad." She watched Winnie collect her belongings, then turned to the washing-up, knowing what was to come.

She didn't have to wait long. In less than half an hour Muriel Withers marched into the kitchen.

"What's this I hear about Mason going home? Is she ill? She should have reported to me."

"No, ma'am, she isn't ill. She heard today her brother's reported missing. She came in, but she was worried sick. Her mother's that upset and she's an invalid. I said to go home – that I'd do her work." Emily waited for the explosion.

"You told Mason to *go home*? *You* told her?" the matron's pale face suffused with angry colour. She scanned the kitchen.

Mrs Meery stood unmoving by the table, and Betty Pritchard who happened to come in at that moment, froze, hand on the doorknob.

"You," the matron jabbed a finger at Emily. "Come to my office!"

She was for it now all right! Emily stuck out her jaw. Would she be sent packing this minute? She trudged after the bristling figure whose snapping skirts were almost visibly shooting out sparks of anger.

Inside the office Emily stood stolidly in front of the desk, refusing to let the blistering tirade get to her. She had explained and that was that. Nothing was going to make her lick this woman's boots and whine excuses when all she'd done was what anyone with a bit of heart would do. She looked across at the chiffonier, piled with files and papers. Always before there had been a bowl of flowers on it, she remembered. Flowers softened a place. None there now.

"You may count yourself fortunate we are so stretched for help," the scouring voice said finally, "I shall not sack you on the spot, which is what you deserve. I can see clearly the mistake I made taking on anyone without a Leaving Certificate. The error will not occur again. As soon as I can replace you I will. Mason should have had more sense than to listen to you. I shall deal with her when she returns. You can go."

Dismissed, Emily worked through a day of disasters – a tray dropped, crockery broken, two saucepans burned dry – so that when she ran to catch her tram home she wasn't surprised to see it move away from the stop without her. A heavy drizzle had started and she had no mackintosh. Walking home she got soaked through, shoes squelching. Turning into her street she saw the poster that said:

EAT LESS BREAD FOR VICTORY

and thought: if we eats much less we won't be far off starving! But when she opened the kitchen door a wonderful smell of frying bacon met her.

"Sit yourself down, your supper's all but done," Mam said.

"Where did yo get that?" Emily was looking at the large slice of prime back in the pan. "Yo never bought it?"

"From our Ernie."

"Oh Mam – he's up to some fiddle, yo know he is, coming here with food and sweets and all sorts."

Her mother turned on her: "Yo don't know that. Get it down yo and shut up."

Emily took off her wet shoes. "I'm too tired to eat."

"And waste good food? Yo'd cut off your nose to spite your face, yo would. That stubborn!" Mam sat down in the wooden armchair by the range as if suddenly overcome with weariness. "We've never had two farthings to rub together, and what we had the war's taken. Our men as well as the bread out of our mouths. We deserve summat."

How did you deal with pity? Emily didn't know. It tangled with her exasperation and wrecked the hard arguments she had ready, threatening to use up the last of her energy, which mustn't happen. She had important things to do.

"Just give me a cup of tea and a slice of bread to take up. Save the bacon and I'll eat it cold for breakfast."

Upstairs she moved quietly so she wouldn't wake Lena asleep in the bed they shared. Taking paper, pen and ink from a box on the chest of drawers, she sat on the floor to write in the last of the fading twilight.

How did you address a Lady? Emily bit the end of the pen. Stared through the cracked window. Watched a pigeon fly on to the roof opposite – a homely thing.

Homely! That was it. Comrade to comrade. Friend to friend. She began to write:

Dear Mary,
   It seems ever such a long time since we marched up Constitution Hill together alongside Mrs Pankhurst. I hope you don't mind me writing now for a bit of advice . . .

She signed the letter, read it through, then putting it in the envelope, wrote the address.

Lady Mary Grant,
Red Cross Headquarters,
Devonshire House,
Piccadilly,
London

She posted it in the morning, and Mam handed her the reply four days later. Her hand trembled as she slit the envelope with her supper knife and pulled out the thick paper.

Dear Emily,
   How good to hear from an old comrade after all this time. It gave a lift to my day. I

will do my best to provide the advice – and will say first of all I think your best chance of getting to France will be from London. There should be no difficulty becoming a VAD nurse here, especially as you say you passed the First Aid and Home Nursing exam. That anyone should have the impudence to turn you down in the first place is a disgrace – but much has changed since this dreadful war began.

So – sign on at one of the Red Cross detachments (a few listed overleaf) and you should soon be placed in a London hospital to learn the basics and with a little luck should get posted without delay. I can't guarantee this, you understand, but the numbers of wounded have increased alarmingly and nurses are needed urgently everywhere. Experience and some luck then – if you can call it luck to be dragged into the Front Line of war!

I hope we find time to meet and talk over old times. If you encounter any difficulties, you know where to reach me. Please remember me to Louise and Una. I was glad to have news of them.

Yours in friendship,
Mary

"Well?" Mam was eaten by curiosity.

Emily passed over the letter. "I'm on my way, Mam. They'll take me for a nurse after all. I'll give in my notice and work out the week, then I'll be off to London."

Lena, elbows on the table as she ate her supper of bread and dripping, began to whine: "Oh our Emmie, yo ain't going . . . I don't want you to go away . . ."

Emily went and gave her a hug. "It ain't for ever, love. I'll be turning up like a bad penny again, yo see!"

Telling Louise was less easy and she had given in her notice before they met briefly a few mornings later, as Louise was going out of the hospital and Emily going in. Emily gave her Mary's letter.

"There you are, what did I tell you! That's splendid," Louise said.

"Yo aren't put out?"

"Why should I be?" Louise seemed amazed.

"Me moving on so quick. I feel I'm letting yo down."

"Of course you aren't. It's what we said before, Pete and me – you'll make a splendid nurse." There was a breath of hesitation before she smiled brightly. "Go ahead – *do* it."

They looked at each other, both aware of a reservation that had not been there in the pre-war days. With a touch of regret Emily thought: we're older – too much has happened. She wondered if the shadow of Peter would always lie between them, and for a moment felt sad, but couldn't stay downhearted.

She didn't see Louise again until her last day at the Tower House Hospital, and even then they almost missed each other. After hanging about for some time, Emily was on her way to catch the tram when Louise drove up and stopped.

194

"I'm so glad I caught you. I was afraid you would have gone – I'm terribly late. I want to wish you good luck."

"Thanks."

"I'd drive you home only I promised Aunt G ages ago to take her to her next precious whist drive, and of course it's this evening!"

Emily smiled. "It don't matter. Me tram's just coming."

Louise squeezed her hand, then impulsively reached up and pulled down Emily's head, kissing her cheek and almost knocking off her hat. "Take care of yourself, my dear, and write – don't forget!"

Emily straightened her hat, cheeks burning, eyes very bright. "And yo too."

"Yes."

"I'll have to go – don't want to miss me tram. 'Bye, Louise!" She turned and ran.

As the tram began to jolt away Emily leaned back against the slatted wooden seat, blinking away unwanted tears. Partings, she thought, this damn war seems nothing but heartache and partings.

~CHAPTER 14~

From the outside the hostel was not inviting. A grey barren three-storey building set in a dusty patch of overgrown garden. Inside wasn't much better, Emily discovered, as she clattered after the housekeeper up lino-covered stairs. The room she was taken into was dingy and uncarpeted, divided into four by curtains that might once have been blue chintz, but over the years had washed down to a universal spotty grey.

"This is yours," said the old woman, pointing to the far cubicle.

A small grubby sash window filtered light on to an iron bedstead, a washstand and a tiny chest of drawers. The only reassuring thing in sight was the old green tin trunk she had sent on in advance.

"I'll be in the basement making a cup of tea if there's anything you want," the housekeeper said.

"Thanks." Emily waited until she had gone, then unpinned her brand new uniform cap, took it off and placed it reverently on the chest of drawers. Buying her Red Cross uniform had left her almost broke, but she didn't care. She was bursting with pride.

The cubicle still looked bare and impersonal. Impulsively she opened the trunk and rummaged about, taking out Vic's photograph in its papier mâché frame. It wasn't a very good likeness, he looked far too stiff and solemn, but it was a piece of home. She placed it by the cap and then found the pincushion Lena had made for her last Christmas – gaudy patchwork bits cobbled together with endearing big stitches. Another bit of home – the sight cheered her. Already she was feeling less of a stranger.

The cubicle was stuffy. Late September rain combining with sudden sunshine had turned the air humid. Undoing the catch, Emily pushed up the window and looked out at the mean little street below. Cockney sparrows quarrelled in the gutter and a totter's cart like a rubbish tip rumbled past. Some children were playing a skipping game, oblivious of the fine drizzle. She watched a cat stalk through the shadow of a wall, keeping a wary distance from the children. A street like thousands, she thought, full of living things – and had the eerie impression that row upon row of soldier's faces, Peter's among them, were pressed against the overlapping panes of glass where a trapped bluebottle buzzed. They seemed to beg her to let them in.

She twisted away, telling herself not to be such a fool – mooning over unchangeable things! At supper she worked to keep her mind on the present, listening to nurses' gossip. Afterwards she nosed about the hostel sizing up the elderly bathroom geyser and deciding to leave well alone.

At five the next morning an alarm clock shattered Emily's sleep. It was still dark. Feet pattered across the boards and the shared electric light was switched on, giving out a hard unshaded glare. Emily got sleepily out of bed, and, pouring water from the enamel jug she had brought up the night before, splashed her face and neck. Putting on the new uniform, she felt a little leap of joy. She was on her way! Only one more piece of luck, that's all she needed.

"'Scuse me," said a voice.

Emily turned to see a long face apparently hanging mid-air between the cubicle curtains. Big brown eyes blinked, reminding her of a friendly horse.

"Sorry if I made you jump. Thought you should know that the tram leaves in half an hour. Mug of tea downstairs. Breakfast's at the hospital."

"Thanks for telling me," Emily said.

"It's raining cats and dogs. I should take spare shoes and stockings as well as an extra apron. I'm Norah Smith, by the way. I was late back last night so we didn't get to meet. Such a to-do in the ward. Priors fainted right in the middle of cupping poor old Moggs. He was so upset. Brought on his asthma. You'll be coming with me to the surgical ward."

Emily rapidly packed the little attaché case she used for carrying overalls and sandwiches in her factory days, then went downstairs for her tea, but had to wait for Norah.

She came rushing up looking harassed. "Sorry to keep you – couldn't find my other shoes!"

"The rest have gone on. Hadn't we better hurry?"

They ran – rainwater splashing shoes and the backs of their stockings, mackintoshes flapping – panting up to the stop as the crowded tram arrived; piling in.

"That's the lot!" the conductress's arm came down like a barrier between Norah, last to climb on, and five other VAD nurses. "Sorry, my loves, you'll have to wait for the next."

"Why is it always on wet days that the tram is choc-a-bloc?" Norah complained as they squeezed between the seats and grabbed at the hanging leather straps.

The answer seemed obvious to Emily, but she didn't say anything.

"Sandcastle's a demon for punctuality. Lucky we didn't have to walk." Rain was dripping off Norah's nose.

The tram began a slow stop-start journey down Denmark Street, and even with straps to hang on to it was difficult keeping their balance.

"How long have you worked in the hospital?" Emily asked.

"Since March," Norah swayed; recovered. "Before that I helped Mother in the shop. We've got a newsagent's. I went to Red Cross in the evenings to roll bandages. Got the nursing bug there, I suppose! What about you?"

"Did all sorts . . ." Emily fell against her. "I'll tell yo sometime. What I mean to do as soon as I can is get out to France."

"Rather you than me. I've heard some tales in the ward about what it's like – makes your hair curl!"

The stuffy air was dank, windows steamed up and ran with moisture. Conversation lapsed and only began again when they got off and reached the entrance of the sprawling general hospital. Under the heavy sky the building rose gaunt and forbidding with rows of identical windows, the red-brick outline saved from total grimness by gables and a wealth of mellowing creeper which climbed almost to the roof.

"There's more than this place," Norah said as they went in. "Huts have been put up in the park, and three schools and a chapel taken over. That's the war for you."

The VAD cloakroom, Emily discovered as they toiled up several flights of stairs, was about as awkwardly placed as it could be – well away from their ground-floor surgical ward. She felt keyed up as they changed stockings and shoes and put on the crisp aprons, pinned caps to hair, and thought of the Tower House Hospital routines which she knew like the back of her hand. Everything about this place seemed different. Long corridors. Countless doors. Nurses, orderlies and porters scurrying about. Rows of empty stretchers were pushed against the corridor walls; others were carried past, their burdens covered with red blankets.

"It'll be in at the deep end," Norah murmured, pushing open the ward door. "We used to have instruction time for beginners, but now we're so rushed it's learn as you go – except for the professionals, of course. *They* get lectures come what may!" She sounded tart.

The ward was whitewashed, with high windows looking down on long rows of beds. The contrast to the cosy intimate little wards Emily had been used to couldn't have been greater, despite flowered curtains and a bunch of chrysanthemums beside a gramophone on the ward table. But she knew the smell – Lysol with that underlying sourness of festering wounds. Any other impressions had to wait, because Sister Castle, square and starched, was there waiting, with a tall pale VAD nurse standing quietly in the background.

Emily knew immediately how the nickname "Sandcastle" had come about – sandy hair, sandy eyebrows, sandy freckles, even the colour of her eyes were the light gold of a sandy beach. She looked down at the silver watch attached to her apron bib.

"Only just in time, Smith," a soft Scottish voice with a hint of steel.

"Sorry, Sister. The tram was slow."

"I don't wish for excuses. Next time get up earlier. Is this the new VAD probationer?"

"Yes, Sister. Emily Palmer."

The sister looked her up and down, while behind her the VAD nurse caught Emily's eye, and a hint of a smile hovered round the sensitive mouth. Strange eyes, slanting and so green, Emily thought, knowing her attention ought to be solely on Sister Castle.

"You – Palmer!"

Emily said: "Yes, Sister!" quickly.

"There's mud on your shoe. Clean it off and make sure you wash your hands afterwards . . . Smith, straighten your cap! A good nurse is a neat nurse. Neat in dress, manner and attitude of mind. The sooner you attend to those three maxims, the quicker we shall make useful nurses out of you. Priors . . ."

"Sister?" the drawling almost insolent voice startled Emily. She had heard voices like that before in Mrs Silver's fitting room and in posh London houses. They found fault, were nit-picking about every last line of featherstitching, and usually had mouths like traps that never offered a smile.

"No fainting fits today, I hope? You are fully recovered?"

"Perfectly, Sister." Thin nervous fingers smoothed the sides of an immaculate apron.

Sister Castle eyed the group. "Three of you, so no excuse for being slipshod. Priors and Palmer, work together. Smith, you come with me. I want as many wounds dressed as possible before Matron arrives." She consulted her watch again.

Emily's stomach rumbled. Breakfast seemed to have been overlooked. But with a flick of her cuffs, Sister added:

"Priors, take Palmer to the canteen after the beds are made. Fifteen minutes precisely, then I want you back here neat and smiling," she gave them a copybook smile. For a whisker of time her hard outer shell seemed to soften and unveil a touch of humour. Then her mouth pinched together. "I said *smiling*," she waited.

The three smiled dutifully.

"That's better."

She moved away and Emily began helping Priors with the bedmaking.

"I can see you've done this before," Priors drawled as they rolled the patient on to his side, smoothed out the first two-thirds of the sheet and mitred the corner before rolling him the other way.

"Once or twice," Emily said dryly, unfolding a clean sheet.

"Lovely!" the wounded man settled with a sigh of content, smiling up at Emily. "We've not seen your bright face in this ward before, have we, Nurse?"

"No," Emily passed a corner of the sheet to Priors.

He rubbed his shadowy chin. "I've not shaved and my old back's murder this morning, so I can't sit up and give you a welcoming kiss." He appealed to Priors: "Nurse, can't you give me something to ease it? Old Satan's got his team mining down there."

"Medicines will be round later," Priors tucked in the blankets.

"Oh, you're a hard one . . . isn't she hard?" he said, turning to Emily. "But I can see your heart is made of softer stuff – you'll tell Sister how I'm suffering?" he smiled coaxingly.

"That's enough of your Welsh charm, Corporal Jones," Priors said crisply. "Watch out for him, Palmer, he's got a tongue like oiled silk."

"Blackening my character!" Corporal Jones pushed stubby fingers through his short dark hair, making it twist in all directions. "And me flat on my aching back!"

Emily couldn't stop the smile, but they were already moving to the next bed and the man lying there had the benefit of it. The quiet slow upward curve of his blue lips broke the lines of pain marking his gaunt face.

"This is our other Corporal Jones," Priors said. "How are you this morning?"

"Still here, Nurse. But how's yourself? You gave us all a turn last night, passing out like that. Poor old Moggsie was right worried. They should let you have the morning off. Here . . . I'll sit out while you make me bed. I'm summat of a weight to haul about."

He sat forward with effort and Emily could hear the breath wheeze in his chest. He was a weight – with great shoulders and huge scarred hands that looked as if they were used to heavy manual work, but now lay limp at his sides. As she helped strip back the bedclothes a sour smell met her and she saw the stained bandages on the stump of one leg.

"Don't you dream of getting up," Priors slid her hand under his armpit, easing him down. "Lie back . . . that's it. I'm fit enough to dance the Highland Fling today. Quite recovered."

He watched them with grave blue eyes. "They call us Jones One and Jones Two," he told Emily. "Just to make sure they don't dose us up with the wrong jollup. I'm Number One because I was here first. He's nobbut a newcomer," thumbing at the Welshman. "Only been in our hotel three weeks."

"That Jones Two is a card," Emily said later over porridge and tea in the canteen.

"He's always complaining," Priors said, stirring sugar into her mug. "But to tell the truth I'm hoping he can feel something, however painful. He was shot in the back and hasn't been able to move or feel his legs since." She took a long drink of tea: "Oh, I needed that!" then attacked her porridge. "I thought those bandages on Jones One were a bit suspect. Niffy and a bad colour – did you notice?"

"A pong like reesty bacon," Emily said.

"Poor fellow," Priors shook her head. "God forbid it's gangrene on top of all his other problems."

"What else is wrong with him?"

"Dicky heart. Emphysema. A wife who has left him . . . and of course only one leg!" Priors ate the rest of her porridge in silence, then almost threw down her spoon. It clattered on the oilcloth. "He used to be a miner, think of that – a big

205

strong man. He once told me he could lift three hundredweight of coal . . . and now it's all he can do to lift his arm."

Emily watched her – eating her own porridge and drinking her tea in silence. She warmed to Priors, but was wary of finally making up her mind about her yet.

Priors let out a short laugh. Her shoulders sagged. "Sorry to go on at you – your first morning too! If you've finished we'd better get back. Sister will want to get Jonesie cleaned up before Matron stalks the ward.

But when they returned to the ward they found the Matron's visit had been postponed, which was just as well, Emily thought, as the day progressed and she managed to drop a full bedpan. The contents splashed over Sandcastle's apron and legs.

"Incompetent and careless!" the scathing look and snapping words were still ringing in Emily's ears when she returned to the hostel.

"You don't want to fret about it." Norah kicked off her shoes and flopped on her bed. "My feet are killing me!" She looked pale and tired, but managed a grin. "We all do daft things sometimes. You see, it'll be peaceful tomorrow. Humdrum, Olivia predicts." She saw Emily's puzzled look. "Didn't you know Priors's name? Olivia ffoulkes-Priors with two little fs and a hyphen – how's that for a signature?"

"She's really out of the top drawer then," Emily said. Yet this wasn't quite right. Something about Priors didn't fit into any kind of class. A square peg in a round hole? That wasn't right either. She was an odd fish.

Emily was made aware of this again a few mornings later when Olivia arrived in the ward with a huge white caterer's box in one hand and a carrier bag in the other. She put down the box on the ward table where Sister Castle was checking the night sister's report.

"Whatever's that, Priors?"

"Chocolate éclairs, Sister," Olivia opened the box. "Do have one. I've brought enough for everyone in the ward . . . and these," producing carnations and parsley, "for Jumbo as he can't take rich things yet."

About to start on the round of bedmaking, Emily waited for the explosion which didn't come, and later was amused to see Sandcastle tucking into her éclair in her office. The incident produced a warm glow, as if she had come across an old friend, a feeling which strengthened as days moved into weeks and the probationary month drew to a close.

"Two more days and you will be a fully fledged VAD nurse. Next stop France!" Olivia smiled across the medicine trolley as they worked their way from bed to bed, Emily passing bottles and pillboxes.

"I hope so." She wished her feet didn't ache so much. The day had been hectic: a new influx of patients all needing rapid attention, on top of which was May's anxious letter about Mrs Silver's stroke. "Jones Two," she said, passing a bottle to Olivia standing between the beds of the two corporals. "Jones One."

207

"Thought so!" the drawl disappeared. "You've mixed up the medicines. Digitalis when it should have been aspirin. Read, woman! You have eyes!"

Emily felt sick and shocked. "I'm sorry." The mistake was *unforgivable*. Shame weighed on her.

"Sorry won't do. Thank your stars I'm not Sister Castle."

Emily followed Olivia in silence, humiliated by the lapse and sure that Priors must think her a fool or worse. But at the end of the day she had another shock.

"Like to come dancing tonight?" Olivia put a hand on her arm. "Do come, Palmer. Life shouldn't be all work."

For a moment Emily was speechless with amazement. All of her ached with fatigue, yet the chance to get to know this woman outside work was very tempting. Hesitating, she shook her head.

"I'd like to ever so, but I've got to write to my sister. She's having a bad time."

"Another time, then," Olivia said lightly.

They parted, and watching her walk away Emily thought regretfully: I've never been dancing in me life!

~CHAPTER 15~

Devonshire House in Piccadilly, classical and imposing in the pale autumn sunlight, seemed less daunting than the first time Emily had confronted it over a year ago. The memory of that visit was with her now. She tightened her mouth. This time she'd make sure nobody gave her the cold shoulder.

She went in through the heavy doors to the large entrance hall. At the far end a stout woman in matron's dress was interviewing someone. Nearer, a girl in Red Cross uniform sat behind a table. She looked up as Emily came in.

"Can I help you?"

"I'd like to see Lady Mary Grant," Emily said firmly.

"Is she expecting you?"

"I haven't got an appointment if that's what yo mean, but she knows I'm coming. She did invite me."

The girl looked doubtful.

"Say it's Emily Palmer, and that I've managed to get two hours off unexpected – she'll understand."

"I'll try," the girl sounded unsure.

"Yes, try." Emily was surprising herself. Last time she had quaked in her boots, and now here she was issuing orders; like Louise might, or Priors. Would Mary also be changed?

She was not kept waiting to find out, and a few moments later was led to an office where Mary was sitting at a typewriter behind an orderly desk framed by the tall window. As she glanced up, Emily saw lines furrowing her smooth forehead, cheekbones prominent under skin that seemed tired, until her face broke into a delighted smile. Pausing only to take off her pince-nez and place them with familiar precision between a carriage clock and an ornate brass inkstand, Mary rose and came towards her.

"Emily!" A warm handshake and an unexpected kiss. "My dear, you look . . . different. More . . ." she put her head on one side, considering, "well, thinner!" She laughed. "Oh it's good to see you. I'm sorry I can only spare ten minutes – the price of war!"

This genuine welcome and the real pleasure Mary showed took Emily by surprise. She wasn't sure what she had expected, but nothing so warmly open.

"Good of yo to let me barge in like this. I came on the off chance . . . yo said we should meet."

"I'm glad you came. Truly. Do sit down – have you heard anything of Louise lately?"

Emily perched on the edge of a chair. "About a week ago. She's well enough, but that restless. Her and Mrs Boston have had words – a real bust-up – and now Lou's got itchy feet."

"That impossible aunt!" Mary shook her head.

As they looked at each other, Emily wondered again at how much could be said without words. In a twinkling her mind had gone through their Suffragette experiences together, seeing them marching up to Buckingham Palace, and before that standing side by side in court. She even remembered the magistrate's bald head gleaming like a billiard ball! And that last encounter at Holland Park with the "impossible" aunt hovering . . .

"I always felt she was too restraining with Louise," Mary went on. "But you haven't come here just to talk about old friends. It's France, isn't it – *your* itchy feet?"

They both laughed.

"I've done everything I can think of," Emily said. "I asked our ward sister and she said apply to Matron, so I did and *she* said wait, so I waited and waited, then asked again and all I got was a telling off for being impatient, and to apply when any notices went up. So I thought I'd push in a different direction," she studied Mary's well-remembered face and thought: there's grey in her hair and she looks that tired!

Mary watched her with curiosity. "Why is it so important to you?"

This time Emily had a suitable answer worked out pat: "Because there's nurses coming home wounded along with the Tommies, and I *know* we're badly needed out there. Plenty don't want to risk it, but I'm keen as mustard." She spoke passionately and saw she had touched some chord in Mary. Oh please, please don't let her fob me off, Emily willed and the burst of urgency brought more tumbling words:

"I know I'm not out of the right drawer, but I'm strong, I've hands, eyes, *experience* . . ." she broke off, alarmed in case she had said the wrong thing.

"Ah, experience," Mary said. She took a deep breath and let it out again. Going behind her desk, she sank down in the chair, propping her head on one hand as if her neck was weary. "To be candid, there are still some people – people in top places – who are absurdly choosy about who is allowed to nurse overseas. It is pathetically snobbish, but facts are facts and I respect you too much to try and pull the wool over your eyes."

"Are yo telling me there's no hope?" Emily asked slowly.

"No, of course not. Nurses *are* scarce in France. My dear, I'll do what I can to hurry things along, but you have to accept what your matron says – in nursing terms you haven't had all that much experience."

Emily got up. "Thanks for listening to me, anyroad."

Mary got up as well and, skirting the desk, came close, putting her hand on Emily's arm. "Don't stop trying. I remember you always had great persistence." The smile had gone and her face had taken on careworn lines.

With a pang of remorse Emily realized she hadn't asked Mary anything about herself.

"What must yo think of me, just begging favours and asking nothing about how yo are?"

Mary smiled. "Burning the candle at both ends, like everyone else. I know it shows," she patted her greying hair, "but at least I have the luck not to have anyone to worry about at the Front," she hesitated, looking directly into Emily's eyes, "nor any losses to grieve over. Is that partly what drives you to try and get to France?"

"Partly, yes – but there's plenty of other things," Emily was careful to sidestep any chance of being trapped into talking about old relationships. The past was gone.

"Yes . . . yes, I see." Mary nodded and glanced at the carriage clock. "I could talk for hours, but I've a meeting to attend." Going to the door she opened it. "This really has been a pleasure, my dear. And I will do whatever I can."

They kissed again, and Emily went back into the sunshine.

Emily looked at what was left of the man's leg, amputated above the knee only the day before. A flap of skin had been neatly sewn either side to cover the severed bone and muscle – no sign of

213

bleeding. She felt a flutter of relief and began to irrigate the stump, pouring disinfecting peroxide over it, afterwards swabbing then redressing the wound with care.

"There yo are. Now let's have a look at your arm."

Under the bandages were a mass of wounds made by flying shrapnel. The worst had been tidily stitched, all were minor compared with the amputation, yet as she dressed them the man seemed to suffer far more. Sweat beaded his forehead and round his mouth. He groaned, eyes glazed.

"Mr Purbeck always does a good job," Emily smiled encouragingly. "Ever such a skilled workman he is. Yo'll heal up nice as anything."

The surgeon always did do a good job, but she doubted that this poor lad could hear what she said, let alone take it in. She had got over feeling sick and dizzy at the sight of so much blood, torn flesh and shattered bone, but hadn't yet learned how to handle the overwhelming pity she felt for the sufferers. She scrubbed up and would have gone to the next bed, but Sister Castle came from behind the screens round Jones One and beckoned.

"There's a crisis in the next ward. I want you to sit with Corporal Jones while I'm away. It's his heart again – a collapse, but he's conscious now. All you have to do is check the pulse and watch for any alteration in his condition. You understand?"

"Yes, Sister." She felt elated; scared.

"Doctor will be here as soon as he can. If you're worried, fetch Priors."

Slipping behind the screens, Emily saw Jonesie wink at her.

"Too . . . many press ups!" his breath was laboured.

"Don't yo talk." His pulse was irregular under her fingers. A bluish tinge spread out from his lips. "I've come to keep yo company."

There was no chair.

He patted the coverlet. "Sit."

"Yo trying to get me into trouble?"

He moved his hand again. "Tired . . . sit," his eyes were anxious; kindly.

Better to break a rule than have him worry, she thought and lodged herself. "I'll know who to blame if Sister catches me!" He had nice eyes, but the skin round looked as if he'd been in a fight!

The bruised lids drooped and he seemed to sleep.

Cocooned from the buzzing ward life, time slowed almost to a standstill. Emily wondered why Jonesie's wife had left him – didn't make sense, a nice chap like him. But what did she know of him? Only how he was now in a hospital bed.

She leaned closer and he woke. "Glad . . . it's you." He was suddenly restless, straining his head, mouth open gulping air.

Alarmed, Emily stood up, but he seized her hand in an extraordinary vice-like grip.

"Don't leave . . . me."

"Only for a minute."

"No!" he hung on. "*Please!*"

For an instant she stood irresolute, weighing up this cry from the heart against fetching help, and in that moment the spasm passed.

"Betty," he said, voice quiet but clear – and relaxed.

Emily took her hand from the loosened fingers and felt for his pulse.

It wasn't there.

Heart thudding, she bent over him, but the name seemed to have taken away the last of his breath.

Now she ran, going to Olivia. "Jonesie . . ." her voice was urgent. "I should've . . ." but Olivia had gone. Emily followed her behind the screens.

Jonesie lay as she had left him, eyes half open. He looked peaceful, yet already the colour of his skin had taken on a darker hue.

Olivia said: "Fetch Sandcastle. Hurry!"

Emily fled to the next ward, explained, and hurried back, feeling bleak and desperate. There was nothing for her to do but watch the two women work to try and revive him. At last Sister Castle shook her head, delicately closing the dead man's eyes.

"I should've fetched Nurse Priors sooner," Emily said, anguished. "He was having trouble breathing, but he begged me not to leave him, and held on to me that tight. How could he have so much strength if he was going? I didn't know if I was doing right. He said:

'Betty' clear as anything – was that his wife? What else ought I to have done?" She felt devastated.

"You did what was right in the circumstances. Not an easy choice for anyone." Sister Castle looked at her steadily.

To be handed praise when she had expected thunderbolts almost finished Emily.

"And now you'd better take over from Priors and continue dressing wounds. I need her help here," the sister's voice was back to its usual briskness.

Emily didn't know how she would cope with the curiosity and questions, but went back to work and found it an unexpected relief. There was no time to brood.

At last, taking round the night-time cups of cocoa, and thinking longingly of bed, she saw Norah come in, speak to Sister, who nodded, then cross the ward.

"Emmie, your brother is in the Royal Warwickshires isn't he? Sergeant Victor Palmer?"

"Yes. Why?"

"He came in on the last convoy. They brought him into our ward. I told our charge nurse and she sent me to find you."

A cold chill settled on Emily. She handed the last cup of cocoa to Jumbo, and still carrying the tray went straight to Sister Castle, passing Jonesie's stripped and empty bed.

"Of course you can go," Sister said before Emily could ask. She glanced at her watch. "You only had ten more minutes before going off duty anyway. I'll see you in the morning, Nurse – but you can give me that tray!"

"Oh . . . yes," Emily held it out. "Goodnight then, Sister – thank yo." In spite of her anxiety she noticed and was warmed by the compliment of being called "Nurse". She saw Sandcastle nod and turn back to her papers on the table.

"Is he bad?" Emily asked, going into the corridor.

"Fairly," Norah shot her a swift glance. "Arms and chest. They fixed him up at a base hospital, but I don't know if he needs more surgery."

"Is he conscious?" she dared not ask if he had lost any of his limbs.

"When he isn't asleep."

They left the main building, running across the road and into the park.

Emily had only once before been inside the ward hut where Norah had been transferred. She thought it more homely than her own. Someone had pinned up pictures of country scenes on the colour-washed walls, and there had been jam jars of flowers on most lockers. But that was summer. It was late autumn now, and she was in no mood to look for anything but Vic.

The charge nurse, small and stout, saw them come in. She pointed to the third bed from the end of one row. Vic was lying half propped up. Eyes closed. Face ashen. Both arms were in box splints, chest bandaged. The sight of him, coming on top of all that had happened that day, was almost more than she could take. Fighting down tears, she told herself he had enough to put up with without having her snivel all over him – and going to him, leaned down and kissed his cheek, noticing with huge relief that all his fingers and both thumbs were there.

She said: "Hello, Vic," before his eyes opened, and saw the lids struggle to raise themselves. "Dropped in for a cup of tea, have yo?"

"Emmie!" His astonishment was almost comic. "Yo *here*?"

She smiled. "I works here. Nursing . . . remember? Yo been getting in a spot of bother again?"

"Third time lucky. Got a Blighty one from a Minnie."

"Third time? I only knows about your leg."

"Had a scratch between. Nothing much – just me hand. They kept me in hospital for a week and then it was off up the line again."

"And yo never told us?" She felt weak with relief that he was home and talking.

"I ain't much of a one for letter writing."

"I've a good mind to tell yo off proper, keeping us all in the dark." she ruffled his spiky hair which was thinner than she remembered, with streaks of grey and a hint of a bald patch coming.

"Yo'd not do that if I had the use of me arms," a faint grin lightened his gaunt face. "It'ud be me nicking your hairpins!"

Memories of the old game made her throat thicken. She had to swallow before she could say:

"I'll keep yo in proper order now yo're safely in that bed!"

He pinched his face together in a sudden grimace of pain, irritably clicking his tongue. "Bloody arms! Emmie, scratch me nose, girl. It itches something chronic."

She scratched the top. "That right?"

"Down a bit . . . left . . . that's it!" His relief was only temporary. He shifted in the bed, trying to find a more comfortable position.

Emily skilfully eased his pillows. "Better?"

He gave a tired sigh. "I dunno."

"Is it just your arms giving you gyp?"

"There's a gash across me chest and belly that don't help. I daresay I'll live." His eyelids closed and she thought he was dropping into sleep when he opened them again. "Emmie, have yo heard from our Dad lately?"

"No." She wasn't going to mention the worrying letter from Mam she had found waiting for her at the hostel last night. Trying to sound easy, she added: "He's like yo, not much of a one for writing letters."

Vic didn't smile. His eyes in their dark sockets looked feverish. "I saw him when I was in camp near Étaples, some weeks back now."

"Tell me about it tomorrow," she said soothingly, but he shook his head.

"Ain't much more to tell. We had a word. Got the feeling he was in a bit of bother, but never found out what. Didn't see him again . . . so I couldn't . . . "exhaustion seemed to sweep over him suddenly and completely.

220

"No more talk," Emily got up, bending to kiss him.

"How's Bella?"

"All right, so far as I know. I saw her once down at the theatre, but neither of us has much time – and I ain't going to say another word!"

His eyes closed but she thought she saw the glimmerings of a smile.

One hell of a day, she thought as she left him and went to collect her belongings from the faraway cloakroom on the top floor. Trudging back down the flights of stairs, she considered going now to the theatre to let Bella know about Vic – but the idea of travelling all the way to the Elephant and Castle while her feet and back were shouting to lie down and all of her was trembling with hunger, was more than she could face. It would keep. Vic was home and alive, that was what mattered.

In the tram, lurching back up the hill to the hostel, she took out Mam's letter to read through again.

Birmingham
16 December

Dear Emmie,

A letter come yesterday from the Army to say your Dad is gone missing. I am that worried because they don't know what has happened to him and our Lena is ever so upset. I have tried to find out more. I went to the Drill Hall where your Dad signed on for the army but the officer said he didn't know nothing and to write to your Dad's CO. I don't know who that is or where to write. I can't ask our Ernie as the army bobbies took him last week for nicking army supplies they says. They come and asked me a lot of questions and turned our house upside down but didn't find nothing. When you gets to France can you look for your Dad? I wish you was here. Two heads are better than one and Lena is too small though handy at washing up and whitening the front step. She says to tell you her teacher give her a piece of ribbon for her hair for being top in class.

Your loving mother
N. Palmer

Emily felt as if a heavy weight had settled on her shoulders, pushing her down through the floor of the tram and on down into the earth. *If* I get to France – it's Christmas in a week and not a word out of Mary Grant. Folding the letter, she put it back in her pocket. One hell of a day!

~CHAPTER 16~

"Well, aren't you going to sign?" Norah asked, coming up behind Emily. "You've been talking about wanting to go to France long enough. Here's your chance. It's not quite New Year, but close enough to make it your New Year resolution!"

Emily had just finished her breakfast in the canteen and had stopped casually on the way back to the ward to glance at the noticeboard.

"Volunteers required for Active Service Overseas," Norah read out. "What are you waiting for, Palmer? Here . . ." ferreting in her pocket she brought out a pencil.

Accepting it, Emily wrote her name with a hand that shook slightly, noticing with a little jolt of surprise that Olivia's name headed the list.

Norah was also surprised. "Didn't know Priors was keen to go to the Front. She never breathed a word about it – but then, she's unpredictable. You can't tell what she'll do next. Come on, Palmer, or we'll be late and nobody will be going anywhere except to stand on Sister's mat and get a dressing down."

Emily returned the pencil, hurrying after her along corridors with their distinctive smell of carbolic and faint lavender. The astonishment whirled in her brain. All these weeks, no, *months*, of trying just about everything including pulling strings, and now just her name scribbled on a bit of paper! She couldn't believe such a simple act could bring results. 1918 hovered. A new year! Maybe that was a good omen? But what if they took Olivia and not herself?

Reaching the ward, there was no opportunity to brood. The place was like a house on removals day.

Jumbo, with a blanket over his pyjamas, was wheeled out as Emily was about to go in. He waved to her. "Tata, Nurse! Going on me holidays. I'll send you a postcard!"

"Fresh convoy and double the usual quota," the orderly pushing him told her. "Trying to squeeze a quart into a pint pot, if you ask me – some hope!"

As soon as they were inside the ward the rest of the day was swallowed up in rushing from one task to the next – stripping and remaking beds, washing the new influx of patients, dressing their wounds, providing drinks and food, adjusting pillows, bedclothes, cradles, smoothing uncomfortable creases out of bottom sheets, supplying medicines, emptying bedpans and sputum cups, rubbing tender flesh with lotions, quietening daytime nightmares – on and on and on . . .

Would there ever be a moment to buttonhole Olivia and have a word about volunteering, Emily wondered as she heated linseed for a poultice. There wasn't, and in the next hectic days they managed only a few snatched words, and those about work. The flow of wounded increased. Two days after the second anniversary of Peter's death, Emily realized with a painful sense of betrayal that she'd been too busy to remember.

Christmas came. Streamers were hung around the ward and a bowl of holly sat on the table. Olivia brought a record of carols that were played over and over again. There was no hope of going home, and now and then Emily was plagued by thoughts of Dad and how Mam was going to manage without him. She couldn't sort out her own feelings and carried around a vague sense of shame that she wasn't more upset. The rare letters from home brought no further news about when or where he had last been seen.

She was reading the latest of these over her stew in the canteen, plunged into gloomy thoughts, when Olivia joined her.

"I've been wanting to talk to you," Olivia put her dinner plate on the canteen table and sat down opposite Emily. "You've heard, I suppose?"

"No." Her mind switched to the volunteer notice, and her heart sank. Being out of the wrong drawer did still matter after all.

"I was sure you'd have inside information. Grapevine and all that. Haven't you noticed rumblings in the newspapers?"

"What are yo talking about?"

"Us getting the Vote, you old chump! What else?"

"I thought yo'd heard about going overseas – that yo'd been picked and I hadn't."

Olivia's piled fork stopped on the way to her mouth. "Well, you were wrong, weren't you? I'm impatient too. There's *no* difference between us on that point, none at all."

Emily coloured. "I hope yo're right. Didn't know yo were bothered about voting, though."

"I am female. I can't be unaffected if I'm to have the doubtful privilege of saying who will govern our country. And I shall have it – there's a Bill on its way through Parliament now."

Emily ignored the mocking note in Olivia's voice. "Oh that's wonderful! I can't hardly believe it."

"It's true, and I'll tell you something else. If we don't hear soon, I'm going to beard Matron in her den and demand to know what is causing the delay."

She would too! Emily wanted to laugh. "I'll come with yo. Nothing like a bit of solidarity."

"I appreciate that," Olivia dropped her joking tone. Her direct gaze was a challenge. "What about after we go off duty tonight?"

All the hounding struggles, the impatience, the compelling need to know about real war, gathered together and burst out: "I'm with yo!"

They got up and walked from the canteen in silence, Emily holding tight to the knowledge that she had crossed an important bridge and there must be no retreat.

Outside the ward Sister Castle emerged from her little office and called to them: "I'd like a word."

They followed her, squeezing round drums of disinfectant, boxes of medical supplies, crowded shelves.

"This order arrived while you were having your dinner," Sister had taken a sheet of paper from her desk and tapped it with a stubby finger. "You are required to prepare yourselves for foreign service, and will join the draft due to sail for France on Monday week."

Emily saw the corners of Olivia's lips twitch, and feelings of near disbelief, then astonishment and triumph swept over her in quick succession followed by a wild excitement.

Sandcastle's light gold eyes creased into a smile. "I would like to say that the army's gain is our loss. I wish you both the best of luck."

The headline VOTES FOR WOMEN leapt out at her. The newspaper had slithered off the old woman's lap on the dressing-room floor, and Emily left off telling Bella all about Vic to pick it up. Since Olivia had mentioned the Bill going through Parliament, Emily had only nibbled at what it meant in the rare moments she had to herself.

Now the impact came like clear sparkling spring water, fresh and reviving.

"Votes for women," she read slowly, savouring every word. Joy tingled along her arms, spreading out over her body. She slapped the paper with her hand. "D'yo see? It's happened at last . . . after all that trying . . . all that struggle. We've got the vote, Bel. Think of it!" Shoving the paper back at the old woman, she seized Bella's thin brown arms and whirled her round. "The vote . . . we've got the vote!"

They were backstage in the music hall where Bella worked in the wardrobe, and a show had already begun. Emily could hear the audience singing:

> "It's a long way to Tipperary
> It's a long way to go . . ."

The old woman sniffed. "Much good it'll do you and me. We ain't never going to end up in Parliament putting the world to rights – more's the pity. Wouldn't be no ruddy wars if we did."

"Oh but we will," Emily was surprised to find how deeply moved she was. All the old convictions seemed to have been fired into life again. Tears came into her eyes. Still holding Bella's arms, she shook them, wanting her to understand. "We ain't finished yet. Yo see!" She saw Bella smile, and knew that however long she lived and whatever else might happen, this was a moment she would never forget. More than gaslight seemed to illuminate the seedy room, gilding the peeling walls, the tawdry spangled costume hanging from its rusty nail, the smears of greasepaint and layers of dirty powder.

"Goodbye Piccadilly, farewell Leicester Square,
It's a long long way to Tipperary . . ."

There was still a long way to go yet – Emily knew there could be no election until the war was over, so it was anybody's guess when women would walk into the polling station for the first time and make that first cross on that first bit of paper.

The marching song plucked at her nerves, reminding her of her other urgent errand and almost immediately the blare of a warning hooter cut through the melody.

"My Gawd, Fritz is at it again," the old woman said. "Well, he can do as he pleases. If I've gotter go, I'd as soon cop it in here as anywhere. I'd feel more at home."

Emily said urgently: "I'll have to go, Bel."

"Oh Emmie, think of Monday! They won't want a bandaged nurse crossing to France!" Bella's dark eyes were anxious.

"I'll dodge!" A faint thunder of guns mingled with the dull explosion of distant falling bombs. Nearer, almost overhead, came the drone of an aircraft. Her feelings of urgency grew. "Yo will go and see our Vic then, Bel?"

"'Course I will," Bella seemed suddenly shy.

"Thanks, love," Emily gave her a kiss.

"Good luck!" Bella hugged her. "Write to me."

"I will."

Emily went down to the stage door. Out in the darkened street the rumble of gunfire was louder, and searchlights made diamond patterns against the inky sky. Bombs were still falling, distant and threatening. The dark shape of a man on a shadowy bicycle rode quickly past. Emily began to walk, the thin wind cutting round her ankles and sending needles of cold pricking through her clothes. She shivered, quickening her steps, driven by a sense of snapping urgency. These precious few hours of free time were almost over. Tomorrow was full – a visit to hospital for injections, another to Victoria station to make sure her trunk had gone on ahead, some final packing, last minute letters to Mam and May – then it would be Monday.

The street wound away, coming out into the Lambeth Road. Turning left, she headed for the river, keeping up the brisk trotting pace to stay warm; hitching her bag more securely under her arm. The hard bulge inside pressed against her ribs and a panicky resistance against what she had to do almost took over. But a decision was a decision. She would not let herself dawdle.

Lambeth Bridge and the Albert Embankment.

There was a spot she knew, a few steps down, where she could tuck herself away from prying eyes. Crossing the road she found the quiet place without difficulty. With the river wall at her back she was sheltered from the worst of the wind. Conical beams of light still searched the sky, while below, the choppy surface of the Thames sparkled with occasional dancing silver as ragged clouds parted to allow glimpses of the moon.

Emily opened her handbag and took out the bundle of Peter's letters. Twenty-six of them in a little cloth drawstring pouch, weighted with the pebbles Peter had picked up from the seashore and given her that long ago day before the war. Opening the drawstring, she pulled out the first letter far enough to see his bold scrawl of handwriting, just visible in the moonlight. It was hard to let go, but at last she pushed the envelope back and, pulling up the string, leaned out as far as she dared, opening her hand. The pouch dropped with a splash that threw up a glittering fountain from the dark water which collapsed back almost at once, and closing over the letters, engulfed them. All that remained to mark the grave was a tiny circle of expanding ripples and a few bubbles – then even they vanished and there was nothing left but the wind-roughened surface of the river. She felt weak and shaken as if a limb of her life had been amputated, yet there was a curious sense of release. From the moment she had learned she was to go to France she knew the letters must be destroyed. The thought of indifferent fingers taking out the sheets, other eyes reading words written only for her, was more than she could face. The friendly Thames along whose banks she and Peter had walked so many times seemed a right and proper burial place.

In her mind she watched herself and Peter, hand in hand, wandering past Cleopatra's Needle, pausing to lean and look down. She could hear his familiar voice and gusty bursting laugh, head thrown back as if it wasn't just his throat laughing but all his body. Sun-stars glittered on the water and waves creamed back from a passing barge.

Yes, a proper place to bury such private things.

With a sigh, Emily tucked away the memories and closed her bag. The loss would always be there, but perhaps the guilt would fade. People did live on after pieces of themselves were torn away. Never the same, but managing.

She got up stiffly and began to walk across Lambeth Bridge. For a while she let Peter's ghost accompany her along familiar pavements. Then, crossing the road, she walked away alone.

~CHAPTER 17~

England was shrinking! Leaning on the rail of the ferry boat, Emily watched the chalky cliffs dwindle to the size of a matchbox then disappear, leaving nothing but a great circle of water. She had left Olivia below, braving the icy sting of the January wind because she couldn't bear to waste a single minute of this chance to watch the sea. Only once before in her life had she seen it – running across Camber Sands with Peter. Now sailing over it, without him, she was touched by nostalgia. But melancholy couldn't compete with the exhilaration that came rushing in as she looked up at the wheeling gulls and huge arch of cloudy sky spanning the blue-grey sea.

The deck was as packed as the saloon below.

VADs and soldiers, with here and there a few civilians – some hanging miserably over the rail as the choppy water slapped the sides of the boat, which breasted a wave, slid down the other side, rose again, dipped again. Emily was glad her own stomach seemed steady! For a while she did nothing but stare out to sea, until from the corner of her eye she became aware of being watched. Turning, she saw a tall woman about her own age, with a thick plaid rug over her Red Cross uniform. Wide thin lips split into a smile that pushed up wind-reddened cheeks until the grey eyes almost disappeared.

"Marvellous!" the woman waved her large hand at the sea, shouting a little in competition with the wind. "I never get tired of watching it, do you?"

Reluctantly Emily moved a little closer. "I didn't expect it to look so big."

"Your first crossing?"

"Yes."

"I've been over for holidays – Paris Plage mostly – but this is my first posting. My sister was at the Front last year, but had to come home, with a bad infection in her hand – almost lost a finger!"

"She's told yo all about it then?"

"A good deal. But it isn't like first-hand experience, is it? By the way, I'm Sarah Potter," she waited, smiling.

"Emily Palmer." Emily was torn between wanting to be friendly, and do nothing but stare about. She did stare – and saw Olivia on deck now, coming towards them with a kind of staggering run.

"We might manage a visit to Paris Plage if we're posted to Étaples. Beautiful woods . . . golden sands . . ." Sarah had her back turned and didn't see Olivia until she grabbed the rail, hung over and heaved.

"Poor love, yo looks like death," Emily said, as she came up grey and shrunken.

"I'd welcome a comfortable coffin," Olivia groaned, hanging over again as the boat sank into a deep trough. Before the sea levelled, she retched twice more, leaning on Emily.

"You'd better stay on deck," Sarah put her rug around Olivia's shoulders. "Keep warm. Seasickness is awful, isn't it?"

Emily said: "There's a bench by them crates. Come on, love, we'll give yo a hand."

Between them they supported her, and the VADs who gave up their places lent another rug and a cushion. Emily tucked her up, then perched on a crate beside Sarah.

As the slow journey stretched out and Olivia dropped into sleep, they chatted fitfully about hospital work, home lives, families.

"Staying on at training college didn't seem right somehow," Sarah said.

Emily was surprised. "I thought they were crying out for teachers with the men gone for soldiers?"

Sarah shrugged. "All those books and essays! Carrying on as if the war wasn't happening made me feel like a louse – a parasite living off others."

"Can't say as I ever thought like that."

"Why should you? All your work has been

235

practical – *useful*. That makes all the difference."

Did it, Emily wondered – and lapsed into silence, looking out at sea and sky; thinking.

"Twenty minutes and we should be there," Sarah glanced at her watch and stood up, shading her eyes. "There it is – France! See?"

At first Emily saw nothing, then a thin grey line like a pencil mark formed along the horizon. The line fattened as they sailed closer, focusing into a straggling mass of canvas against winter sky. The darker cluster of buildings in the heart of this camp was Boulogne itself, Emily realized, as the canvas separated into tents and marquees spilling down from hilltops to lower sand-dunes and stretching out either side of the harbour as far as the eye could see. There weren't that many tents in the world – yet she was looking at them!

"The edge of war," Sarah said.

Slowly the ferryboat sidled into the harbour and docked. Gangplanks were lowered. Trunks, crates, tea-chests, sacks, were unloaded on to waiting trolleys and trucks. The quay was like an ants' nest, the harbour almost as busy. Leaving the boat for the quayside, Emily found the sight of fishing boats gently rocking at anchor curiously reassuring. Ordinary life was still going on.

Waiting to meet them was a Red Cross official who introduced herself as Mrs Goodrick. Stout and cheerful, with the plump red-veined cheeks of a ripe English apple, she surprised Emily by rolling off names of places and streets as if she had lived in France all her life – the Red Cross headquarters was in the Hotel Christol in Place Frédéric-Sauvage, and their lodgings would be in the lower town, a short walk across the Liane river . . .

By the time they had been through customs, walked to HQ, had a meal and faced more official forms, over which Sarah's pen squirted blots of ink, Emily couldn't hold back. She burst into helpless laughter. Sarah laughed with her – they couldn't stop.

"Where do you find the energy?" Olivia had shadows of exhaustion circling her eyes. "I'm off to bed!" Out of pity, Mrs Goodrick had found her a place in the hotel among the crush of nurses on leave and anxious relatives here to visit wounded in the base hospitals.

Emily, with Sarah and four others, had to trudge on, crossing the bridge into a street of tall shuttered houses. As they plodded up the uncarpeted stairs of their lodgings, the last of the silliness subsided, leaving her flat and uncertain.

Sarah pushed open a door. "This is us, Palmer – second floor first right, the concierge said."

Emily had to believe her. The gabbled words flowing from the wizened little woman who had answered their knock had meant nothing.

"Double bed, cot under the window," Sarah dumped her bag on the floorboards. "You choose."

There was a table as well, with a blue washbowl and hissing oil lamp that lit up the room and showed faded violet-sprigged wallpaper, a bright rag rug by the bedside.

"I'll take the cot." She disliked the idea of a

double bed without the comfort of Lena's little body snuggling up.

In her nightdress, long fair hair loosened, Sarah looked younger. Emily paused, brush in hand, before starting on her own hair. They looked at each other.

"Well, we're really here," Sarah said.

"Almost. We ain't reached the hospital yet."

They were silent, reality reaching out with a foretaste of what was to come.

In bed, light extinguished, Emily lay staring into the darkness, sifting through the day. After all the planning and scheming, the dogged determination not to give in, she'd *done* it. Peter's war was waiting somewhere out there. The thought was awesome. Her stomach clenched.

And there was Louise driving her ambulance and based at Étaples – her last letter had said as much.

Emily turned over and closed her eyes.

The train wound south, following the coastline. As the track curved, Emily had a brief glimpse of slatted cattle trucks rattling behind. They were filled with troops and she shivered in sympathy, though her compartment was damply warm – VAD nurses and women from the army corps sitting squashed together on the wooden seats. Moisture ran down the window panes and she rubbed a clear space, looking out at the fresh snow which had fallen overnight and camouflaged the ugliness of the endless camps snaking between railway and sandhills. Winter sun glittering on sagging loops of whitened canvas, reminding her of icing on a Christmas cake.

Sarah, opposite, had also made a hole to peer through. Next to her, Olivia was dozing. None of them felt talkative.

The frosted tents gave way to snow-capped roofs and chimneys as the little locomotive ran into the town of Étaples, halting in the new siding tacked on to the old station. From quiet apathy the compartment suddenly came to life. Everyone stood up, talking, reaching for bags, shuffling out on to a platform already crowded with soldiers, nurses, women in army uniform, porters, kitbags, trunks, boxes of medical supplies, of food, of every kind of army stores.

"Make your own way to your hospital at Étaples," had been Mrs Goodrick's parting instructions. There was no transport, and leaving trunks to be collected, they crossed the icy cobblestones of the little square, looking for the Camiers road. A curious assortment of vehicles passed – army lorries, a London omnibus packed with Tommies, a converted baker's van from Luton. Doors were opening into shops and cafés; there were old men and women in clogs, heads covered with black berets or shawls; soldiers everywhere . . . town muddling into country with the tentacles of camp-life stretching out either side of the dirty snow-packed road.

They found their hospital – a stark collection of marquees and wooden huts sitting in a wilderness of churned snow, unfenced, ungated, and with nothing to distinguish it from the others except a board with the number – arriving at the same moment as a hodge-podge of ambulance cars, waggons, vans and horse-drawn carts, which made up a convoy of wounded. Emily looked at each driver as they passed, thinking Louise might be among them, but didn't see her. They trudged up the track, watching stretchers being unloaded by nurses and orderlies swathed in scarves and a strange assortment of coats.

"Now what?" Sarah said.

A nurse in wellingtons, fur coat over her uniform, paused, pointing: "Green door. Dump your stuff with Bryant. She's a good egg – she'll show you the ropes."

They skirted the convoy and found a bundle of scarves and cardigans perched unsteadily on a stool behind the door. Stubby arms reached to lift a box from a high shelf.

"Oh Lord!" said a muffled voice. Bulging green eyes that reminded Emily of gooseberries looked down at them. "Matron's doing the rounds, I'm afraid. She'll raise Cain if you don't go and see her first. All newcomers have to." Thick woolly legs in stout boots scrambled to the floor.

"Should we look for her?" Olivia put down her bag.

"Or we can wait here if yo likes," Emily was already warming herself by the little oil stove.

Bryant rubbed her mittened hands, shaking her head. "Better to get settled in your quarters. Goodness knows when she'll be finished. Hut five has a couple of free beds and Calder had to go home in a hurry, so there's her bed in the bell tent next to it. Sleeping quarters are across the track. If you get lost ask for Petticoat Lane. You can get a mug of tea in the mess, if you want. Good luck!"

They got their tea after locating their lumpy beds and tossing to see who would sleep in the bell tent. Emily lost, but didn't mind, and, coming out of the mess, was first round the end of the hut, meeting a tall slender woman in a dark cloak and the unmistakable ruffled cap of a matron. Under it, wings of black hair looped back from a remarkably young-looking face.

Too young, was Emily's first thought – yet authority was obvious in the set of the woman's shoulders, the poise of her head and the cool steady eyes.

"I hope you were on your way to see me," Matron said. "And what are your names?" She paused while they told her – then carried on: "When you have quite finished your examination, Palmer, take yourself to Ward 8A. Ward rows are numbered in sequence from the road side." Strongly marked eyebrows met over the high-bridged nose. The voice was cuttingly precise.

Realizing she must have been staring, Emily reddened but wasn't going to look away as if ashamed.

"Priors and Potter to Wards 10A and B respectively. See me directly all casualties are settled for the night and before you have supper. I need details of your work experience." She watched them hurry off and then continued on her round.

Emily lifted the flap of the marquee, found a

blanket hanging in the way, lifted that and was hit by muggy air laced with smells of Lysol, cigarettes, paraffin and the stink of festering wounds. Through groans and the buzz of conversation, a high clear tenor was singing with gusto:

"Take me back to dear old Blighty,
Put me on the train for London town . . ."

Three suspended hurricane lamps revealed a scene of near chaos. The usual two rows of beds, aisle between, had become a crazy-paving of extra mattresses and stretchers lying on rough boards. The singer was propped up in bed halfway down the ward, bandages wrapped round his dark hair and across one eye, while two beds further on a diminutive sister was swabbing the chest of a burly soldier lying flat on his back. With no room for any locker, she had lodged a tray holding dressings with her scissors and forceps on the next bed where a young Tommy, buried inside an enormous khaki jersey, was watching everything she did as if his life depended on it.

Winding through the muddle of beds, Emily had almost reached the sister when there was a sudden loud crash. She looked up as the bundle of khaki dipped over the side of the bed.

"Bloody 'ell . . . bleedin' bloody 'ell . . ."

"THAT'LL DO, Fred me boy! LEAVE IT!" the sister's powerful penetrating voice was far more of a surprise than the falling tray, "And I won't be having LANGUAGE, not if I have to stop your mouth with a poultice. You hear me now?"

Emily thought: they'll about hear yo in Dover!

Fred had pulled himself up again, saying sheepishly: "Sorry, Sister. Me leg just give a twitch, Sister. Didn't do it on purpose," as she disappeared between the beds then rose again holding the tray. Her sharp eyes looked over the top of the burly soldier and directly at Emily.

"Mary and Joseph, they've sent some help at last! Well, you look strong if nothing else. I'm needing some clean dressings, Nurse, and look slippy – we've a full house tonight. Take yourself behind that curtain at the end – left as you go in. They'll be in the bottom cupboard."

In her anxiety to be quick, Emily hitched up her skirt to step over and round the stretchers, aware of showing more leg than rules permitted, and heard the swarthy tenor begin a different song:

"She's my lady love, she is my dove, my baby love. She's my girl . . ."

"SNOWFLAKE!" roared Sister.

Emily nipped behind the curtain and found the dressings in a converted orange box. The little kitchen/storeroom was a marvel of trim neatness in contrast to the ward, but she couldn't really take it in. Too much had happened in the last twenty-four hours. She was beginning to feel as if she had been blindfolded, spun round, then left to get her bearings as best she could. She would have given almost anything for a good meal and some sleep. Instead, she braced herself for the return journey down the ward.

It was ten o'clock before the last dressing was done and the last man settled for the night. In all that time Emily had learned that the sister's name was Kelly, that this was her third year in France, and not much more except that her energy seemed boundless. But even she seemed tired when they finished.

"We deserve a mug of tea after that lot." Kelly rubbed her cramped back.

The idea was wonderful, but Emily's heart sank. "Matron said I've to report to her as soon as I go off duty, Sister – before I have supper."

Kelly looked hard at her. "And who says you're off duty yet? The soiled dressings haven't been cleared. Leave them inside the door flaps for an orderly. I'm not having you break your legs hunting for the sluice in the dark tonight. We've enough compound fractures as it is." She moved briskly towards the kitchen. "And see to the sergeant – him next to Fred. Neat as a pin he was when I left him, but just look at him now! Don't forget, I want to see you before you leave, Nurse."

The night sister, fat with clothes, had come on duty, and gave Emily a sympathetic smile. She struggled to smile in return, but everything was beginning to be too great an effort. Thinking was impossible. Straightening the rumpled bed, she helped the restless sergeant to a drink of water – Fred watching every move. As she was about to go, he said:

"*He* shouldn't be here by rights. He's a real bad'n, Nurse. *Real* bad."

The sergeant turned his head and glared at him. A guttural sound came from his throat and he strained from the pillow, neck muscles like whipcords.

Alarm overcame Emily's fatigue. She tried to coax him to stay down but he resisted. A pulse throbbed in his temple. Suddenly the pressures of the day, worries about Dad, and her own exhaustion rolled together.

"Give over – like silly kids, the pair of yo!" She grasped the sergeant by his shoulders, leaning with all her weight, and felt him collapse back against the pillows. He let out a hard gasp, forehead pricked with sweat, and for an awful moment she wondered if she had done him some damage. Straightening the sheet again, she sponged his face, then turned on Fred.

"Don't matter to me who he is or what he's done. My job ain't to judge folks, it's to help mend 'em, that's all." She saw him flush, but didn't care and picked her way back up the ward.

The night sister was thinner by two coats, a cardigan and long khaki scarf, but was still a big woman, with a jaw like an overhanging cliff. "In there!" she smiled again, jerking her head at the kitchen.

Without a word, Emily went inside and found three steaming mugs and a plate of thick sandwiches on the table. Slices of fruit cake were in an open tin.

"Sit!" Kelly commanded.

Emily sat, knees buckling, head thick as a coal bucket.

"Now eat. It isn't your supper so you won't be breaking any commandments." Kelly's sharp face was stern but her small eyes twinkled.

Emily took a cheese sandwich and nibbled.

"I'm not letting you out of my sight empty. A healthy body is a well-fed body. You are on duty, Nurse, until you have put away two sandwiches and one mug of tea at least. If you don't stoke the fire the engine won't work."

"Our Mam says that."

"Sensible woman. Sugar?"

"Two, thanks." Taking the mug she drank, realizing immediately that this was more than ordinary tea as the liquid ran warmly down her throat and glowed into her stomach. She finished the sandwich. Managed another. Ate a piece of cake. Drank a second mug of Irish tea, and felt sleep overtaking her in leaps and bounds. She stood up before it caught her.

"Is there anything else, Sister, before I goes?"

"Only this," a torch was held out. "Turn right as you go out. Matron's office is first hut on the left at the end of the row. A very goodnight to you, Nurse. You deserve it." Kelly gave her a brusque nod. "See you in the morning."

Collecting her coat, Emily pushed through the tent flaps, switched on the shaded torch and, turning right, began to follow the tiny beam of light.

~CHAPTER 18~

As Emily pushed through the canvas flap the following morning, the smell that met her was just the same, but the transformation in the ward was astonishing. Overnight, chaos had resolved into order. She could see some of the wounded had gone because there were spaces between every bed, but the men left on the floor had mattresses properly made up, while the hospital cots had been pushed apart and their lockers restored. Over all lay a sense of peace. Remembering the havoc, it was almost as if she had stepped into the wrong ward. The patients lying deeply asleep were scarcely recognizable as the lice-ridden haggard men plastered with trench mud and stinking bandages. Even those awake chatted quietly.

Kelly was at the table, writing. As if she hasn't been to bed at all, Emily thought. But though her eyes looked tired, her cap and apron were spruce. The only concession she had made to the raw cold were boots and mittens. She gave Emily an approving nod.

"That's what I like to see on a frosty morning . . . fresh as a daisy, and the sparkle of your eyes saying you're raring to go."

Emily struggled with this bright picture – head muzzy from all that had happened yesterday; eyes still gummed with sleep despite the icy water she had splashed over them.

"You've brought the luck of the angels with you," Kelly went on. "Chalkley's on loan from the kitchens for two hours as we're short-handed, so the scrubbing is all but finished. I want you to fetch what we need for the dressings. I've made a list," and she held out a sheet of paper. "Anything not in the kitchen you'll be finding in the tunnel."

Emily took the paper. "Where's the tunnel, Sister?"

"Outside to your right. Between this ward and the next."

The list was long, but Emily found a good-sized basket in the dim space that was roofed with canvas and whistling with draughts. She found Chalkley there as well – tall and gaunt with hands cracked by chilblains, a dewdrop hanging from her beaky nose. She was pouring disinfectant into a bucket.

"I was going to top up the stove for you, but the last drop of paraffin's been pinched." She flicked away the dewdrop.

"Who'd do a thing like that?"

"Anybody who's short. It goes on all the time. They'll put it back when supplies come through, but it's a nuisance all the same."

Chalkley went out and Emily filled the basket, lugging it back into the ward. She had already placed on the table a prepared tray and smaller basket, and now set beside them drums of peroxide and Eusol, some ether soap and packs of dressings.

"We'll see to the corporal first," Kelly whisked up the tray. "He'll be needing all the hands we've got. Bring that bucket and the basket, Palmer."

Dark eyes watched them through peepholes in the bandages and as they uncovered what remained of the corporal's jaw and nose, unruly pity thrust through Emily's hangover of weariness. These were folk like Vic and Dad, like Pete had been, their tough courage and smiles reached out and tore at her.

Moving on she swabbed the hole in the docker's bowel, syringed the stumps of a gardener's arms, dressed the raw meat where the stable-lad's buttocks had been shot away, bound up the deep shrapnel wound of the dour unpopular sergeant – all the time alert for warning signs of haemorrhage or the telltale green stains of gas-gangrene. All the time chatting about families and home; listening to the chipping and jokes. All the time raging; battling . . .

"Change your apron and get the boys and us workers a cup of tea, Palmer," Kelly boomed as Emily secured the last bandages of the last patient whose boozy nose and twinkling grey eyes reminded her disturbingly of Dad.

The break was a relief, and in the kitchen over teapot and mugs Emily managed to stuff away the troublesome pity. Afterwards she scrambled more or less under control through the doctor's round, feeding Reggie the gardener, doling out bedpans, finding the sluice, helping Reggie write to his ma, and preparing Fred for his operation – then special diets, a haemorrhage alarm, linen checked, hot water bottles filled, suppertime cocoa . . .

"A nice quiet routine first day to cut your teeth on," Kelly said at the end of the shift when Emily was putting on her coat and steeling herself for the wintry blast outside. "We'd better pray to the saints to keep it this way."

But the next days and weeks brought one crisis after another and Emily lost what little faith she'd had in the saints. Even Kelly's prayers didn't pull any strings. There were many small emergencies – severe overnight frost turned water to ice, burst bottles of castor oil and lotions, and froze hot water bottles; then the newly repaired coke stove refused to light and the old paraffin one sent out clouds of black smoke; the spring of the gramophone broke; there was an invasion of mice but only one small syringe for a batch of typhoid injections. And of course, the deaths, the gloomy war news, the endless flow of new wounded.

Coming up out of a heavy restless sleep one morning, Emily heard the haunting notes of a bugle playing Last Post over some freshly dug grave. The sound was a regular part of every day and she thought she had grown used to it. But the poignant notes struck deep and mingled with the remnants of a dream she couldn't quite remember. Irritated, she forced herself out of the warm bed and began to throw on clothes, noticing the scrap of paper stuck to her trunk with butterfly tape only when she went to take out clean stockings.

"Got a parcel from home today," she read. "Help yourself to some fudge from the blue tin. Thought of waking you when I got up for the night shift, but you were sleeping like a baby! Do you think we shall ever get to talk?

Gwen T."

Emily helped herself to a piece of fudge, tucked a note of thanks into the tin. They seemed destined never to meet. In the four weeks they had shared this tent all she and Gwen knew of each other were mounds of snoring bedclothes and a stack of scribbled notes! She pulled on her stockings and hooked them to her suspenders, grabbed coat and wellingtons, bracing herself for the Arctic outer world. Crossing slippery duckboards, she found Sarah already in the draughty ablutions hut, a mist of cold water hanging from her eyelashes.

"I keep having hallucinations about lying on a hot sandy beach being cooked by the sun. Some hope!"

"Paris Plage?" Emily suggested.

"In February? You must be dotty!" Sarah rubbed vigorously with her towel. "Mind you, I'd welcome a visit anywhere. We haven't had an hour off since we've been here. Thursday is supposed to be my free halfday."

"And mine," the coincidence struck Emily as too good to miss. "We could go out together, even if it was only a walk. I'll ask if yo will."

"Right right *right*!" Sarah beamed.

The sight of her in chemise and drawers, big mud-splashed boots, fair hair dangling in ratstails, made Emily laugh.

Sarah shovelled on her coat and pulled her watch from a pocket. "You'll be laughing on the other side of your face if you don't get a move on. In twenty minutes we should be in the ward."

A flick of the flannel and Emily ran – scrambling through breakfast; coming into the ward on the end of the night sister's account of what had gone on in the small hours.

". . . that sergeant wouldn't stop swearing in his sleep – every other word was blasphemy!"

Kelly said briskly: "He's nothing but trouble . . ." and noticing Emily: "Make tea for the boys, Palmer. Breakfast's late again. What they get up to in that canteen kitchen I don't know at all – racing cockroaches, I shouldn't wonder."

Putting on the kettle, Emily had the impression Kelly might have said more about the sergeant if she hadn't come in. Since that first night she'd avoided asking questions, but now curiosity gripped her. What was wrong with him? Nobody had a good word to say. She felt a touch of pity.

252

Carrying out the first tray of tea, she paused to chat with a soldier who had come in overnight.

"They say you get concert . . . parties sometimes, Nurse. That so?" his chest mewed and rattled, telling her he'd had a dose of gas.

"Yes, but not since I've been here."

"I like a laugh . . . songs . . ."

A cold blast of air interrupted. Someone bellowed: "Look out!" and she spun round.

Lumbering towards her was a man brandishing a bayonet. Built like a weightlifter, he was naked except for bandages around his torso – face all ruts and stubble, wild eyes. She saw Kelly and the night sister frozen against the table; Fred swinging forward on his crutches; several patients urging each other to "Get the bastard!", while the sergeant was trying to roll off the far side of his bed. He was the target! She put down the tray, and as the man roared by, launched herself, scything him down with a sweep of her leg that sent agonizing pain skimming along her shin as bone cracked against bone. As he fell she dropped on him, knee in his spine, grabbing then wrenching up an arm to lock it behind his back; leaning with all her weight as he began to heave and thrash.

The pain in her leg was excruciating. She shifted her knee. Put every last ounce of strength into leaning down, greasy hands slipping.

"Can't hold him . . ."

Hubbub all round, with serge skirts and khaki legs crowding close. Somebody knocked against her. Two orderlies flung themselves on top of the massive shoulders.

"It's all right now. We've got the beggar!"

Awkwardly, gasping, trembling with effort, she got up.

"Well done, Nurse! You're quite a wrestler!" Dr McBride, the new MO, squatted down by the prisoner. A wry smile creased his craggy face.

Everyone seemed to be staring at her. The wish to fade into the canvas wall was strong, but instead she rescued her cap and did what she could to tidy herself.

Dr McBride straightened up; the man was suddenly quiet. "Orderly, make this fellow decent and get him on a stretcher." He gave the syringe he had used to Emily.

In the kitchen she took longer than usual to deal with the syringe, steeling herself to go out again.

Kelly was waiting, curiosity beaming like a searchlight: "Where did you learn such tricks, Palmer?"

"I had . . . lessons."

"And you only a slip of a girl?"

Emily nearly laughed, but kept her mouth firmly shut. Let her stew! She met the keen gaze. There was a brief silent tussle. Then Kelly's lips twitched.

"Mary and Joseph, didn't I say you were the strong one . . . stubborn too!"

News of what had happened crackled through the hospital. Within an hour Emily found she was famous. On her way to fetch supplies from the tunnel, she was stopped by a canteen cook, a nurse she had never seen before, and Olivia on a similar errand.

"What's all this about being one of Mrs Pankhurst's bodyguards? You never told me!" Olivia gave her a quizzical look.

"Who told yo that?"

"One of the orderlies – a new chap. I don't know his name."

"How does he know?"

"Your guess is as good as mine."

"Damn cheek! What's it got to do with *him*? Wait till I catch the blighter!" Emily scowled.

"He wasn't scoffing," Olivia said mildly. "He sounded full of admiration."

"None of his business what I did."

"All right, all right . . . you aren't ashamed of it, surely?"

"No!"

Throughout the day the questions went on. Even bed was no escape. A note was anchored to her trunk.

"Who says women are the weaker sex! Well done – and how *did* you learn what to do anyway?

Gwen T."

Emily undressed. What a day! *And* she'd forgotten to ask for time off!

"They say you trained . . . as a bodyguard," Fred said next morning.

Emily swore to herself. "Who says?"

"The lads – it's all round the ward."

"Who told *them*?"

"That new orderly. One of them as held that bloke down."

"You're upsetting her, mate. You want to watch what you says!" warned the corporal from the next bed.

Emily pulled herself together and finished dressing the corporal's shoulder, then helped him back into his pyjama jacket and warm cardigan.

"What was it you used to do, then?" the corporal asked, forgetting his own advice. "Was you ever in a real barney?" His weathered face broke into a grin.

"Once, if yo must know!" A vivid recollection of hecklers closing in and scrambling on to the platform in Glasgow; Mrs Pankhurst standing, frail and indomitable. Abuse slung like stones. Punches thrown.

"Go on, tell us – was it a right ding-dong?"

She pushed away the images. "Not that bad. A bit of shoving . . . and who's being the nosy parker now?"

The corporal eased his shoulder. "Know what the lads have been saying?"

"What?" she gathered up the soiled dressings.

"They feel safer . . . having you here."

She almost laughed, it was so ridiculous. "Don't talk daft. Yo boys have seen more trouble than I have in a month of Sundays!"

"They mean it."

"The sergeant as well?" She could joke about him now he had moved on.

"Oh *him*," the corporal lost his grin. "Dunno what that beggar thought – *if* he thinks! Used to be one of the NCOs at the Bull Ring. About says it *all*!"

"The only Bull Ring I knows is back home in Brum – where the market is."

He let out a snort of laughter. "The Eetapps Bull Ring's a bit different. Not so bad since all the trouble, but it's still a hard place. They lashes you to a wagon wheel if you so much as look the wrong way. Can't brush off the flies nor have a drink nor nothing. Number One Field Punishment. They say that's what he give the poor bloke what came in raving yesterday. Twice on the trot they says."

Silently she went on working. She felt depressed.

The shrilling of a whistle and familiar shout: "CONVOY IN" came as a relief.

Sister Kelly boomed across the ward: "Palmer, take yourself with the orderly here down to the convoy. I'll manage the rest."

Outside, the orderly asked:

"Aren't you the nurse that legged over that bloke with the bayonet? They say you learned that stuff as a Suffragette."

"Is there anybody who don't know about it?"

"The whole hospital knows about it."

Emily felt furious. They walked on through a thin mizzle of rain that was crazing the ice in the puddles. The rough track from the road was skimmed with sticky French mud and a straggle of ambulance vehicles was parked along it. Hobbling towards them was a group of Tommies, one with his arm round the neck of an orderly. Emily and the man with her stepped off the duckboards to let them pass.

"Thanks," the orderly winked, and with a sense of shock Emily realized she was looking at an older version of Gordon Box. His callow boyish face was lined and thinner than she remembered, the jug-handle ears even more pronounced. For a moment she felt bewildered, seeing him here. And then she caught sight of his hand spread against the muddy khaki of the wounded soldier. Where first and second fingers should have been were two pink scarred stumps. As they passed, the orderly with her pointed at Gordon's back.

"That's him, Nurse. That's the feller who's been telling everybody your history!"

She stared after him, annoyance and pity tangling. He'd no business to tell what he must have learned from Pete. But she couldn't shout at him now – not here.

She slopped on through the mud and saw Louise, thinner than ever and with a pale, strained face, opening the back of her ambulance car. Extraordinary how this great big war was somehow small enough to keep throwing neighbours and friends from back home together. So far she and Lou had only glimpsed each other – no time for a chat. But now Lou was beckoning; urgently.

"I need to talk to you," she said. "When does your shift end?"

"Eight – sometimes later. Why?"

"I'll be at your tent at eight thirty. I don't mind waiting."

"PALMER!" The sister in charge was standing between a military policeman and two stretcher-bearers carrying a still figure under a red blanket.

"This isn't a vicarage tea-party, Nurse! Take this patient and the sergeant to Ward 10B."

"Yes, Sister."

Ten B was Sarah's ward, and Emily found her there alone, temporarily responsible for twenty patients and fifteen empty beds that were rapidly filling.

After a swift inspection of what lay under the stretcher blanket, Sarah looked up in dismay, knowing she didn't have the time to deal with him. "Can you see to this one for me, Palmer?"

"Don't you trouble with him, Nurse." The MP picked at his teeth. "Just tell us where to put him – floor'll do."

Emily was outraged. "I'll see to him. We'll take the bed in the corner."

The MP eyed the clean linen. "He's right mucky."

"Aren't they all," Sarah said tightly, and hurried away.

"What's he done?" Emily asked, cutting away the stinking dressings.

"Deserter." The MP was careful to keep his eyes averted.

She didn't ask any more, she'd heard what that meant. Men shot for refusing to go "over the top"; others shot in the back running in panic. Deserters wouldn't stand a chance. A wave of anger engulfed her. He couldn't be more than nineteen. She smiled at him and saw tears well and overflow into his ears.

He didn't make a sound. Wiping his face she went back to trying to clean up the pus that kept oozing from what looked like caverns of putrifying meat, raging at the mindless cruelty of having to bind him up ready for the firing squad.

She was still sick with fury when she went off duty. The rain had stopped and stars glittered in a sky of such intense deep blue another time she would have been stopped by its beauty. Now all she could think of was the poor kid on the hospital bed. From the distance came the usual grumble of gunfire. She didn't notice that either, or the army bike lying in the grass, and pushing through into her tent, momentarily surprised to see the candle alight and flickering in its bottle. There was a mound heaped over with blankets and coats in her bed and as it shifted she remembered.

Louise sat up. "You don't mind me crashing in like this, do you?"

Emily did mind. Very much. She ached in every limb and her eyelids felt like ton weights. "No, course not. Want some tea?" Luckily there was water in the little tin kettle. She lit the primus.

The stove helped to take away the worst chill, but there was still a chill of tension. Taking a blanket from Gwen's bed, Emily bundled it round her shoulders. When the kettle boiled, she made the tea and waited for it to brew.

Louise watched silently.

Emily held out a mug. "Sorry, no milk."

"That's all right."

"Help yourself to sugar – in that jar."

"Thanks."

The silence descended again.

Sitting on her trunk, Emily warmed her hands round her mug, too tired to ask questions. If Lou had something to say, let her get on with it.

"Was that lad the MP brought in a deserter?" Louise avoided Emily's eyes.

"Yes." She didn't want to think about it.

"I wonder why they chose to bring him to this particular hospital?"

"I dunno."

"I suppose it's pot luck . . ."

"Oh for heaven's sake!" Emily burst out, resolutions going up in smoke. "What else could they do – leave him to rot? Sometimes I wonder what goes on in folks' heads – sending lads who never left home before to this hell, then acting as if they've committed murder when they can't take it and go on the run."

"Sorry, sorry – *all right*!" Louise hunched knees to chin and balanced her mug on top.

But Emily, launched, couldn't stop. "Nobody seems to care. That poor lad – what he told me. So scared he wet himself and the shakes so bad he couldn't hold his rifle. Shell shock, I reckon, only nobody . . ."

"I'm pregnant," Louise interrupted baldly.

Emily stopped mid-sentence.

"Did you hear what I said?"

'Yo're . . . *pregnant*?" Emily couldn't believe she had heard aright.

"In the family way, as they say. Put into an interesting condition. Lost my virginity and gained

261

a brat!" Louise stabbed her teaspoon into the jam jar of sugar, transferred it to her mug and stirred viciously.

Emily was astounded, remembering the times Lou had sworn she would never have children . . . "Marriage is a trap to catch women and bind them for ever" . . . she could hear those words Lou had said so often.

Louise put down her mug. In the candlelight she looked suddenly small and defenceless. "Oh Emmie, what am I going to do? You will help me, won't you?"

"I'm not a midwife," Emily said stupidly.

Louise shook her head impatiently. "To get *rid* of it, I mean. You must know about those sort of things."

For the second time that day Emily felt outraged. "Yo can't mean that?"

"What else do you expect me to do?"

Emily took a deep breath to steady her voice: "Same as most women – go through with it." The sharp feeling of insult was overlaid by unexpected creeping jealousy.

Louise let out a mirthless laugh. "I can't stand babies. Smelly little brats – all wet bottoms and yowling mouths."

A vivid memory of the row of cots in Sylvia Pankhurst's nursery back at home filled Emily's head. She could almost feel the small bodies pressed against her as she dried them after their morning baths – smell their sweet skin and hear the gurgling laughs.

"A live baby, Lou – yo can't kill it!"

"Oh, don't drivel, Emmie. You aren't going all sentimental on me surely? It isn't a proper child yet. Besides, it's my body; I've a right to decide!" Hysteria edged Louise's voice.

The row of baby cots switched to a row of hospital cots filled with shattered dying soldiers. They had been children once – babies with mothers. "Nothing but killing – and yo holding a life. Yo're so *lucky*!" She couldn't control her envy and thought: she must've heard . . . she'll guess!

In the sudden silence, Louise pushed back the heap of bedclothes and got off the bed. The primus hissed. She stood trying ineffectually to smooth creases from her rumpled clothes, hair tangled. The powerful mix of envy and insult began to wilt inside Emily and change to pity. Poor Lou, to get caught . . . and in wartime . . . what if it had been me and Pete . . .? She felt unutterably bleak. What a mess it all was.

Louise bent her head suddenly, and, covering her face with her hands, burst into hard sobs.

The trickle of pity turned to a flood. Emily shook off Gwen's blanket, dumped her mug, and going close, gathered her up in a hug. Louise buried her face in the hollow of Emily's neck, tense and jerking, then gradually relaxing into the release of more abandoned easy weeping. Emily stroked her beautiful hair, rubbed her cheek against its softness, and as the sobs began to quieten said gently:

"It ain't just your problem, love – takes two, yo know. Who's the dad, and what does he say?"

Louise sniffed; gulped. "Rob Cathcart, and I haven't told him. I'm not going to either."

"Don't yo think yo should give him a chance? Yo always was strong on people's rights!"

"Call yourself a friend!" Louise sniffed, but stayed where she was.

Emily kissed the top of her head. "If I weren't I wouldn't be trying to make yo see all sides. Besides, I only knows Ma Nailor back in Brum. They say she's helped a few girls in trouble – if yo can call it help! I wouldn't let yo go in half a mile of that boozy old bag."

Louise made a sudden explosive sound, half sob, half laugh. "My nose is running," she pulled away. "I'm ruining your collar."

"Bugger my collar."

"What would Matron say?"

They laughed together shakily, some of the tension gone, but not all.

Emily said: "I ain't been much help."

Louise blew her nose hard, mopped her face and began to repin her hair. "You are the only person I've told. I'm trusting you not to breathe a word to anyone. I'll . . . think over what you said. I can't decide anything just now. You do understand?"

Emily couldn't speak. Her feelings for Louise were extraordinary, and had come pouring back in these last moments as if someone or something had smashed down barriers and let in the past, making it the present. Friendship. Love. Admiration. All these and something more which she couldn't pin down. To think that she had ever imagined she could shut the door on that part of their lives they had shared. She must have been daft!

Louise had put on her coat and tied a scarf over her head. Resting her hands on Emily's shoulders she gave her a little shake. "Promise!"

Throat still thick, Emily nodded.

Louise held her for a moment, looking at her intently, then leaning forward gave her a smacking kiss and hurried out into the wintry night.

For a long time Emily stood by the tent flap watching, until the slender figure perched on the battered old army bike disappeared and was lost in darkness.

~CHAPTER 19~

The young deserter died in the night, and Emily
felt a strange relief which disturbed her and was
still nagging when she walked to the Stores and
saw the shed door swing open. Gordon Box came
out, arms full of blankets.

She shouted at him: "Hey – I want a word with
yo!"

He halted, his homely face breaking into a smile.

She marched up. "Yo've got a cheek, going
round spreading rumours about me!"

"Rumours?" He was taken aback.

"About me being a bodyguard in the Suffragettes."

"You mean you weren't?"

"I didn't say that."

"What, then? Cap'n said . . ."

"Blow what he said! It's what yo *shouldn't* have said I'm talking about. What I did before the war is none of your business. Understand?"

The smile died and his ears reddened. "Clear enough. But I don't see as you can say it ain't my business when the cap'n was for ever mentioning you. I can't forget what he said, can I?"

"No, but yo could keep it to yourself."

"I never meant to upset you. Cap'n was so proud of what you did. I thought you must be proud an' all. Going to prison for what you believe in takes nerve."

She snapped at him: "I suppose yo'll shout that from the housetops as well!"

He looked hurt. "I wouldn't do that, but if I did, you should be proud of it. Ain't everyone has that sort of courage. I'd be proud of meself in your shoes." He sounded almost indignant.

Emily glared, about to let rip again, but his scarlet ears, blunt nose lodged on the blankets, startled eyes above, cap rakish on the back of his head, looked so funny a snort of laughter burst from her instead.

His face crumpled into a smile. "Here, miss, you had me worried for a minute!"

"Quite right – all the trouble yo've caused!" but she couldn't keep her mouth straight. "And yo'll have Sister on to me if yo keep me talking!" She turned away, going into the Stores to collect some hypodermic needles, and finding none. Gordon had gone when she came out again, but she didn't spare him another thought, too bothered about what Kelly would say.

"We've not a single needle that isn't as blunt as an old nail," was Kelly's reaction. She pursed her mouth. "You'll have to see what you can scrounge . . . and it's no use looking like a constipated hen. Doctor will be here as soon as blink. He can't give a typhoid injection with *that*," holding up their one tired syringe with a thread of cotton wound round its plunger in an attempt to make it work. "While you're about it, we need more iodine."

Emily retreated from the ward. Everybody "pinched" and returned the goods later, but there would be a right royal row if she was caught in the act. Heart in mouth, she went into the two nearest tunnels, rummaging in the boxes but finding nothing. She couldn't help thinking of Ernie doing time for nicking army stores – enough to make anyone laugh on the other side of their face the way he kept himself safe in jug, when Pete and Dad had come out here and given their lives . . .

A solitary hypodermic lying in a box put a stop to the uncomfortable thoughts, and feeling like a criminal she sneaked out of the third tunnel, returning to the ward to find the MO already there. Not Dr McBride, but another newcomer – tall and rangy with a narrow face and thin fingers that drummed irritably on the table top.

Sister Kelly said: "I want that syringe sterilizing ten minutes ago, Palmer."

Emily retreated to the kitchen, coming out again after what seemed like far too long with the syringe in the ward pie-dish used for everything except baking pies. Putting it on the prepared table, she was conscious of the doctor's air of nervous hurry, and of the first man waiting with resigned patience. As she wasn't needed to help with the inoculations, she went to the bedridden Tommy who was calling loudly for a bucket because he felt sick.

Fred was in the next cot, lying against his pillows, looking wan.

"Not dressed yet?" Under pressure herself, Emily was a trifle sharp.

"I'm cold," he glanced at her furtively. "Can I have a hot water bottle?"

"Yo'd be warmer over by the stove. Yo know yo're supposed to be up for most of each day."

"I feel bad. I think I must have caught something."

She put a hand on his forehead which felt clammy. Then took his pulse, which seemed normal.

"I won't be well enough to go back up the Line, will I? Not if I'm poorly?"

So that was it! She knew he had missed out on the Blighty ticket when Dr McBride had come round yesterday. "I can't say. Doctor will have to decide." She saw desperation come into his face and fetched the bottle, tucking it under his bedclothes.

He was overwhelmingly grateful. "You're a proper rose," and grabbing her hand, kissed it.

"Give over!" She pulled away, aware he was trembling.

"Palmer!" Sister Kelly's voice carried through the ward.

Oh Moses, she's been watching, Emily thought – but hurrying to the table she found all that was needed was a cup of tea for the doctor who had missed his dinner and had had nothing since breakfast.

Later, when the inoculations were finished, Kelly bellowed at her again: "Nurse, why didn't you tell me this man was running a high temperature? A hundred and three!" She was standing over Fred, a thermometer in her hand.

Another scurry across the ward.

"I'm sorry, Sister. He said he didn't feel well, but his pulse seemed normal. I didn't think to take his temperature."

"Hmm!" Kelly took hold of Fred's wrist, then gave him a long searching look. When they were well away from his bed she touched Emily's arm, murmuring: "You'll have to keep your wits about you better than that, Palmer. So shall I! Some of them will try anything."

The story was too good to keep to herself, and after supper when she and Olivia were sitting by the stove in Olivia's hut, she told her what had happened.

"Cooked the thermometer on his hot water bottle?" Olivia stopped pouring Cointreau into Emily's tooth-mug and burst out laughing. "He deserves top marks for ingenuity! Careful how you drink this stuff, it's got quite a kick."

Emily took a sip. She had been invited in specially to try out this liqueur which was a new experience. "Nice. Like a warm worm going down."

"One way of describing it, I suppose," Olivia said drily. "That Fred of yours . . ."

"Not mine," Emily interrupted. Over the last few days she had noticed Fred watching her all the time, trying to catch her attention whenever he could. He was becoming a nuisance. Another time and place she would have told him where to get off, but out here . . . She sighed.

Olivia lifted one eyebrow. "Showing too much interest, is he?"

"Yes – but he's not much more than a kid and he's going back up the Line. There's no way he'll get home."

"That's your answer then, isn't it? Be kind. He won't be here much longer . . . oh hell, what am I saying?"

Emily stared into her mug, trying to fight off the feeling that it was a cheat to let Fred go on dropping deeper into a mushy attachment to her when she couldn't give anything back – but how did you turn away from a cry for help?

She glanced at Olivia and saw she had her eyes shut and was huddling down into the blanket round her shoulders.

Sarah bursting in, apron full of letters and parcels, shattered the edgy silence.

"I found a stack of mail in reception and I've been doing the rounds. All these are for us now."

They fell on her and she beamed, cheeks and nose glowing with cold, passing out mail with raw bony hands.

"Two parcels for you, Priors. One, two, no *three* letters for Palmer. And I've got a letter from my

271

sister. D'you see what that means? She's able to write again; her hand must have healed!" She twirled round, stubbing her toe, swore and collapsed on the end of her bed.

"It's always the same," Emily said, shuffling her envelopes, scanning the handwriting. "Give us a few bits of paper from home and we all go daft!"

Olivia was tearing open a parcel. "Stockings . . . ginger cake . . . toffees *and* chocolates! Have another drop of liqueur. Help yourself to the goodies. Where's your mug, Sarah, my poppet?" She added to her own drink, holding it up. "Cheers to us all . . . what's wrong, Emmie?"

Emily looked up from the official letter in her hand. "No more than I expected," her voice was husky. "It's from the Bureau at HQ. I wrote to them asking if they'd try and trace me dad. Well, they did. Some stretcher bearer found his identity tag in a shellhole," she had to blink before she could read out the words: "There were no survivors, and as it had been a direct hit, identifying the dead individually was not possible . . ." she couldn't go on – bile rose in her throat and she covered her face with her hands. Two hard sobs forced out between her clenched teeth.

Olivia said gently: "They'll let you go home to your family in the circumstances. They won't argue about breaking your contract or anything like that."

Emily fumbled for a handkerchief, couldn't find it, and, accepting Sarah's, blew her nose. "No point. There's nothing for me to do." She scrubbed at her wet cheeks. "Me sister May has gone back home anyroad," tears kept on rolling down her cheeks. "He was never anything but a load of trouble . . . I didn't even like him very much. But he was me dad."

She thought: I've shocked them. But trying to explain and make them see, would mean going over a lifetime of family rows. It was all too complicated – besides, she couldn't be bothered.

Opening the other letters, she tried to concentrate on what they said, but it was difficult with watering eyes and dripping nose. She blew hard into the handkerchief again until her ears hurt. "It ain't all gloom and doom," she said shakily. "The other letters are cheery. Two out of three – that's not bad!" she tried desperately to stop the sobs that would keep jerking out.

"Who are they from?" Olivia asked, helping her along.

"Bella – a friend back home. She's got engaged to me brother Vic. The other is from Louise Marshall – yo remember her? Used to be with the Ambulance Corps in Étaples. She had to go home a week or so back for . . . family reasons. She's written me all the gossip about Brum. She took the trouble to visit my family," but there wasn't a word about the baby.

"I think," Olivia said firmly, "that for all sorts of reasons we could do with another tot." She poured out generous measures.

"Put this round you," Sarah took two blankets from her bed and gave one to Emily. "I've got another bit of news. Nothing important, but

Matron's decided I should go into the German ward. I'm to have tomorrow afternoon off. How about that! I'll be starting on Friday morning."

Emily was prised away from her troubles. "Them prisoners in that ward on the other side of the Mess?"

"That's right."

"Do yo mind?"

"Why should I?" Sarah seemed mildly surprised. "So long as I can make out what the poor things need. I can't speak a word of German."

"You seem to be taking it like a positive lamb," Olivia's drawl was exaggerated. "If Matron had approached me with the suggestion I nurse those dirty Huns I would have chewed her up and spat her out!"

Emily was startled. "I didn't know yo felt like that."

"Well, there you are. A little bit of me you didn't know existed. Have another piece of ginger cake and don't look so shocked. Sarah's shocked, aren't you?"

Sarah didn't answer. For the rest of the evening she was very quiet. It wasn't until Emily got into bed that she realized quite how silent Sarah had been.

"I could have thumped her, if you want to know," Sarah looked across the little table at Emily. "And I hate violence! But I wanted to lean over and give her a real good *thump*. The only way not to was by shutting up. After all," she added, "Priors has every right to say what she thinks."

"But she doesn't know how yo felt . . . unless yo've told her."

"Are you angling for me to explain to you now?" Sarah looked amused.

"No . . . well, yes!" Emily grinned. "Can't say as I haven't been wondering."

They were sitting over a meal of omelettes, crusty French bread and a rough red wine, in a small café in Étaples. The food and wine tasted like heaven after hospital meals; the tablecloth was clean and crisply ironed; a log fire burned in the grate throwing out pleasant heat and brightening the room as daylight slipped away. Emily thanked her stars that Kelly had let her have these few hours off duty. Being here wasn't Sarah's dream of roasting on hot sands, or walking through the pine woods to Paris Plage – rain and a chance lift to Étaples had changed those plans – but she wasn't sorry.

Sarah drank some wine and put down her glass. "All right, I'll tell you. My cousin was engaged to a German. A really nice fellow. She brought him to our house a couple of times. Of course he was called up," she twisted the stem of her wineglass between her fingers. "He was killed at Passchendaele. I don't mention him because I might be seen as a risk. I know you won't gossip."

Emily was moved by her trust. "Shan't breathe a word!"

Slowly they finished their meal, revelling in each leisured lingering moment, but at last it was time to go. As they went into the street the café doorbell tinkled behind them, and as if it was a signal, the sun chose that moment to sidle between heavy clouds, casting shafts of light and long angled shadows across the wet cobblestones. People hurried and dawdled – in uniform; in peasant black. Boots and clogs clattered past, the sounds mingling with the rattle of cartwheels and the more distant clanging of a tramcar crossing the town square.

The last of the sun was just dropping behind the rooftops when Emily pointed. "Look, a chemist! Yo wanted some lavender water. I'll come too . . ." she broke off, staring.

"What is it?" Sarah tried to follow where she was looking but could see nothing unusual. "Emmie . . . *wait!*"

But Emily had already nipped between a lorry and a cyclist, hurrying after the soldier. She could only see him from the back – a stocky figure in shabby battle dress, puttees and boots, forage cap tipped forward on sparse greying hair, but she knew that bull neck, the set of the shoulders and lumbering walk. The street curved left. A group of Australians in rakish khaki hats burst from a side street, full of boisterous laughter. They mingled with the people already on the pavement, blocking him from view.

In desperation Emily shouted: "DAD!" and speeded up, trying to run between the bodies, brushing against shoulders and arms, knocking baskets – convinced she saw him turn left. Reaching the corner she scanned the narrow street which was scarcely more than an alley. Poky shuttered cottages; a thin grey cat licking its poor fur on a doorstep; a girl with a shawl over her head dragging a small boy by the hand. At the far end two old men in black berets were loading a handcart. Midway, a knot of women with windmill hands gabbled in strident French.

No soldier. No place for him to have gone. It was a cul-de-sac.

"Emily!" Sarah came up behind, panting. "Whoever are you chasing?"

Desolate, Emily went on staring down the dingy street. "Just a ghost, that's all." She took a long deep pull at the damp air, then let it out in a jerky gasping sigh. "But I was so *sure* he was me dad . . . the way he walked an' everything! I called, but he didn't take no notice. D'yo think I'm going barmy?"

"War," Sarah said simply, as if this was the answer to everything. She grasped Emily's hand and felt the pressure returned. They stood for a moment, saying nothing. Then Emily gave herself a little shake.

"Come on, we'd best get back."

~CHAPTER 20~

Since Easter, the streams of wounded had swollen to a flood, and rumours invaded every crack in the hospital.

"I've never known the boys so gloomy before," Sarah said as she and Emily were on their way to snatch a few hours' sleep. "Usually they're cock-a-hoop to be in hospital, but not now. Even a Blighty ticket doesn't seem to cheer them up."

"You don't have to tell me! Bailleul's copped it, a whole division of them Portuguese wiped out at Neuve Chapelle, and now they're saying Fritz'll be marching up to Buckingham Palace before you can say knife – it's all round the ward." Emily yawned, almost staggering with exhaustion.

Sarah patted her shoulder sympathetically. "Haven't they found anyone to give you a hand yet."

Kelly had fainted in the ward three days ago.

"Sort of. That orderly, Box, has been doling out meals and helping those as can't help themselves."

"Sister Kelly won't be back for a while, I suppose."

"Not with everything coming out both ends at the same time and a temperature near boiling!"

Inside the bell tent Emily found Gwen in chemise and drawers, stockings undone, collapsed forward across her camp bed fast asleep.

"Wake up!" Emily gave her a shake. "Yo'll catch your death like that."

Gwen stirred. "Oh it's you, love. There's silly I am. Must've dozed off for a minute."

Tired though she was, Emily couldn't repress a smile. One of the few good things to come out of the chaos, with everyone doing what they could when they could, was meeting Gwen awake.

"Don't go off again! Up yo get . . . into bed!" a shove, and Gwen half shuffled, half fell on top of the bedding. Emily dragged the blankets from under Gwen's considerable weight and tucked her in, then undressing, fell into her own bed, asleep so quickly that next morning she had no memory of even lying down.

"Thanks for putting me to bed. Fancy me dropping off over my prayers! But I daresay the Lord won't take it too hard!" Gwen opened the tent flap, and Emily glimpsed a clump of primroses nestling in

279

the grass outside. A bird was singing – liquid trilling notes. The clean yellow of the perfect flowers, and first peppering of new buds thrusting along the branches of a tree, lifted her spirits.

There was life after all – things being born again – she thought on her way to the ward, and wondered briefly what Louise had decided about the baby.

Going in, she found the night sister gathering her belongings.

"I'll see if someone can be spared to help you. I couldn't get through everything . . . it's been Bedlam!" She went out.

Emily scanned the dishevelled beds and stretchers; the piles of filthy cast-off clothing. Only one other mobile person here besides herself – Alf on his crutches! Not knowing whether to laugh or scream, she loaded a basket and began the round of dressings. No nurse appeared, but Gordon walked in about an hour later, crossing to the bed where Emily was working.

"You'll have to make do with me, there's nobody else free. Tell me what you want and I'll do me best," he smiled wryly.

"Help me with Cyril here," she looked encouragingly at Cyril. "This'll hurt a bit."

"I can take it!" Cyril clenched his teeth hard, but couldn't hold back the shout as they slowly rolled him on his side. The shout dissolved into a groan, joining other shouts, other groaning that troubled the ward.

Emily cut away the bandages, cleaned and redressed the gashes and sores. "We could all do with a bit of cheering up if yo asks me. Pity that gramophone bust." She looked at Gordon. "Corporal, would yo empty this bucket and bring some more Lysol from that drum on the table?"

He did as she asked and, coming back, picked up where they had left off: "Where is that gramophone?"

"Somewhere. I don't think it was ditched . . . pass me them swabs would yo? Thanks. Now if yo could go to the kitchen and see what's happened to the boys' breakfast, it would be a help."

Gordon went out again, and breakfast appeared in a very short time. Pressurized though she was, Emily noticed he did everything quickly and without fuss. More than that, he used his common sense about what was suitable to give to each patient. She was grateful.

When breakfast was over and cleared away, he came back to her, going on talking as if nothing had interrupted.

"A concert party. Now that would really cheer up the lads. Take their minds off the war."

"Yo ain't serious? Singers and comics an' that from home, with the state things are out here? They wouldn't be allowed."

He went out to the sluice and back before answering her. "Don't have to be professionals. There's plenty of talent round the hospital. I bet you could do a real eyecatching turn if you put your mind to it."

She gave him a quick scouring glance. "Yo pulling my leg?"

"As if I would!"

He looked as innocent as a lamb, but she wasn't convinced. "What about yourself, if yo're so keen? What sort of turn could yo do?"

"Me? A bit of a sing-song, like we used to down at the local, me and the lads. After we'd got a few pints down us we'd sing fit to bust." He sighed with pleasure.

"He used to be in the church choir," Alf called across to her. "I was there meself, so I know. We're both Coventry kids!"

Emily handed Gordon yet another bucket of soiled dressings. "I can imagine yo as a choirboy," his jug-handle ears sticking out above a white ruff – face scrubbed to a shine with soap and water.

"Well, they let you go to the outing if you turned up to the services regular . . ." he was interrupted by a shout of panic from the other side of the ward:

"Nurse . . . Nurse . . . me leg . . . Nurse . . ."

They both dashed across to the big man, face like chalk, who was clutching his thigh, Gordon reaching him first. Pulling back the scarlet sodden sheet, he used both thumbs to press down through bandages on the pressure point between hip and groin to stem the pulsing blood. Everything was forgotten in the emergency.

But the next morning as Emily went into the ward she was greeted by a burst of music.

"My old man said follow the van
And don't dilly dally on the way . . ."

"Ain't he a marvel?" Alf had set the gramophone going, timing it for her entrance. "Boxy fixed it last

282

night for us. He nosed out where it had gone. That Nurse Bryant had it in reception. Took it all to pieces he did – fix anything from a steam roller to a cigarette lighter. Just the same when he were a nipper. I knew him at school, see. We were in different standards, but he were just as clever with his fingers then as he is now."

Much cleverer now, Emily thought. "Where is he?"

Alf shifted his crutches. "He only popped in to leave the gramophone and a couple of records, and to say tell you he's been put back on stretcher duty. He's sorry but he don't know if he'll be sent to our ward again."

"I see. Thanks." Emily wished she could thank Gordon personally and kept looking for him, but it was several days before they came across each other.

"That's all right, miss," he said after she had told him how much everyone was enjoying the music. "But it's only second best. I'm not giving up on us having our own show. I've got a few of the lads interested, so don't forget – we need all the talent we can get hold of!" he winked, saluted and went on down the duckboards.

She smiled, and went on smiling at intervals, telling Olivia about him later in the mess. It was the first time in weeks either of them had managed to snatch time away from the ward for food at midday. Kelly still wasn't back, but Chalkley was on loan again from the kitchens twice a day.

Olivia had picked up a plate of thin gravy in which floated a few lumps of grey meat and potato. She glanced coldly across the serving table at the cook. "What is *that*? Antique rabbit or army mule?"

"Rat," said the cook cheerfully. "Be thankful it ain't mice. Rats are bigger so you get more!"

Olivia shuddered, but Emily had to laugh.

"It's not funny," Olivia said as they sat down.

"Well, I'm that hungry I don't care what it is."

Olivia picked at her food. She was very pale, with deep shadows under her slanting eyes. "This *war*!" she almost spat out the word, startling Emily, but seemed to recover straight away. "Before I forget, there was a Tommy asking for you today."

"Who was it?"

"He didn't say. He wasn't a patient. I told him your ward, but said you were on duty and was there a message? He said no, and walked off." She shrugged. "What else could I do? You know how stuffy Matron is about men friends invading the hospital – definitely *no* admirers."

"I ain't got none." Emily chewed the tough meat.

"The fellow seemed very keen. A *secret* admirer, Palmer my pet."

"Oh, give it a rest, can't yo!" Emily said irritably.

"Merry as a tombstone, aren't we, dear girl?" Olivia's thin eyebrows lifted and she looked down her nose, back straight, making full use of the fact she was inches taller than Emily even when they were both seated. Then, putting down knife and fork, she rubbed her hands over her face. "Ignore me. I've just been laying out one of my nicest

284

officers. I do wish I could learn not to mind so much when they die. It doesn't help at all."

All the exasperation drained away. Emily touched her hand. "I knows what yo mean."

Olivia forced a smile. "Never mind, chin up, *we're* still alive and kicking . . . oh Lord, can't we even have five minutes peace?"

The familiar whistle was shrilling. Shouts of: "CONVOY IN, CONVOY IN," broke into the mess. Chairs scraped back from the trestle tables. Leaving her food half eaten Emily fled back to the ward, catching a glimpse of a straggling row of ambulance vehicles rolling up the track as she went through the tent flaps.

Chalkley had already made up the two vacant beds, and they began hurriedly to lay out everything they would need on the table, finishing only just in time.

"Here's our first new lodger," Chalkley put down the last drum of disinfectant with a thump as a soldier supported by an orderly stumbled into the ward.

Busy removing the rough field dressing, and lice-infested clothes, Emily didn't see the second arrival until the stretcher was close to her.

"D'you want this one putting on the bed, Nurse?" Gordon had helped carry him in.

Emily glanced round. The wounded man's body was swathed in muddy blanket with rust patches of dried blood. His head was partly bandaged, eyes closed above a blunt, veined nose.

Waves of shock went through her. For a moment she couldn't think or speak. Her ears buzzed.

Dizziness gripped her and she struggled not to faint.

'What's up?'' Gordon looked at her with concern.

She almost said: "He's me dad," but at the last instant held back. Something she couldn't pin down warned her to wait. With effort she shook her head. "Put him on the bed." She fastened her attention on the blanket being rolled back; saw the box splint round his leg, the scarlet-bordered field card that warned of possible haemorrhage. It was pinned to her dad's filthy shirt next to his identity tag. She read the card. He had severe gunshot wounds to his back and right leg, which also had a compound fracture of the femur. She saw the identity tag in passing:

"Pte Frank Enderby . . ."

He opened his eyes, which were glazed and feverish, his gaze wandering until he focused on Emily. A look of utter astonishment passed over his grey stubbly face and was chased by a feeble smile. "Emmie," his voice was hoarse but quite clear, "I never thought to see my gal over here."

The other stretcher-bearer had turned away, but Gordon had heard – one glance told her that . . . oh God, she must make Dad shut up, at least until she could sort out what he was doing here as somebody else. But how . . . *how*?"

"*Private Enderby*," she stressed the name. "I'm going to do what I can to clean yo up and make yo comfortable, ready for the doctor to take a look. We'll have a chat when I'm not so busy," and don't say another word, *please*, yo silly old fool, she begged silently.

Whether or not he understood, or whether his grasp on reality had slipped away with the pain of having his wounds dressed, Emily didn't know, but his eyes closed. Having to move on and leave him without a chance of a private word made her deeply uneasy, but there was a ward full of wounded all waiting, all needing her help.

The next few days turned into a small nightmare. Coming into the ward each morning she dreaded finding some overnight crisis. There was no one she could confide in, and the lack of privacy in the ward made a quiet word in Dad's ear almost impossible.

Then a chance arrived out of the blue. She came to give him a blanket bath minutes after the man in the next bed had been taken away to the operating theatre. Under cover of Vesta Tilley's cheery voice blaring out from the gramophone, Emily was able to whisper:

"Where yo been? They told us yo was most likely dead."

"Living rough."

"Everyone lives rough out here."

"On the run. Trenches. Woods," he muttered.

"Yo mean yo . . ." she bit back the dangerous word "deserted".

He gave a sly nod. "Fighting's a mug's game. Wasn't alone. There's hundreds. Heard of the Eetapps battle?"

"Yo were in that?"

Another nod.

"But how did yo keep from starving?"

"Nicked from farms and such. Sometimes we went into Eetapps. Ain't difficult if yo knows what yo're doing. So much muddle yo gets lost in the crowd."

So she had seen him . . . perhaps. It was on the tip of her tongue to ask about that particular day, but the record came to an end. She finished bathing him and collected up basin and towels, almost reeling. The implications of what he had said trebled her anxieties. A *deserter*! Deserters had only one fate. The old fool – the stupid crazy old bugger! But she didn't blame him.

"Where did yo get that identity tag?" She managed to slip the question as she collected his bedpan next day.

"Took it off a dead bloke in a shellhole," he told her.

That was all she learned. Anything else would have to wait. She thought fiercely: if the old sod gets away with it, I'll make him tell me every last detail when we get home.

But home and safety seemed like a distant dream. She went over the situation in her head – frantically at first, then forcing herself to stand back and take a cool look at the facts.

Dad, known to the army as Private Palmer, was *officially* "missing", the army said so, it was on their records. But really the old dafty had deserted and had been scuttling about with lots of other deserters. Then, somehow or other, he'd taken himself back into the Front Line, stolen a new identity from a corpse, got shot up and finally arrived here in this hospital, in this ward. Here he was Private Enderby, wounded but alive, and yet the fact was Private Enderby was dead. It wasn't likely he'd chatter on about being a deserter but would he keep quiet about being her dad? Gordon had already overheard him call her "my gal". And his wounds looked bad enough to give him a Blighty ticket which is when all the *official* questions would start flying. If he stuck to being Private Enderby he might get across the Channel and find Mrs Enderby waiting to meet him. That was too horrible to imagine. She would need to talk him into owning up to being Private Palmer, no longer missing, just wearing the wrong identity simply because he was a stupid, blundering, bloody old idiot!

Then it dawned on her that even if luck was on their side and he got home safe to Brum, the problems still weren't over. She could just imagine what would happen when he went down to the George and Dragon and met his pals. A few pints inside him and he'd be boasting about how he diddled all the Brass Hats! Everything would come tumbling out. What a mess! She was no longer cool but frantic again.

After days of these worries, Kelly came back – a bag of bones but as needle sharp as ever. She took one look at Emily.

"Take this afternoon off and see that show."

"But, Sister . . ."

"Now don't you be arguing with me," her hard gaze bored into Emily. "I know when someone's at the end of their tether. If it eases your conscience, you can push one of the wheelchair boys. That's an order!"

Emily gave in. For an hour or two Dad would have to take his chance . . . so would she!

~CHAPTER 21~

The mess was fuggily warm. A makeshift stage had been erected at the far end where a door led into the kitchen beyond. Faded red curtains hanging from a rod in the rafters were looped back. A white sheet had been pinned up backstage. Front left was a battered upright piano, with a stool in front, on which sat "Our Yorkshire Lad – A Joke, A Laugh And A Song". He had come to the end of his patter and sat strumming the keys, singing with gusto:

"My Girl's a Yorkshire Girl."

"I'd rather have a Birmingham girl any day of the week," said a voice in Emily's ear.

She twisted round and saw Fred grinning at her from the row of chairs just behind.

"Where in the world have yo sprung from?"

"Camp. Over by the Bull Ring. Thought I'd drop in and say tata as we're off up the Line tomorrow. I came before but you were busy." His voice was jaunty but his eyelids kept flickering and blinking. He leaned forward:

"How about a bit of a walk after?"

"I can't. I'll be back on duty," Emily murmured.

"When you've finished, then? It'd be something good to keep in me mind in the trenches – remembering you."

Blackmail and a cry from the heart.

"I'm not allowed to walk out. I can't promise . . ." Emily wished him a thousand miles away but couldn't throw off the truth of what he'd said. It could be a last time. All he was asking was the chance of a kiss and a cuddle, and she'd never been one for bothering about rules. Who was she saving herself for, anyroad? She felt his hand on her shoulder.

"Say you will!"

"Can't you shut yer great trap," said his neighbour. "Some of us have come to see the show."

Fred subsided and Emily tried to fix her wavering attention on the stage, wondering if Dad was all right. The singer had gone and a trestle table brought on. Orange boxes behind were stacked with army clothing. In front a banner proclaimed:

DEALER IN CAST OFFS.
DRESS UNIFORMS A SPECIALITY.
OLD BOOTS COLLECTED
G.E.T. A C.H.I.T.

The audience dissolved into appreciative laughter, but Emily couldn't concentrate. The sketch finished and she sat through two monologues, a barber's shop quartet, Juggling Jack Throws Things About – then the corporal compère came to the front of the stage.

"And now, ladies and gents, our old mate Corporal Orderly Box is about to burst into song. You will most like burst into tears . . . but give him a big hand anyway!"

As the audience clapped and whistled, Gordon walked to the middle of the stage and gave a jerky little bow. Emily sat up. "Our Yorkshire Lad" had settled back on the piano stool.

"What's it to be, Boxy?" called a voice from somewhere in the audience: "Pack up yer stretchers in yer old kit bag and groan groan groan?"

Howls of laughter.

Gordon held up his hand, and the pianist played several rousing chords before melting into a familiar sentimental melody.

"There's a long long trail a-winding
Into the land of my dreams . . ."

Gordon's voice was an untaught baritone, clear and true, and he sang with feeling. Emily was surprised to find herself moved. The shuffling audience fell silent and as he came to the end of the song there was a moment of utter stillness before wild applause and shouts of "More . . . more . . ."

She hadn't realized how popular he was.

Gordon had a quick word with the pianist, then raised his hand again. Emily found herself sitting forward, eager to hear what he had chosen this time.

"There's a Rose that grows in No Man's Land
And it's wonderful to see . . .
Tho' it's sprayed with tears
It will live for years
In my garden of memory . . ."

She had heard the song often enough. It was a favourite record in the next ward – but she had never paid attention before. The tune was not so much sad as downright drab, yet Gordon was managing to put heart into it, plucking at her feelings.

"It's the one red rose
The soldier knows . . ."

The cloying words and humdrum tune suddenly sickened her, triggering off a burst of anger that had been rumbling around for a long time. This little lull in the war had brought a few precious moments of sharing with the genuine warmth of being together. She wanted to stand up and shout:

"We should all go home. Put some of them Brass Hats in the trenches and let 'em fight it out if they wants war. Wouldn't last long then!"

Was that how Dad had got to see it and had run

to save his skin? She felt tossed by anger, forced to sit and listen without protest.

"In the War's great curse,
Stands the Red Cross Nurse,
She's the Rose of No Man's Land . . ."

Gordon held on to the last note, letting it die and drift into utter silence that lasted for several seconds before the audience burst into a thunder of clapping.

Over – what a relief! She listened to the cheers and whistles, the stamping of boots on boards. Gordon gave his jerky little bow, and, straightening up, smiled directly at Emily. She joined in the clapping, raising her hands to him, but as soon as she could she stood up, intending to collect the wheelchair and the man she had pushed in to enjoy the show.

Olivia was there first. "I'll take him back. You stay and have a word with your friend," she glanced at Fred. "By the way, Palmer, I wrote to another friend of yours today. That ambulance driver, Louise Marshall."

Emily was shaken out of her annoyance. "Why?"

"A patient asked me – a Major Cathcart. They brought him in a couple of days ago. He's in a bit of a mess."

"Poor Lou! Is he very bad?"

"Multiple fractures, a lung puncture – touch and go at first, but he seems to be holding his own," Olivia began to manoeuvre the wheelchair into the bandaged crowd, steering towards the door.

Emily was left with Fred.

They joined the queue, inching along. Outside, Emily halted. "I'm that pleased to see yo again, Fred, specially looking so fit. I must get back to the ward now. Goodness knows when I'll finish – yo understand?"

"Are you telling me there can't be no walk?" The teatime light of the May afternoon showed his disappointment clearly.

Knowing what he faced, she almost crumbled and gave in. But honesty was all she could offer. "Yes, that's what I'm telling yo. Goodbye, Fred. I wish yo all the luck in the world."

He grasped her hand. "Owrecvoyer, as the Frenchies say. I don't believe in goodbyes. You see, I'll be turning up like a bad penny to plague you again one of these days!" His thin freckled face split into a grin. He shook her hand several times before letting go, then walked away without a backward look.

Bloody war, Emily thought savagely – and went back to worrying about Dad. She was so engrossed, she didn't see Gordon come out of the mess kitchen. He touched her shoulder, and she jumped.

"Hello, miss! Did you enjoy the show?"

"Lovely! The boys had a really good time," she didn't want to admit that during most of the turns her mind had been on other things. "And yo sang beautiful. I never would've believed . . ." she broke off in embarrassment.

"Thanks!" He grinned, his cheerful face shining with such infectious good humour that she felt heartened.

"And all that hard work yo did behind the scenes, getting everything together."

"The lads needed something to buck 'em up. So did I."

She laid her hand on his arm. "Lots of folk talk about what they mean to do. Not many *do* it!"

He glanced down at her hand, then up and directly into her eyes. He didn't speak, but she was aware that something had sharpened between them. Her face warmed. She said hurriedly:

"Sister's all on her own. I mustn't stop here chatting," and dashed away, reaching the ward just as Olivia came through the flaps.

"Palmer – I've just had a thought. Would it help if I went to see Louise when I get back to Blighty? What d'you think?"

Emily gazed in blank astonishment. "Yo're going *home*?"

"Oh, of course . . . you haven't heard. Mother's had a stroke. Nothing desperate, but she needs me," Olivia shrugged. "Means breaking my contract but it can't be helped. I'm leaving as soon as the travel arrangements are settled."

~CHAPTER 22~

Emily emerged from the ward tunnel carrying a loaded basket and stopped dead. "What in the world . . . I thought yo were in Blighty!"

Louise came and kissed her. "I'm here to see Rob – just been with him as a matter of fact. I pulled some strings, got a pass and crossed the Channel yesterday. I stayed overnight at a hostel in Étaples." She looked drawn and pale. "Don't stare at me as if I'm mad! I'm perfectly safe and so is the baby. How are you, Emmie?"

"All right. Nothing a year's sleep won't put straight. But yo've no business over here in your condition," relief and exasperation collided. "It's not safe. Fritz is moving this way. We may have to pack up the hospital. Lou, I can't stop now.

It's chaos. We're having to shovel the boys around because a new lot has come in . . . gassed, poor beggars. How long are yo staying? Shall I see yo again?" Emily felt torn – yearning to stay; having to go.

"I'll remain until Rob's well enough to travel." Louise's bright front suddenly crumbled. "Emmie, I'm scared. He's so *ill*. He could hardly get enough breath to speak." Her voice broke and she pressed her hand to her mouth. "Tell me he'll come through."

Emily was wrung with pity which clashed with growing impatience. "Where there's life there's hope. Have yo told him about the baby?"

"Yes."

"How did he take it?"

Louise flushed. Her mouth trembled slightly. "His face was a picture! But he was pleased," she took a deep breath. "He wants us to be married."

"There yo are, then. Yo've given him something to live for." Emily's heartiness was put on. Too much was happening. She felt driven to get back to the ward. She saw Louise's eyes grow moist. "Don't give way. There's two depending on yo now."

"Nurse!" Kelly's head, skin like paper tight over protruding bones, craned between the flaps of the marquee. "Nurse, I'll be thanking you to move those sprightly legs of yours, there's work to be done."

Emily left Louise standing forlornly on the duckboards, and scurried into the ward.

There was no dinner break. Emily and Sister Kelly ate sandwiches sent round from the kitchen, snatching bites between one patient and the next. By the end of the day Emily could scarcely drag herself to her tent.

Inside she found Gwen in much the same state.

"It'll take more than Gabriel blowing his old horn to wake me in the morning." Gwen said, easing off her shoes, and falling into bed with a groan. "I swear my poor old toes are twice the size they were this morning. Nothing but run run run – over here, Nurse . . . the Lysol, Nurse . . . fetch my forceps, Nurse . . . I hope you've got a stick of dynamite up your drawers, Palmer. You'll need it to get me out of bed tomorrow."

"It's me as'll need dynamiting!" Stretching out on her hard bed, Emily revelled in the sheer joy of being horizontal. She didn't want to do anything. Even talking was too much effort. From outside came the thuds of the heavies starting up and the screaming of shells. She told herself not to listen – long slow breaths, that was the way.

"'Night then, Thomas!"

A rumbling snore was the only answer.

Emily smiled, for the moment almost content. Dad was bound for Blighty – tomorrow maybe, or the day after – perhaps with Olivia to keep an eye on him? Though she still had to work out how to ask without giving the game away. Drowsiness was stealing in – the thunder of guns, Gwen's regular snores merged and dwindled to a pinpoint . . .

She was blasted awake by some colossal noise she didn't understand, heart hammering against her ribs with fright. How long she'd been asleep she didn't know.

"God Almighty, what was that?" Gwen was out of bed, standing barefoot on the strip of matting between their beds before her eyes were properly open.

Another shattering roar shook the ground, rending the canvas and making the tent bend and groan. Flashes of brilliant light flared and went out. Flared again.

"We're going to die . . . I don't want to die . . . oh Lord, save us!" Gwen let out a screech, covering her face as a machine gun stuttered low in the sky.

Emily fell out of bed and began piling on any clothes that came to hand. Thrust her feet into shoes. Laced them with trembling fingers. Started for the outside world.

Gwen seized her arm and hung on. "Don't! You'll be killed . . . don't leave me!" She burst into hysterical tears.

Emily tried to shake her off. "Pull yourself together, can't yo? It's no good giving way. We've got to help them boys."

But Gwen only clung tighter. "No . . . I can't . . ."

"Yes yo can – they'll all be frying in their beds."

"Jesus save us!" Gwen screamed as the ground shook with another explosion.

A violent jerk and Emily had freed her arm. Leaving Gwen to fend for herself, she dashed through into the smoky night. Beyond the track a red glow spread like a halo lighting up the marquees

301

and sheds. Other nurses were tumbling from huts and tents. All around, noise and confusion – the flicker of fire, shouts, roar of aircraft overhead. Emily began to run across the track, trying to work out what part of the hospital was ablaze. The line of marquees seemed to be all right, but some of the sheds opposite were smoking. She thought of her dad, guts tightening . . . and speeded up; slipping; righting herself; seeing the wings and underbelly of a plane illuminated briefly by red light as it banked and came in again with a rattle of bullets.

Silhouetted against the backcloth of firelight, people were scattering – stumbling as they ran for shelter. Tongues of orange flame from behind the black pattern of marquees licked at the sky. Emily heard a thundering crash as a roof caved in, with a belch of smoke and cascade of glittering sparks. Another plane was circling and she could hear the harsh sputter of its engine growing louder. From nowhere a wall of hot wind came to meet her with such hurricane force she was blasted backwards, jarring her spine as she fell, all the breath knocked from her body. Through dazed eyes she saw light spear upwards and vanish. A shattering roar sent shafts of pain deep into her ears, and a rain of mud and burning debris stung as it fell. For a while she lay, unable to move, but at last managed to drag herself on to all fours.

Somebody bent over her, grasping her arms. "Are you hurt? Can you stand?"

Olivia. Nightdress kilted up under a coat. Hair wild.

Emily gasped, coughed, and staggered to her feet, ears ringing. "Nothing bad – just winded."

"If you're sure, I must go. Sarah's on night duty."

"God – is it her ward copped it?"

"Don't know."

"Yo go on. I'll manage. Catch yo up."

Olivia was already running, long legs taking her quickly away round the end of the marquees. Emily tried to run after her, but the shock of the fall made her tremble. Shooting pains stabbed the small of her back and her ribs felt cramped and beaten. She dropped into a stiff walk.

A human chain was forming; buckets of water passed from hand to hand – the chain growing away from the inadequate water tanks towards the marquees and on, aiming for the heart of the fire. Somebody shouted to Emily to come and help, but she took no notice, quickening into an awkward run again. At the end of the marquees she got her first impression of the main fire – it wasn't Dad's ward but the next one which was ablaze. Then relief gave way to a fresh surge of horror as the fog of smoke and dust thinned long enough to show that the shed hadn't escaped damage. Where the back wall should have been was a jagged gaping hole.

Instinct took her the shortest way, stumbling across churned earth and rubble, all that remained of last summer's vegetable patch which ran along the back of the wards. Close to, the yawning hole exposed a twisted iron bedstead with the mattress spewing flock, a litter of smashed wood, torn electric wires, broken glass, and a dead man

hanging head down over the side of his bed like
a grotesque rag doll. There was life too – cries, the
shuffle of boots and bodies, hazed images of people
and stretchers. The stench of burning hung in her
nostrils.

She gauged the hole, thinking to climb in, but
had enough sense left to recognize the hazard of the
jagged splintered edge and bare nails. The sensible
way was to make for the other side where all ward
doors opened on to duckboards.

She broke into a stumbling trot. A lifetime to
get round the end of the sheds, dodge people and
stretchers, avoid the burning wards, the red-hot
embers of wood and ash blown on the wind. But
at last she was there.

Above, on the roof, little fingers of flickering
green and gold were already reaching along the
felting, spreading at a frightening rate. As she
glanced up it split and curled back, exposing the
wooden supports. She thought: Christ, any minute
and the whole lot'll go up.

A couple of orderlies came through the ward door
carrying a man on a stretcher. She had to wait for
them to be free of the door, and in those seconds
Gordon came at a run towards her. He caught her
arm.

"Your dad's still in there. We'll get him, don't
worry. Breathe as shallow as you can."

She accepted that he knew and understood
without any surprise, and they went in together.
Many of the beds had been emptied. The remaining
helpless cried out for help. Nurses were there;
orderlies; Bryant, grimy and coughing, supported

a Tommy with only one leg. Through the mist of dust and smoke, Emily glimpsed Olivia and Sarah trying to heave a giant of a man on to a stretcher. Beyond, Dad sat bowed over on the edge of his bed, clutching his belly with both hands, his broken leg caged in splints, heel resting on the floor.

Flakes of charred felt and sparks dropped from the roof where fire had begun to nibble at the beams.

Olivia looked round, eyes streaming, breath coming in wheezing gasps. "Lend a hand, Boxy." On the other side of the unconscious man Sarah was coughing, straining at the dead weight.

Aware of his hesitation Emily said urgently: "Go on – I'll manage Dad," caught Olivia's quick glance but didn't stop.

Spears of flame had begun to stab through the end wall.

"Dad!" she went to him, seeing his distress. "Put your arm round me shoulders. We'll make it together."

He looked at her, tears running over the muscles of his face that were knotted with pain. "Good gal!" a hoarse whisper as he let go of his belly, inching his arm upwards until she was able to slide beneath.

"That's it . . . up . . . rest on your good leg. Lean on me," she coaxed and coughed – thankful to see him stand, however unsteadily. "Hold on to the end of the bed." She had no free hand to rub at her watering eyes, and coughed again. The animal urge to run for safety, to drag him with her anyhow, was so strong she could scarcely control it. His weight crushed down on her shoulders as he shuffled the good foot into a better position, hung on to the bedrail and tried to hotch forward.

A moment of panic when she thought he was going to fall, but he steadied himself, frowning down at his legs. "Buggers won't go."

She eased him on to the nearest bed, almost at the point of despair, and looking round for Gordon, found him behind her. "We need a wheelchair."

"Ain't none. We'll give him a hand-chair." Gordon grasped his own wrist and held out his damaged hand to her, and as she hesitated shouted: "Come on, come on!"

Somehow they levered Dad's awkward bulk into place, lifted, and began the tortuous journey towards the door and out into fresher air.

"Can you keep going?" Gordon asked.

"To the bunker? 'Course!" But Emily's shoulders were burning with strain, her fingers painfully cramped. The fifty yards to the shelter of the bunker in a small copse on the edge of the hospital seemed double the distance.

They found Kelly there with another sister, and a group of nurses all busy with the steady trickle of patients being brought in.

"Put him over there," Kelly ordered.

They laid Dad on a bare mattress. Emily looked at him anxiously.

"I can't stay. I'll come back as soon as I can."

Gordon had already gone and Emily followed, passing Sarah and an orderly going in, between them lugging the giant on a stretcher.

She called out: "Where's Priors?"

"Left her in there with the last man. He can't move," Sarah shouted. "She wouldn't leave him."

Zigzagging on and off the duckboards to let the line of stretchers and shuffling wounded get by, Emily became aware that the noise of aeroplane engines had ceased, though anti-aircraft guns were still firing. Any relief that the raid might be over vanished at the sight of the ward. Despite a jet of water now playing on it from a hose, the wood was well alight. She saw Gordon go in. Somebody shouted, but she went after him.

Heat struck her like a blow. Swirls of smoke billowed down from the roof beams and through cracks in the burning wall boards. The gaping hole at the end of the ward let in the wind, fanning the flames. Through smoke haze and a blur of tears, Emily saw Gordon with Olivia by a bed. He was heaving the helpless man over his shoulder, arm under one dangling leg, hand grasping the limp arm. As he turned away, she saw Olivia stagger and grab the bedrail. He brushed by, coughing at Emily: "Get out . . . out . . ." but didn't stop, lurching towards the door with his burden.

Ignoring the warning, she caught Olivia round the waist. She was coughing badly but managed to drape one arm round Emily's shoulders. Together, choking, eyes streaming, they made for the door. They were almost there when part of the roof collapsed with a grinding crash and a shower of red-hot debris. The door fell sideways, and the beam above came with it, catching Olivia a hard glancing blow to her head. The impact flung her forwards, dragging at Emily who lost her balance and instinctively put out her free right arm to save herself as they both pitched out on to the duckboards – Olivia falling partly across her. There was a sharp snap as a bone broke and pain flared along Emily's forearm, jabbing into her elbow, sending needles of fire to sear her hand. She cried:

"Me arm . . . oh God, me arm . . ." agony blotting out everything else.

People crowded round. The weight of Olivia was lifted away, but she still couldn't stir, sick with pain and shock; refusing offers of help because to move was unthinkable.

"You must move, Palmer. It'll all come down on us any minute."

She realized hazily that Chalkley was squatting beside her.

"Grab hold of me!" Chalkley's arm circled her waist.

Crying, screwing up her face as she made herself cradle her damaged arm, Emily struggled to her knees, was partly lifted . . . and at last was standing.

They had moved Olivia further along the duckboards. Illuminated in the firelight, she lay on her front, quite relaxed. Her nightdress had been pulled straight and decent over her bare legs and wellingtons. She might have been resting, except for the unnatural angle of her head, her unseeing eyes, and the blood making a dark wet patch as it seeped through her pale hair.

Still crying, Emily went to her, awkwardly crouching down, but there was nothing she could do. Nothing anyone could do.

~CHAPTER 23~

They took Olivia's body to the mortuary shed, where all the dead lay until there was time to bury them – and Emily, waiting her turn in the first aid post set up in the mess, couldn't stop thinking about her . . .

Olivia lying on the duckboards, neck twisted, life-blood trickling away.

Olivia being loaded on to a stretcher with the firelight dancing on her pale calm face.

Olivia becoming a bundle shrouded in grey blanket . . . The images mingled with the relentless throbbing of Emily's arm so that in her distress the two seemed to merge into one intolerable ache. How could someone so brimming with life and go, so special, so full of stubborn grit – how could someone like an instant? The thoughts churned. She'd known enough of the dying and dead since the war began, but this was different. She'd been there, helping Olivia . . . they were almost outside . . . another minute . . . another *second* . . .

"Get this down you, love." Chalkley again, with a mug of tea. "And put this round your shoulders." She had brought a cardigan from somewhere. "Hope you don't have too long to wait."

"Thanks," Emily took the mug with a shaking left hand. Earlier Sarah had roughly bound her arm and put it in a sling. Emily sipped the tea gratefully, but had to keep resting the mug on her knee because all her strength seemed to have drained away. When Gordon came in, bringing her a hot water bottle to hug, it was hard not to cry.

He squatted by her. "Is the arm bad?" He looked tired and strained.

"Aching . . . nothing I can't put up with," her voice shook. How kind he was.

"Can't stop. We're moving the lads out of the bunker now the raid's over. But I wanted to see how you were and let you know *he*'s all right."

Dad! She hadn't given him a thought for hours!

"Which ward will he go to?"

"Four C. I'm going back for him now."

"Tell him I'll be over as soon as I can." She thought for a moment Boxy was going to argue and tell her she should go straight to bed once her arm was fixed, but he didn't.

He nodded. "You watch yourself." As he went out the other implications of this terrible night came tumbling in. She was still too thick in the

310

head to make much sense of it, but one thing stood out sharp and clear. She couldn't put up with the mess Dad had made for himself *and* her a moment longer. A glimmer of an idea hung in the back of her aching skull, and she determined that the moment the MO had finished with her, she was going to find Dad in his new ward and tell him so.

She finished her tea and sat on, waiting until her turn came.

"I'm sorry," the MO said, "but we've run out of anything to dull the pain," and then later: "I must say you're a tough one, Nurse," as he finished strapping the splints into position. His harassed face eased into a tired smile of admiration. "Glad to tell you it's a nice clean fracture – just the ulna, about two inches above your wrist. We'll have you back at work in a couple of months! Meantime you've earned yourself a holiday in Blighty."

Head swimming; sweating with pain, Emily was aware that this was meant as some kind of reward, but couldn't summon up the least flicker of pleasure.

"Sister will give you a sedative. Then I want you to go to bed and get some sleep. With a bit of luck there might be a place for you on one of the hospital trains tomorrow."

Emily took some deep breaths to steady herself. "I'd like to stay on till . . . Nurse Priors, my friend . . ." she couldn't sort out her words.

"Oh yes – the funeral – of course, but don't expect to work, will you!" His tone was jocular, but his mind was on the next patient. Emily recognized

311

the signs, and in any case wanted to go and find Dad, but knew she must conquer the faintness first.

She followed the sister, sitting down at one of the trestle tables where the medical supplies were laid out. Watching the sedative powder being measured, she added: "If it's all right, I'll take that when I'm in bed," and catching the questioning glance: "I promise not to forget. Just want to keep awake till I get there." Some of the truth at least.

She took the powder in a mug borrowed from the kitchen, and after a short rest went outside before the last of her strength deserted her. A heavy acrid stench of scorched wet wood and smouldering cloth hung in the air. People were already working to salvage what they could from the wreckage.

It was only at the door of the ward that Emily thought: what if Dad's asleep? And then: what do I say to the sister about turning up at this hour?

But luck was on her side. Two orderlies carrying a stretcher were on their way in, keeping the sister fully occupied. She found Dad without difficulty. He was only lightly asleep, and woke when she whispered his name.

"Emmie . . . your arm. That bloke, he said . . ."

"Sssh! I shouldn't be here. Just listen, will yo? I'm going to sort out this mess yo're in. Sshhh . . ." as he threatened to start talking again. "Can't explain now, but whatever yo do, don't say a word about the . . . yo know . . . running off. Yo understand?"

She could see he didn't, but he nodded.

"I'll see yo again soon as I can." She swayed and leaned against his cot, briefly closing her eyes.

312

"Here, gal, sit down!"

But she shook her head, and unable to say any more, left him and went back to her tent. Undressing was awkward, but somehow she managed. At the last minute she remembered the sedative, and taking it, passed immediately into heavy stupefying sleep.

There was no coffin. After the air raid, the carpenters were too busy with repairs to make such a luxury. Olivia's body lay on a board draped with a Union Jack. Behind the mourners in their starched caps and aprons, the rough graveyard field stretched away to the horizon where yet another funeral was already taking place – a little group of figures dark against the bright early summer sky. Beyond them, a diminishing line of telegraph poles leaned drunkenly. Guns rumbled in the distance. Nearer, perched on a wire, a thrush was giving a dazzling solo performance, while nearer still on duckboards beside the open grave, six orderlies, Gordon among them, stood holding ropes that would lower Olivia's body into the French earth.

Emily forced herself to concentrate. She *must* attend to what was happening. Someone slipped in beside her, and she saw Louise.

"Thanks," she murmured – though what for, she wasn't certain.

Louise took her undamaged hand, whispering: "How's the arm?"

"Aches something chronic, but I'll manage! How's Rob?"

"Surviving. I left him asleep."

The padre had arrived and any murmurs subsided. Looking at the impersonal flag, Emily felt glad that she and Sarah had got permission to lay out Olivia in VAD uniform instead of the easier nightgown. A mark of respect to her worth as a nurse – but more than that, it had seemed a last touch of friendship, just as the bunch of wild flowers they had found later were a final tribute. There had been no need for explanations. "In uniform?" Sarah had said, and that had been that. They worked together – though being cack-handed, she hadn't been much help. The burden had fallen on Sarah.

Emily glanced at her now and saw that Sarah was crying quietly. On the other side of the open grave, Matron was staring down at the scattering of freshly dug earth at her feet; hands clasped; a slight frown knitting her dark brows.

The padre raised his prayer book, pushing his steel spectacles further up his blunt nose:

"I am the resurrection and the life, saith the Lord; he that believeth in me, though he were dead, yet shall he live . . ."

The warm breeze, catching his surplice, made it billow and dance. The sun was polishing his bald head to a fine sheen.

Emily couldn't keep her mind on the words, which seemed to have nothing to do with Olivia. She found herself remembering the time back in London when Olivia had brought in that enormous box of éclairs; she saw the long fingers with tapering nails working twice the speed of her own, and heard Olivia's cackle of unladylike laughter so nearly real she caught herself looking round.

". . . suffer us not at our last hour, for any pains of death to fall from thee," the padre intoned, raising his hand, and the orderlies lowered the body out of sight. A small shower of earth and stones tumbled after it and the padre threw in another handful.

The nurses looked melancholy. Some wept with Sarah. Emily could not make herself feel any emotion except a faint sense of how ridiculous all this was – nothing to do with Olivia – and some astonishment that so many bunches of leaves and flowers had been found to lay on the ground.

"Forasmuch as it hath pleased Almighty God of his great mercy to take unto himself the soul of our dear sister here departed . . ."

Emily thought: *hath pleased*? . . . *great mercy*? – and couldn't go on listening. The thrush had the right idea, trilling away. Olivia would have liked that. She fixed her mind on the birdsong, waiting for Last Post to sound – watching the taut muscles in the young bugler's cheeks, his lips tightening against the mouthpiece, eyes squeezed into slits with musical effort, his spit-and-polish boots glittering in the sunlight.

Afterwards, when the padre had closed his prayer book and moved on to another graveside, Louise and Emily stood for a moment as the duty squad moved in with shovels. Matron, sisters, and nurses had hurried away, and for the first time Emily experienced the strangeness of not hurrying with them. A different future seemed to open out. She felt a stir of anticipation penetrate the layers of flat sadness.

"I feel guilty," she said.

Louise looked mildly surprised. "Why?"

"Because I'm here. Alive."

"That's nonsense and you know it. That's utter balderdash . . ."

It occurred to Emily that Louise was protesting too much. "Don't yo get that feeling ever – why wasn't it me?" She pointed at the grave where earth was flying in.

"I've only got room for what is," Louise said, and put a hand on her waist that was not as slender as it used to be. "I can't handle more than that for the present."

They began to walk at a leisurely pace.

"Strange to hear them words coming out of your mouth," Emily said. "Yo were always so set against home life."

"I'm still alarmed by the thought of it – shall I be able to make Rob happy? And a toddler staggering round my ankles – shall I love it or find it nothing but a thorough nuisance, an intrusion . . . what *will* I be like as a mother?" she pushed her fingers through her hair with a rueful laugh. "I tell you something this war's taught me, Emmie – there's no going back!"

"No. Yo can't go back – never!" Emily shivered, touched by a chill that had nothing to do with the summer air.

Louise caught her hand again, pulling her to a halt. "There's something I ought to . . . no, *want* to tell you. Something I've been meaning to say for a long time, but hadn't the nerve," she hesitated, colour rising up her neck into her cheeks.

Emily looked at her in surprise – Lou, embarrassed? "Spit it out."

"I'm trying to apologize."

Mild surprise turned to astonishment. Emily couldn't think of a single thing to say.

"Well, come on, help me get it out."

"How can I, if I don't know what yo're on about? What have yo got to say sorry about to *me*?"

"I suppose I should be grateful. I can't believe you didn't notice what a bitch I was about you and Peter. It was wrong of me," Louise paused again, as if trying to assess how Emily was taking this, and when she didn't respond, forced a laugh. "You aren't making it easier . . . no, that's unfair . . . oh Lord . . ."

"Am I that much of an old dragon?" Emily asked with a touch of impatience.

"No no *no*, it's me! I don't find it easy to eat humble pie. Oh, I was so *green* – yes, I know I'd been to prison and wasn't wrapped in cotton wool. I'd had plenty of experience in some things, but it hadn't taught me not to be a snob. When you and Pete met me out of Holloway, it was as plain as a pikestaff there was something between you two; something different that had happened while I was inside. I could see it was serious . . . oh, don't get me wrong, I'm not suggesting that other things weren't serious – all our work for the Vote and equal rights. That goes on. But when I saw the way you two were, I was carrying so much rubbish in my head – your not being out of the right drawer for my brother; fury at him for playing around with you and coming between you and me . . ." another pause when she seemed to be mustering strength. "The plain truth is that I was jealous. I didn't want to be second to Pete in your affections. I didn't want him pushing in and turning you away from us as friends . . . as a *team*." Louise sighed.

Emily wished Lou hadn't chosen this particular moment to raise the ghost of Peter. But perhaps trailing ghosts of the past were part of the price to be paid by everyone lucky enough to stay alive.

Louise began talking faster, as if a spring had been released: "I don't suppose I shall ever say these things again, but I want you to know that there is nobody like you, Emmie. Nobody at all. What we've been through together – prison, hunger strikes, propping each other up, the fun and agony, loving Pete and each other, now the war . . . there aren't words to describe all that and what it means."

A year ago such an open declaration of loving friendship from this woman would have filled Emily with joy. Now she felt sad, as well as tender, towards Louise. That glimpse of a new future by Olivia's grave only moments ago, blank though it seemed, was all to do with a part of her Louise knew nothing about. I've changed, she thought. I'm not just her dependable old Emmie any more. The war had opened up vistas never dreamed of in her dressmaking days, and she was determined not to waste a single chance, whatever lay out there waiting for her.

She said with brisk gentleness: "Nobody is like anyone else. We're all different – but we've had some rare old times together, yo and me, Lou. Whatever happens, I'll never forget a single one . . . and as for forgiving yo – well, the way I sees it there's nothing to forgive. The past is finished. Never forgotten – but it ain't worth a candle looking back over your shoulder. Never was."

Louise burst into unexpected laughter. "Oh Emmie, you are a treat! When the baby arrives, if it is a girl, I shall call her Emily – there's no better name."

Emily's eyes filled with sudden tears. She was more touched by this one thing than anything else Louise had said. She had to blink and swallow before she could say: "I hopes she takes to it when she's old enough to think. When I was a nipper I always wanted to be called Gyp same as the dog next door. I loved that dog."

Louise began laughing again, and they walked on across the track, halting by the first marquee.

"Shall I see you before you leave?" Louise asked.

"All depends. I've got to go and have a word with the chief MO, then do me packing. You get that man of yours on his feet and safe back home. He's had far more than his fair share of bad luck."

"I'm going to change all that," Louise's chin went up. "Bad luck has to end sometime – I shall *make* it end!"

They kissed, holding each other for a warm moment, then went their separate ways, Emily walking slowly towards the shed where the chief medical officer had his office. Walking slowly was a luxury, though she still felt strange when everyone else, except the wounded, were scurrying about – then reflected that she was one of the wounded now and would be for the next two months! It was time she got used to the idea. She went over in her head what she had to say, rehearsing the words so there would be no mistakes, and her heart began to pound.

He wasn't in the office – an anticlimax she had to put up with for the next hour and a half, whiling away the time with a visit to Kelly and the boys in the old ward, then to the mess for a cup of tea. When he did arrive her heart again began pounding and again she felt slightly sick. Again she went over in her head what she was going to say.

"Nurse Palmer, isn't it? You wanted to see me?" He opened the door and allowed her to go in. "Sit down. How's the arm?"

"Going on all right, sir. It ain't that I've come about." She tried not to be put off by his brisk manner, nor by his rank of brigadier.

"How can I help you?"

He was very courteous, but she could hear an underlying impatience. She said: "It's a bit of a muddle, but I'll be as quick as I can. I knows how rushed yo must be," and was rewarded by an unexpected smile that transformed his stern face into something far more friendly.

"I've come about me dad who is here in the hospital. He was brought in wounded, and there ain't nothing strange about that. The problem is he's come in under the wrong name. A while back he got separated from his battalion and got lost – he'd even lost his identity tag somewhere in the mud, and he got into a proper panic and couldn't think straight. He got it fixed in his head he'd be in real trouble when he did get back, and cooked up the idea that if he passed himself off as somebody else, then he'd be all right. So he took an identity tag off a dead man in a shellhole. Then he got shot, and was brought here." She looked at him apprehensively.

"I see." The smile had gone. He picked up a pencil, tapping it on the table in front of him. "What name is he listed under?"

"Private Frank Enderby."

"And when was he brought in?"

The question she dreaded. "Ten days ago."

His tufted eyebrows rose in surprise. "So long? Why didn't you come and report this before?"

She licked her dry lips. "Because I was rushed off me feet and couldn't think what to do. He is me dad, sir. He's a stupid old fool doing what he did . . . but I was afraid for him. Then when I thought things over I realized there was more than one side to it – the real Private Enderby's family for one thing. It's not right they shouldn't know what's happened to him. Another thing was, me dad was reported missing when he got himself lost. We got a letter at home, from the army. It's a proper muddle."

"Oh, so this wasn't recent?"

"No, sir."

He was silent for a moment. The pencil went on tapping. Emily sweated.

"He's being sent back to Blighty. I did wonder if I might travel with him?" she said tentatively.

"I think that's doubtful. I shall have to report this. There will be an interview, of course. He will be sent home eventually, but when . . ." he shrugged. "Leave it with me, Nurse."

"Thank you, sir."

He stood up as she did, going to open the door for her. The smile had come back. "Don't worry too much. A lot of men make fools of themselves in the hell out there. He may get a reprimand, but I doubt if it will be more than that."

She thanked him again, and went straight to see Dad, telling him what she had done and dinning it into him that it was for the best. All he had to do was be honest about taking the identity tag, tell them anything they wanted to know about the fighting, and keep his trap firmly shut about the rest.

"Yo've dropped me in the muck heap this time, gal," he muttered.

"No I ain't. It was the only way. Plenty of Tommies get lost and turn up in the wrong regiments. It happens all the time – *and* they panic. Yo ain't alone. Just stick to the facts about the fighting and taking that bloke's tag, that's all yo got to do."

She went over it all again, adding: "The MO said there'd be a bit of a wait before yo get on that hospital train, but yo will be going. Come on, don't look so fed up."

"Wouldn't yo be fed up?" he looked furtively round the ward, refusing to meet her eyes.

"It's going to be all right, I tell yo. Cheer up! I'll meet yo at Charing Cross. I'll get Nurse Potter to

let me know the time and the day and everything."
She would have to hang about in London, but she
knew she could always stay with Sylvia in the Old
Ford Road. In some ways she was glad of an excuse
not to go straight back home to Brum. She needed
time to herself.

"Now have yo got it all straight in your head,
Dad?"

"I'm not a bleedin' fool," he said. "I took it in
the first time."

"Right – I'll be off then. I've got to get packed
and everything." She pecked his cheek.

The touch of affection seemed to stir something
in him and for the first time he looked directly at
her. His eyes were moist. "Yo're a good gal, our
Emmie," he said gruffly.

Sarah managed five minutes away from the ward
the next morning to say goodbye and reassure
Emily about her dad. "I'll keep an eye on him
and let you know as soon as he's on his way. I've
got the addresses you gave me and I'll drop a note
to both. We're all going to miss you, Emmie. Me
most of all. Keep in touch."

"I'll do more than that," Emily said. "Before
yo know it I'll be back at work – that's if them
bigwigs don't manage to settle the war before my
two months is up."

"Mind you make the most of Blighty!" Sarah
smiled, and with a last wave, dashed away.

"Anybody would think I was going on holiday,"
Emily said to Gordon as she climbed into the
borrowed van.

"You are! Home. Nothing to do except mend that arm of yours and see your family and friends . . . what could be better?" Gordon put her carpet bag in the back of the van next to her old green trunk, then went to wind the starter handle.

"It don't feel like a holiday," Emily said when he climbed in beside her. "If yo wants to know, I'm a bit scared. Over there don't seem real somehow. Does that sound daft?"

He didn't answer until they had driven down the track and out into the Camiers Road, heading for Étaples. "I don't think it's daft at all," he said seriously. "The way it is out here and the way people back home see the war don't match up. But that don't mean it ain't good to be home with your folks. And don't forget, your mates over here stay the same. They know what it's like and are always ready to share with you whenever you meet up. This one will, anyroad."

She glanced at him quickly, but he was looking through the windscreen at the road which wound away over the flat landscape. They were quiet for a while. Emily stared out at the carpet of canvas stretching across the French fields – flapping tents and marquees; soldiers like ants scurrying about. She felt very easy riding along in the van with Boxy. They were somehow comfortable together, she decided – he didn't make demands. She glanced at him again. As usual his cap was pushed to the back of his head so the peak stuck up, hair refusing to lie down. He was whistling through his teeth, but when he noticed she was studying him, broke off and grinned.

"Cap'n said the same thing about Blighty and going back."

Emily was startled, but not unpleasantly. Talking about Pete seemed natural. "I know. He once tried to explain, but I couldn't understand. I wanted to, though. Badly. That's part of why I tried so hard to get out here . . . so as to find out for myself."

"And do you think you did?"

She considered this as he changed gear to negotiate a sharp curve in the dusty road. "Some things. All the misery and mess and terror and uselessness, *and* the courage of them Tommies that takes your breath away, as well as how it seems to draw folk together. But not the flying part. I'll never know what that must've been like. Pete didn't talk about it. I think he wanted to, but he couldn't."

"Only another pilot could ever understand. Someone who'd been up there," Gordon thumbed at the sky. "We once had a few drinks together, the cap'n and me – and you've seen enough of the army to know *that* was against all the rules – anyroad, there we were in his billet, downing these whiskies, and he eased up enough to try and describe what it was like flying them kites. Heaven and hell rolled together, was what he said. Taking off was like shedding everything foul and dirty that the war had pasted over him inside and out. He felt washed clean, he said. It was beautiful up in the sky, he said. Like being a bird. But the cold was hell, and being shot at, and all the strains that flying at speed puts on your body, shoving it about in a way it was never meant to be . . . that's what he

325

told me," Gordon shrugged, looking at her. "Just words, though, ain't it, miss? For us, I mean. We ain't been up there."

"I know what yo mean, but I'm glad yo told me all the same."

He blew out his cheeks, letting the air gush out again. "That ain't half a relief!"

She laughed. "Treading on sore places – was that what bothered yo?"

"Something like that."

"Well, yo needn't have worried, though I know it's because yo've a kind heart. It's two and a half years since Pete was killed, don't forget. It's good to learn things about him I didn't know and talk about him with someone who was his friend. Because a person ain't here no more don't mean we should tiptoe round with hushed voices like we were in church. Pete'd be the first to go off into a great cackle at the idea!" She smiled.

Gordon smiled with her.

They were coming into Étaples – narrow cobbled streets; gabled houses with the pale sun sparking off window panes; cafés, their doors wide open; shops and people; bicycles, army lorries and the London omnibus; the little town square and, at last, the railway station. Gordon drew up outside.

"Wait," he told her, and scrambling out, went round to open the van door.

"It's ever so kind of yo to take care of me like this, giving me a lift and everything." She climbed down, nursing her damaged arm.

"No trouble. I'm glad to help. You go through to the platform while I see to your luggage, miss."

"Emily," she said.

About to walk to the back of the van, Gordon paused and looked at her. He began to smile. "Emily," he repeated, and for an instant she experienced the same sharpening of new understanding between them that had come when she had praised all he'd done for the concert party.

She walked on to the platform and found the train hadn't yet arrived. Groups of Tommies loaded with kitbags, rifles, tin hats, gas masks, stood chatting and smoking. There were a few women from the Army Corps and some nurses Emily had seen about the hospital, but didn't know particularly well. After a few moments Gordon joined her, carrying her carpet bag. Then he went back for her trunk. For the first time she realized that in another twenty-four hours she would be back amongst the rush and bustle of London streets. The thought made her feel strange and very uncertain.

"You look serious," Gordon had found a trolley, loaded on her trunk and wheeled it round.

"Just came home to me that this time tomorrow I'll be in London."

"You should be laughing, then!" He looked at her carefully.

"The way I feel now, I wish I was staying. It's like I'm letting down all them boys in the ward. But I'll make sure I come back if this war keeps on."

"I'll be here to meet you, unless I follow you back to Blighty first. They say since America joined in and sent over the Doughboys, we've turned the corner. They say our side's winning."

"Ever since I got over here there's been rumours of one sort and another." Emily eased her arm and tucked in a loose bit of the sling. "That's another thing I've learned – not to believe in rumours."

"Tell you something that ain't a rumour," Gordon said firmly. "Once this lot's finished and I've paid a visit to me mam back home, then I'm off to Canada. Me uncle runs a bicycle workshop out in Toronto and he's offered me a job. New world. Fresh start. Reckon I can teach meself to work with a hand and a half!"

"That's really good news," Emily said, pleased for him.

"You think I'd be doing the right thing, then?"

"Of course – if that's what yo wants."

"That's good," he grinned at her. "That's very good!" And just then the nasal shriek of the French locomotive sounded as the train came round the curve and drew to a halt, steam hissing. Emily went to pick up her bag, but Gordon grasped the handle.

"You stay here. I'll find you a seat. No point in risking that arm of yours getting a knock." He disappeared into the crowd converging on the carriages, leaving Emily to battle with the growing feeling she didn't want to go home at all, and was going to walk out of the station, climb into the van and demand to be driven back to the hospital.

"I got you a seat by the window. Your bag's there and I'll see your trunk is put in the luggage van. There's no rush, the train isn't due to leave for a few minutes."

She watched him wheel the trunk down the platform and wait until it had been loaded on to the train. She smiled to herself at his thoroughness, knowing this was why he was so good a mechanic – why he was always so dependable. Pete had thought so too.

"Thanks," she said when he came back. "I couldn't have managed without yo."

They began to walk towards an open carriage door.

"About Canada," Gordon blurted out. "It'd be even better if you'd come with me."

Emily stopped, taking a second to register just exactly what he was proposing. Then looked round at him, flabbergasted.

He was very red, but his grey eyes met hers without flinching. "What d'you say? It's a bit of a bombshell, I know. I've been trying to think of ways to ask you for weeks – trying to screw up me nerve, but somehow there was never a right moment and I kept thinking it all seemed a bit of a cheek. Now it sort of . . . well, just tumbled out!"

Emily tried to gather her wildly spinning thoughts and feelings, knowing he was waiting for an answer, but couldn't find what to say. All she knew was she had to be honest. Impulsively she put her free hand behind his head, pulling him close enough to kiss his cheek.

"I do like yo," she said. "More than just ordinary liking, but *Canada* . . . coo . . ." she puffed out her cheeks. "I need more time to think. Yo've blown away me wits!"

He laughed, took off his cap and scratched through his spiky hair as if he couldn't believe what he was hearing. Then settling it back again, he kissed her in return. "I'll wait as long as you like . . . just so long as ever you like!" Sliding his arm round her waist, he walked with her to the train, beaming as she got in, and was still beaming as she looked at him through the window – waving and beaming as the whistle blew and the train lurched then gathered speed, heading down the coast to Boulogne.

Lions Tracks

A Question of Courage

Marjorie Darke

Em could hardly credit her own daring – here she was, Emily Palmer from the back streets of Birmingham, carrying a placard that boldly read VOTES FOR WOMEN in a bicycle parade, and on a Sunday too! But Em had been swept into the cause by the eloquent Louise Marshall, and though their lives were worlds apart, Emily knew she'd had enough of being a 'bloomin' slave'. Already she'd spent five years sewing for a pittance and she was only eighteen.

The night that Emily and Louise were caught red-handed painting slogans on the golf course sealed both their friendship and their fight. Then came London and Mrs Pankhurst's Suffragette Movement, and the cloak and dagger fun was over. Now it was rallies, imprisonment, and most terrible of all, force feeding. But as the movement and its violence grew, so did Emily's self-doubts, and for her the choice of continuing the fight became a question of courage.

Lions

The Fox in Winter

John Branfield

When Fran's mother, a district nurse in Cornwall, first took her down to Penhallow Farm to help on a visit to old Tom Treloar and his wife, Fran had no idea how close she would become to this old man, his home and his past. While Fran's visits fast become the most important event in old Tom's day, he opens up new interests and pastimes for her, and when he tells her about the seal cave, Fran decides to enlist the help of fellow sixth-former Dave in a search for the old carved fox-and-geese pieces that Tom Treloar had found and left behind so long ago.

In John Branfield's sympathetic hands the positive and life-enhancing aspects of a relationship between young and old are convincingly portrayed.

'The story is a love story, of a teenage girl's awakening to awareness of adult emotions . . . The contrast between the stark reality of the hospital world and the wild beauty of a hidden Cornish valley is yet another delight in this book which excels at so many levels.' *British Book News*

'Easily John Branfield's best to date . . . Its admirable honesty make it both touching and amusing.'
Books for Keeps

Lions Tracks

It's My Life

Robert Leeson

"You're playing hard to get," Sharon had said as Jan walked off, away from school and from Peter Carey's invitation to the college disco on Friday night. Was she? Jan didn't really know. She wanted time to think things out, ask Mum what she thought.

But when Mum doesn't come home, Jan finds her own problems taking second place, as she is expected to cope with running the house for her father and younger brother Kevin, as well as studying for exams and trying to sort out her feelings towards Peter. Slowly she realises what sort of life her mother led, the loneliness and the pressures she faced, and with this realisation comes Jan's firm resolve that despite the expectations of family, neighbours and friends, she will decide things for herself; after all, "It's my life."

Lions Tracks

A Star for the Latecomer

Bonnie and Paul Zindel

Brooke Hillary is an attractive, sixteen-year-old girl whose mother, Claire, is ambitious for her daughter to become the star dancer she herself wanted to be. Brooke loves her mother dearly, and does her best to make her dreams come true by working hard at the special school for talented young artists she attends in Manhattan. But secretly Brooke has her own dreams – of falling passionately in love with a fabulous boy and having three kids of her own. To her, love comes first and success in dancing second.

Then, tragically, Brooke learns that her mother is fatally ill. It becomes a race against time to make a success of her dancing while her mother can still enjoy it, and Brooke's first love affair looks certain to be nipped in the bud.

"A beautifully crafted piece of fiction. The language and plot are fast and lean, and yet carry a story that reaches into our quieter, thinking parts." *Reading Time*

Lions Tracks

Hey, Dollface

Deborah Hautzig

How do you separate loving as a friend and sexual love – or do they cross over sometimes? Val Hoffman knows that there is nothing wrong, or bad, in the way she feels about Chloe. They are friends, and their friendship has a trust and intimacy which is special for both of them. But sometimes outsiders, even family, can misjudge and label such friendships and labels are frightening because they distort the truth. In this perceptive, funny and wholly convincing novel about two teenage girls, young, unsure, and on the brink of sexual awakening, Deborah Hautzig charts that all-important time between adolescence and adulthood – that fragile moment when we first begin to learn about loving other people.

"This excellently constructed book is an honest documentary of the tribulations of becoming an adult. It is a sharp, credible and moving book." *Learn*

Lions Tracks

A Sound of Chariots

Mollie Hunter

Bridie McShane grew up in a village in the Lowlands of
Scotland after World War I, the noisiest, most spirited
and also the most sensitive of five children. Her father, a
veteran of the war, died when she was nine, and Bridie
was shattered by grief. She was also possessed by the
consciousness of time passing and the reality of her own
eventual death, and haunted by the sound of 'Time's
winged chariot hurrying near'. But Bridie was a gifted
child, and gradually she was able to come to terms with
her grief through her desire to be a writer.

'This moving story, told with deliberate simplicity, is shot
through with tenderness and insight.' *Glasgow Herald*

'An exceptional book which shines light on the clouds of
glory without dispelling them.' *Sunday Telegraph*

'Tough, yet tender, humorous, yet tragic, sometimes
horrific yet always compassionate.'
Times Literary Supplement